'. . . neither will I compare the friendship between us to a chain, for the rain may rust it, or a tree may fall and break it, but I will consider you as the same flesh and blood, the same as if one man's body were to be divided into two parts . . .'

Wm Penn

A
Tree
May Fall

━━━

JONAH JONES

THE BODLEY HEAD
LONDON SYDNEY
TORONTO

To Judith, with love

British Library Cataloguing
in Publication Data
Jones Jonah
A tree may fall
I. Title
823'. 9' IF PR6060.052/
ISBN 0-370-30320-2

Printed in Great Britain for
The Bodley Head Ltd
9 Bow Street, London WC2E 7AL
by Redwood Burn Ltd
Trowbridge & Esher
First published in 1980

PART ONE

The entire process had taken a mere ten minutes, though for him personally it was a matter of life and death, of peace or war. He could not think of the thousands of other men who were committing themselves likewise every day. He was too wrapped up in his own dread decision. After the awful months of debating, of hesitating, then of finally deciding, the actual committal seemed banal. The clerk at the table in the church hall was in uniform and could not have appeared more bored with the momentousness of it all. He had two stripes on his sleeve. The pearl globe on the gas light over his head bore ample evidence of the depredations of the common house-fly.

'Name?'

He had half-expected 'Sir'. After all, he was volunteering, he was offering his life for his country, or at any rate for Little Belgium. Reared neither to use nor to expect titles, nevertheless he was a little put out by the casualness.

'William Dobie,' and the clerk, or soldier, wrote it down on the appropriate line on the buff form. Two men waited behind Dobie, holding their cloth caps in their hands. Had their decision too meant such an agony of conscience? He rather doubted it as he heard them cracking a joke and lighting cigarettes to ease the tension.

'Address?'

'Penn House, Magnolia Avenue.'

'P – E – N, Sir?' and he winced as he guessed the address gave him away. The clerk looked him up and down, almost insolently.

'P – E – double N.' Should he have replied 'Sir'? What did the two stripes, precisely, signify? The clerk dipped his pen in the ink-well and wrote out the address painstakingly.

'Education, Sir – school, certificates, college?'

'Friends' School, Floxham.'

'Friends?'

'Yes, Friends', with the apostrophe after the S.'

'Are you sure, Sir? If the school's named after a man called Friend, surely the apostrophe should come *before* the S.'

He would have to insist – but how not to condescend?

'Well, no. You see, Friends' is in the plural. The Society of Friends.' As the clerk seemed still unsure, he added 'Quakers – a religious sect', and winced inwardly at the commonness of it all.

'Yes, I know. Apostrophe after the S, then.' Was the clerk trying to tell him that he too had had an education? He looked up from the form as though to challenge Dobie. 'College?'

'Emmanuel – Cambridge.' It was becoming a sort of auction.

The clerk refused to be impressed. Barely audibly he spelt it out as he wrote – 'Coll-ege – Cam-bridge'.

'I'm surprised you haven't applied to the local OTC, Sir. In Cambridge, I mean. Surely the college has one.' Dobie was finding it difficult to weigh up this man. Was this an accusation, or simply good advice? Then he remembered that in fact the clerk was right – it would have been simpler at Cambridge. What the clerk would not realise was his own inward debate – and the fact that he was not at all sure whether or not he should apply to an OTC to train as an officer. It was one thing to volunteer, quite another to volunteer to lead. 'Thank you, Sir. You'll be hearing soon about a medical – a week or two, I expect. I should think they'll be interested in you applying for a commission, Sir. Sign here, please.' Then the clerk looked past him for the two friends who seemed determined to do and die together, come what may, for as he turned to leave, there was some jostling as to who should approach the table first.

'After you, Captain!' said one, graciously giving way to his partner with a mock salute.

'Jaysus, Dermot, would ye be after puttin' me along wi' the quality,' his comrade replied with a cock of his thumb over his shoulder at the retreating Dobie.

'Name?' The clerk was quite unperturbed.

Dobie fled. Why must he suffer all this? He might have made it all so much easier by enlisting at Cambridge. Why wait till he got home after travelling nearly two hundred miles? Yet he recalled that as he left Cambridge for a weekend at home, his mind had been far from made up. As he got off the train it was, and he had resolved that if he saw a recruiting station on the way home he would blaze in and sign on the dotted line and that would be that. No more wavering. It had been agony enough and there was no need to prolong it.

Yet nothing could minimise the agony. Remembering the two recruits behind him, unmistakably Irish, he almost wished he could have taken the whole matter light-heartedly in his stride like them. But to have reached the advanced age of nearly twenty-one with a staunch pacifist upbringing behind you was not the easiest way to arrive at conclusions on enlisting for His Majesty's Forces. The shades of cowardice weighed heavily in his mind – to deny this conscience or that, to deny all that he had hitherto believed on the futility of war, or to deny his most recent conclusions concerning the dangers to Belgium and France from the German advances. The entire journey north had been given over to the debate and he had resolved that, with so many decisions pending on his mind (for this was only one), on this issue he would reach a conclusion before arriving home to face his guardian, Miss Pomfret. And he knew well enough that if cowardice was anywhere involved, it was in this, that if he was to have the courage of his new-found conviction and to enlist at all, then he must do it *before* he reached home.

He reckoned the conclusion to enlist had been reached before York. Careful by habit, he would place it before rather than after York. York onwards had been engaged with *how*. He had decided to walk from the station rather than use the tram, and Kitchener's finger might have been pointing at him personally as he sighted the church hall with its recruiting placard: 'REMEMBER BELGIUM – OFFER your services NOW – There's still a place in the line for YOU'. That particular agony was now over. The Allies had failed yet again at Loos. Belgium was worse off than ever and France, nay Europe, might once again be threatened were not the Germans pushed back from French and Belgian soil. Britain would be next, especially if her armies continued to be decimated as of late. Her Empire would be of no great help if the heart was gone. Indeed as an Empire it would disintegrate without the authority of central imperial government, and though he abhorred the idea of empire, he believed the freedom that ought to be accorded to the subject races could only be given fruitfully in an act of political maturity and not simply thrown at them in a state of chaos. Even Home Rule for Ireland, the eternal question in British politics, had been shelved for the duration, and that state, he knew from his reading, would not endure indefinitely. The two Irishmen at the recruiting station were symptomatic of only half the problem – the other half would welcome the disintegration of Empire, and heaven knew what might be going on over St. George's Channel. So the deed was done. It was no time to stand aside, or to hesitate, and within himself he felt a surge of pride. Patriotism had never pulsed in his veins

11

before. The real test would come once he was inside the house.

And once inside the door, and the effusive welcome from Sally the old Labrador was over, the atmosphere changed at once. Miss Pomfret detected the change in him. She knew, with an instinct as sharp as a scalpel, that their former tentative debates on the dreadful issues of '14 – '15 had hardened on his side into something more definite. The customary tenderness was there, of course. Nothing could impair that. But she knew. He did not have a chance to declare himself – or so he told himself. She had just read *The Times* and the casualty lists had so manifestly upset her that there seemed no arguing a case for striking yet harder at the Germans and getting it over and done with. He tried to steer a way towards the subject of his personal position, but there was no holding her in her contempt for government and the generals who were throwing the life-blood of Europe away in a mad suicidal rush of heroics and raw patriotism. As she looked up suddenly and seemed to question with her eyes where he stood just now, when things were so bad, he felt the world turning over. Any moment, he felt, his relations with this dearest of women threatened to fall, so to speak, out of his hands to smash on the floor.

'It's out of my hands now', he even said.

'Out of your hands? What can you mean?' Did William Dobie detect contempt?

Miss Pomfret did not favour such expressions, which she regarded as mere circumlocutions, designed to obscure the truth. The truth, as far as she was concerned, was that the former serenity of their life together might never have been. His stubbornness, his insistence on debating what for her was beyond debate, had already begun to dismantle what had built up so beautifully, so perfectly, since his days as a mere boy in short breeches. Perfectly except, of course, that he had to grow up and the effect of that was sooner or later to introduce a third person into their lives.

That was always there, impending. There was nothing she could do about that – it was simply biology. What she would mind was who it might be and how it was done. But that, strangely enough, was not the present issue at stake. Although she more than suspected it was there, he had not even hinted at it – though she knew there were letters.

It was this other issue, of peace or war. For once he was unable to look her straight in the face and was aware only of the glint of her

12

silver-rimmed spectacles as he slowly and restlessly paced the room. When had they not looked each other squarely in the face and advanced this or that subject with a candour and plainness that became their calling as Friends? And could he really claim any longer that he remained a Friend – or even a friend?

'There is no such thing as out of our hands', she continued, no more anxious than he to catch an eye in this uncomfortable confrontation. She hoped it was not going to develop into a quarrel, their first. 'That is an abdication of responsibility for our own lives and those of others. Not unless you're talking about an Act of God – and I don't see one.'

From a gesture of hands spread in a rare moment of demonstrativeness she gathered them tidily over her breast as though to compose herself – as indeed she did. They had both gone too far. Both issues, the one now tormenting them, the other as yet undeclared but *there*, her every womanly instinct told her, both issues disturbed her deeply.

He had advanced only the one of peace and war – and on that she was implacable and he knew it. On the other she was ignorant, could not be said to have views beyond the who and how, and for some reason she was conscience-stricken about it, as though she might just have omitted some small area of his education.

But what was it now that was 'out of his hands'? She dared not probe too deep. It might be some irrevocable move on either issue. Yet however much he argued about it, she hardly expected the irrevocable concerned his present arguments about war – more likely the other. On war, she could not imagine the irrevocable. After all, he was an undergraduate, a Quaker, and since conscription did not apply, there was no irrevocable stand he need take – yet. But he was dogged, slow and dogged as only William could be when he got on to something.

'There *is* such a thing as a just war, surely,' he persisted, 'and if ever there were, surely this one . . .'

He had been about to declare the truth. His voice trailed off weakly. In a way, he might never have gone beyond his first intimation, some weeks before, that he could imagine a situation that vindicated a just war. He had not advanced the current situation in Belgium, had talked only in the abstract, feeling his way with the gentle but implacable Miss Pomfret. But they both knew what was meant. The newspaper headlines saw to that, and they seemed to get worse. Yet each time he tried to take the debate further, to explore unknown territory in his own feelings about the matter, she was quite adamant, in a way that was so uncharacteristic as to make a greater impression.

13

She probed at once, sensing that, compared with the summer vacation, things were somehow and decisively different between them. Since the news from France got steadily worse and the autumn failure at Loos to make any impression on the German lines was a depressing factor that even her pacifist conscience must allow, she had to allow too that any young man of twenty, whether he be committed to war or to conscientious objection, must be in torment unless he were quite devoid of feeling. She could even allow him that, whereas former wars had been by comparison mere military adventures, this one was different in kind in the sense that it was becoming a people's war. The humblest and more unlikely candidates were leaving the community; the postman – poor, slow, ineffectual Mr Charlton – had not merely left, but had already given his life. This involvement of the total community may have complicated the Quaker position to some extent, but not, of course, the ultimate stance of the Quaker, which must be steadfastly set against war as a way of settling international and internecine quarrels. That was how she saw it.

She knew however that the call on the people rather than, as formerly, on a soldier minority, was affecting individuals like William, who could feel only more isolated in conscience by the dreadful scale of casualties on the Western Front and the response of the whole people to the call of duty. It was not an army, it was a whole nation which was bleeding, and Belgium was so obviously an example of flagrant military occupation and (here she had her doubts) of German atrocities, that it was no wonder people answered the call.

Yes, she sensed the difficulties, but she also sensed a clouding of ultimate objectives. War was creating its own abstract of right and certitude, whereas in fact the longer it went on, the more it exacerbated the very problems it pretended to solve, and shored up a failing structure that depended on the returns of war.

With William therefore she could sympathise, but felt that he was allowing the truth – of love and peace – to slip away too easily in the present turmoil of conscience. Young men were too easily got at.

Because it was a people's war, a total war, then it was important at this stage, now, that the generation of William's who had been reared to resist war as a solution should not disappear for ever. She had no illusions that mankind would continue to find reasons for war, but after this war it would always be a total war, involving the whole people and ultimately the world, as men became ever more ingenious at devising weapons of destruction.

'War is clearly wrong', she said. 'You're only complicating the argument.'

'Maybe,' he replied, 'but surely no one believes war is anything but wrong, so let's not simplify too much. Let's leave it now, shall we?'

He turned to a favourite picture of his on the wall, away from the fireplace.

'I think of all the pictures,' he said, trying to get Miss Pomfret away from what had now divided them for weeks, 'I like the Peter De Wint best of all. I still claim it's Swaledale. But we'll never know. It's just a view of hills. You may say it's not Swaledale. You could be right. So there's no more to say. Is there?'

'Yes, there is. And don't change the subject. War is wrong, that is clear. So why do we continue with it?'

Miss Pomfret, by now at an age when you could not guess at it, treated him like a son. Though not related, the loss of his mother when he was four had flung him as a child into this Quaker friend's loving arms. All her diffident overtures to his bereft father having proved unavailing, it had become established that the orphan boy's welfare was her personal concern.

The Dobies were not great survivors. At fourteen he had lost his father too, and Miss Pomfret welcomed this even greater dependence on herself. When he returned from Friends' school, it was to Miss Pomfret always. That was home now. Technically he still owned the large house in the city's most respectable suburb, but it was forever shuttered now. Other Dobies did not abound apparently, and with each year the ritual established itself that at holidays he should go to Miss Pomfret's.

The young man's dependence on Miss Pomfret was almost complete.

Miss Pomfret's house was spotless. The mahogany gleamed darkly in contrast to the prevailing whiteness, for Miss Pomfret liked white, its purity. The walls were white, the better (she considered) for showing off her one indulgence: a fine collection of English watercolours.

The whole aspect of the room where they both paced uneasily, each afraid to sit lest the tension be allowed to slacken and things be left as unresolved as ever – its whole aspect was that of a Dutch interior by Pieter de Hooch. And that Miss Pomfret liked, for what could be plainer, simpler, more befitting her idea of life than those bare, clean interiors by painters whose genius for the plain truth was so palpable?

A rare Cotman, two Varleys, a Turner, three David Coxs, the de Wint – a fair sampling of the English water-colour school gleamed in their frames round the plain walls. They seemed meant for just such an interior, and if indeed they might be judged as an indulgence in one devoted to the simple life, the choice was interesting, for each provided in its different way a contemplative focus. Even the Turner seemed muted for the occasion: a single great elm in mid-ground and a sky behind that simply glowed. Not one picture could be termed effusive.

'Ah, there's nothing worse than getting old', she said wearily, quite out of tune. ' "Time's winged chariot hurrying near . . ." '

On this he caught her up. They were moments when they could turn towards each other again, as though no argument had happened. But it was clutching at straws now.

'Nonsense! You're not old, Nonnie. For that matter there's nothing worse than being young. Here I am, twenty, over two years at Cambridge, and what have I done? What am I good for? Europe is about to go under to the Germans, all the things you and I live for are in danger, men are dying to defend them, and here we are arguing about pacifism! What good am I . . . ?'

He had never dared go so far. Her Quaker philosophy was paramount in her life, its implicit pacifism unassailable in her view. Even to question it amounted to treachery, a heresy not to be hinted at.

She came from a long line of Quakers, while his own parents, ever diffident and earnest in their search for truth, had been 'Attenders' only. He too was an 'Attender', a position either of preparation for full membership, even a sort of initiation – or an ambiguity offering easier release from the gentle constraints of this most tolerant of faiths should they prove too great in their inward dictates.

'I suppose you will ask me next,' she replied with an asperity even more uncharacteristic, 'what we should do if the Germans rape our grandmothers. Or should we call them Huns?'

He had not seen her quite so roused, ever.

'Let me tell you, William,' she went on, 'that I've seen what happens. I'm old enough to have seen and remembered. That silly Boer War! And look at the present situation in France. Whole nations locked together in a hopeless state of attrition, solving nothing, losing everything, throwing young lives away. Pride, sheer national pride, that's all it is – when a few words of peace on either side would solve more. Whoever wins this war will prove only one thing: who is

16

strongest. Truth won't prevail, only strength, only he who can last it out.'

He had not realised she could be so angry. And she was right – if only it were as simple as that. But it wasn't. He felt the betrayal of his stance, his particular treachery. He knew how deeply his arguments must wound her, yet he was determined that this issue should be brought out into the light and debated once and for all, however difficult she made it. The second issue could wait a while. He wondered guiltily if Nonnie knew what was going on in the streets, what ordinary people were thinking and feeling.

As she confronted him now, with back straight and head high, she looked through the plain silver-rimmed glasses at him and thought how like his father he was in many ways – how unlike in others. There was the same heavy lick of dark hair across his forehead, the same dark brow that almost met over the long straight nose, and with it all, a certain tautness of the skin that made a smile almost unnatural, as though requiring a physical effort to transcend its constraints. The grace and yet austerity of late Gothic, she thought.

She could detect no sign of actual unhappiness in the dark face, but there was something, the way he hung his head slightly to one side and let his shoulders hang loosely, which as far as she was concerned was a fall from grace, and made her want to tell him to brace up. Yet there was something hard and military about telling a young man to brace up. Miss Pomfret was an example of constant self-discipline and self-correction – and she wished William to be likewise.

Had she failed him in some respect? At twenty, he ought to have looked happier. She did not know whether he was happy or unhappy. Why think in terms of either? Happiness was not a right, after all, and despite his deprivation of parents, she felt in all honesty and humility that she had given him everything she could, had eased life for him in such a way that all things might be possible. Yet in relation to both William and to his father earlier, she would admit to a certain impatience on her part, which deeply disturbed her desire and pursuit of the whole. Was it not true that both father and son exuded a feeling that the gods were against them? A tinge as though the universe might have been arranged a little better for them personally . . . That was a wicked thought, which she quickly corrected. After all, in each case Providence might have been kinder; the father losing his wife so early, the son losing both parents. How much she might have helped had she been allowed.

17

So the moments of impatience came inevitably – and were duly corrected. There were moments when her daily habit of self-command gave way, however. If she had loved the father quietly, deeply but unrequitedly, did that disqualify her from what she could only think of as the secret of life, since the here and now were quite as important, certainly more vital to present living, than the hereafter? Her slight unorthodoxy, her independence of the more ready consolation of religion, her rejection of what she called 'its sillier side', were in one way a bulwark, but left her exposed to these almost irrational moments of impatience.

Yes, his father in many ways. And her heart went out to him. There were the same endearing intimations of an incapacity to cope with life's rough edges, inviting protectiveness, a womanly firmness and control. But in William she detected a slight difference here. Whereas the father had been quite, quite ineffectual, burning away his shortened, anxious life with an unbending routine and regularity that it would have seemed sacrilegious to disturb, the son showed a streak of stubbornness about certain things – the things he cared for – about being selfish even where his personal interests might be at risk. And that, so far, had been fine in her view, except for a momentary irrationality about it on occasion, very rarely, but most noticeable when it flashed through him.

In effect, it led him inexorably towards mistakes that her instinct and normal protectiveness would have prevented, but when those moments came she detected the slight defiant stiffening, almost a declaration that, despite her moral and legal guardianship, he was, or was about to be, a man of independent means. At such moments, she knew that anything she might say to protect him would be misconstrued, would be counter-productive, and was better left unsaid, to dissolve if possible into a Quakerly silence.

To words he would react, whereas silence at least would give him pause and *ex opere operato* would heal the impending breach between them. For however upright she might be, both in posture and in moral rectitude, and indeed in a certain imperviousness to life's barbs, it would be heartbreak for her should this son of his father in the least thing turn against her.

In one respect alone the darkness in him, the withdrawn stubbornness that held her off with an abruptness that augured hostility should she be foolish enough to press, descended when the second issue might just occur: of a girl, of love, of romance – she was lost for a verbal

18

image of it and never quite put it to herself frankly, except to remind herself that he was, well, nearly twenty-one.

However it might be, however it was said, Miss Pomfret knew it was to be the second issue between them. That was a pity, for should it not have been a matter for ease and rejoicing? But it had become difficult, without even being mooted.

She sensed a certain little deception, could not quite put her finger on it. She had not handled it well – in fact had not handled it at all, out of ignorance and incapacity she now regretted in more ways than one. She evaded it. Yet in her position as surrogate parent, nay mother, she felt some guilt about it, as though there were some duty she ought to fulfil, perhaps some advice to offer, an opportunity to provide for meeting somebody, if indeed there were somebody, and she half suspected there was. The guilt (or, less harshly, the want) she felt in herself was not over the will to help or advise so much as not knowing the first thing about it. She felt she ought to know more, to discuss it with somebody else. She felt short on what she could only think of as actual motherhood, and she felt the want keenly at certain moments when he returned home and discussed this or that aspect of his life at Cambridge, in particular his fellow undergraduates, with an ease and assurance she found comforting.

But when, having completed the first hour or so in light conversation, he excused himself and retired to his room, he would not appear for as long as two hours or more, and when finally he did, it was with a letter in his hand which obviously he did not wish to discuss in any way. Of course, he had every right to such privacy – that she realised, and would not infringe in the least detail. It irritated her however. It was just the fact that he so obviously did not wish to discuss it that gave her unease.

On the first occasion, she had innocently suggested that Mary, their ever-faithful maid, would post the letter for him if he left it on the hall table, but at once the slight darkness appeared on his face and he insisted on taking Sally, the old Labrador, for a walk while he posted the letter. It happened on several occasions; he established the ritual so firmly that she dared not interfere, indeed would not wish to, except that at those moments the question arose in her mind of her incapacity to guide or assist should the need arise. She could not even imagine quite how the need might arise, but felt it might and she would not know how to recognise it and respond to it. She hoped that whatever or whoever the letters might concern, he would one day wish to talk it over with her. It was the circumstances in which they might begin that agitated her.

She found herself, in the usual silence between them, dwelling more on this second issue, when what he was constantly broaching lately was the first. Was that the female in her, looking for the problems of ... romance? ... when what men worried over, especially these days, was war. So she held her peace mostly, and fretted over it quietly out of a sort of conscience.

She dared not admit it, he was her all. In some ways she had pared life to the bone, sloughed off any possible indulgence beyond the water-colour collection and certain books, till she was in a way unassailable. That she might be vulnerable in her purity and austerity was of course just apparent in the way she picked up the end of a sentence before you could quite finish, in the occasional flash of her eyes, defying challenge to some extreme stand she might have taken.

That the austerity did not extend downwards to living without cook, housemaid and the general accoutrements of middle-class, or rather merchant-class life as she would have preferred to call it, was something that increasingly disturbed William on his side as political awareness gradually informed his slowly developing sensibility.

The causes of separation and division, of class distinctions, worried him – of Miss Pomfret's and his own station above those who ministered to their daily needs. Of the effect that immediate cancelling of it might have he did not think: of Cook's possible unemployment or Mary's being put out on the street. It was the faint distaste of privilege that rankled rather than the dependence of the underprivileged.

Except for rare glimpses of the occupants of Miss Pomfret's home for 'fallen women', of whom he heard occasional remarks (since this amounted to her vocation, her good works, the other side to her absolute purity and spiritual essence, the Martha side complementing her more natural Mary side) he was carefully shielded from the question or the touch of poverty. In his rooms at Cambridge he might ruminate on the essential comfort of their life, and contrast it with a few sights he was beginning to register on occasional visits to London. But in her presence, under the steady gaze of those penetrating blue eyes under the glasses, he had never dreamt of questioning. She was ageless, alert, strangely imperious, even in her silences and composure. But the contradictions within himself disturbed him even more deeply. He did have questions, but her eyes, and the quick arrest of any breath of discomfort in the air, silenced them even when he felt them on his lips.

'I've never accepted that old chestnut about Huns raping our grand-mothers', he replied suddenly, out of a deep, deep silence. 'You know that, Nonnie. All the same, the nations are locked in a war of attrition with neither side able to move – but regardless of grandmothers, what about Belgium? She's being raped, if you like. What do we do about that? Tell me!'

He realised he was almost shouting, here in this lovely room over-looking the old walled garden in the winter light, with the water-colours glowing in their exquisitely lined mounts all round the walls.

Here they had discussed the virtues of Cotman's early work, and the vices of his later use of body-colour and the consequent loss of transparency. That too was a heresy, Cotman's descent from the limpid purity and transparency of water-colour. And they had loved every minute of that. She had been more than a mother in some ways, she had been teacher of facts, mentor of life's ways. Her work on the home for 'fallen women' had always moved him. He knew how much of her heart she gave, how much of her inherited wealth and privilege she wished to share with those who had 'fallen', and yet how much of both love and inheritance (though he had little need of the latter) was held back for him.

'William,' she answered, only half patiently, 'you've had a hard term, I'm sure. Let's leave things awhile. Ring for Mary. Let's have tea early, while this light holds. Shall we?'

The crocheted antimacassars over the chair-backs held his gaze. The argument was too quick, all this of grandmothers and rape, requiring an answer, was too precipitate for him. He dwelt a moment on the comfortable old chairs whose black horsehair provided such sharp contrast to the white antimacassars, so white as almost to hurt in this strange late light.

He wanted to slow things down, to think it all out, aloud if neces-sary, and used as both he and Miss Pomfret were to silence between them, she allowed him the time. The drawing-room gave directly through tall french windows on to a walled garden.

For a moment, he ceased his restless pacing and looked out. Even a sparrow scuffing up grass sweepings would be something to dwell upon. But no, not even a sparrow was about at this dead period of the year. He moved on, lightly he fingered the marble bookend which with its partner clamped the few books of daily reading on the maho-gany table: William Penn's *A Collection of the Works*, George Fox's *Journal* and *Advices and Queries*. Were even these to be denied, the *vade mecum* of the Quaker way of life?

Slowly he moved towards the fireplace, slid a finger idly along the mantelshelf as though to catalogue its burden of two great bluejohn vases and a brass chiming-clock and to take in the Turner water-colour which held pride of place overhead.

How strange that the breach between them had grown so quickly and so deep. It was unthinkable; he was unprepared for it. As well as Miss Pomfret, Friends' School had been the gentlest of educations for life. In his rare contacts with boys of other denominational schools, he had realised how undogmatic his own schooling had been when he came to Miss Pomfret. There was no great gulf dividing the two halves of his life. His various preoccupations caused her no disturbance, and if his option for History proved no great link between them, at least they shared an interest in landscape and enjoyed together a great feeling for it in their different ways, especially in summer.

They would retire to a small house she had in Wensleydale. It took most of the day in the train with three changes, but they both exulted in it once they arrived. Daniel Crowther, the neighbouring farmer, was always warned by letter the previous week and met them at the station on their arrival with his sturdy cob and float. Miss Pomfret, despite her modest needs in life, always took Cook and Mary, and except that they spent most of their days outside when it was fine, life continued much the same. Only vaguely remembering his father, and his mother not at all, it never struck William as strange that he should spend his life with a lady who could be described as 'of advancing years'. Her gentle, yet trenchant way of speaking and her flexibility of mind were in some ways younger than his own. He spoke slowly, hesitating just slightly, articulating every phrase.

She dabbled, as she put it, 'in the most appalling water-colours'. He, clad in his knickerbockers, woollen stockings and fell-boots, climbed the moors and spent hours among the limestone scaurs that rose, like a final rampart, over the dale. Looking back, this solitariness, arising out of orphanhood, was his real life, his inner life, a life which Miss Pomfret discerned quite clearly from the beginning when, bewildered but only somewhat bereft (he and his father had never been close), he was finally committed to her care as a boy of fourteen.

His quietness, even his slowness of speech, augured well for an adventure in education and upbringing which she had never dreamt would come her way. Until he was fourteen, he had called her 'Miss Pomfret'. She had not demurred at the implication of formality. Then, as fourteen was the age when boys were 'breeched' and donned long trousers, and he was now, so to speak, completely hers, she had tackled him that first Christmas after his father's death.

As soon as he returned from school for the holidays and the first greetings were over, she said, 'Do you not think, William, that the time has come when you might *not* call me "Miss Pomfret"? This has been your home for some time now, you are no longer a child, and it is good to start as we mean to continue.'

'It has never occurred to me to address you otherwise. But I would love not to, if I may.'

She had always encouraged candour, and it was a start to call her nothing. She had always ended her letters 'Affectionately yours, N.M.P.' And for the life of him, he could not remember her being addressed, even among friends and Friends, other than as 'Miss Pomfret'.

'We have a difficulty there, I'm afraid', she replied. 'For some reason my parents named me Non McKenzie. N-O-N. From what I've never discovered, unless it were to be different from any other name – and I can believe *that*, remembering my parents. I've learnt since that it was a Welsh saint's name. I'll believe anything of the Welsh! But where my parents got it from I cannot think . . .' She smiled a little, in memory. 'They were both great eccentrics. The McKenzie came from one of my father's best friends, an Edinburgh Quaker. I often thought he wished I'd been a boy, to use it as a first name . . . As you know, most people insist on calling me "Miss Pomfret". Do you recall hearing me called otherwise?'

She was curious to know. Was it a sign of a want of intimacy in her life that so few, or none, got beyond the formality of her surname? Or was it that the rather odd forename presented some difficulty to Friends, whose normal usage was simply to use forename rather than Mr, Mrs or Miss, among themselves?

He hesitated, trying to remember.

'I'm afraid not,' he said, not looking her in the face, for fear she might feel hurt.

'I rather thought so. Perhaps it's my own fault. Do you never recall your father calling me anything?'

The memory hurt as she passed it across her mind in this exchange with his son. As she searched William's eyes, she reflected that they were both orphans: he sadly so young, she expectedly so since she was, well, 'getting on in life'. They were alike in their solitariness, their essential privacy.

Again he took his time, searching in his mind back over what years he could remember. He could see things, meetings, mutual house visits. But he could hear nothing.

'No, I can't remember how my father addressed you. Was it not "Miss Pomfret"?'

'No, my dear', she replied. 'He was one of the very few who called me Nonnie. That was my name among my childhood friends and my family. As I've grown older, fewer and fewer people seem to have taken the privilege – if it *is* a privilege', she added shyly. 'Perhaps your father refrained from using it in your presence. That was just like him. He was so very reticent.'

The boy did not quite grasp the impact of that, but the sadness of it struck him. Young though he was, he sensed that it mattered, was a *cri-de-coeur*.

The silence between them, like this one as he simply stood there, presented no difficulty. Stillness, quietness of the spirit, the indwelling, were in fact quite the opposite, and if during Sunday meeting at Friends' House only one spoke during the entire hour, no one thought anything of it. It was the patient sitting in silence, waiting on the spirit, that mattered and provided the *raison d'être* of a gathering of kindred souls.

'Well then,' she said, hands clasped in her lap, and with a loving smile through her plain spectacles, 'I think you might honour your father's memory by calling me "Nonnie", as he did. Do you not think it right and proper?'

'Nonnie, I will,' he replied with a simplicity and directness she approved.

It had been broken, the last barrier between them; the formality of 'Miss Pomfret' had been a barrier in a relationship that had had to grow from the first assumptions of adoption rather than from the nursery. For him, she was parent – both father and mother in one.

It was always a joy to return to her, yet he missed the 'Father' and 'Mother' of other boys and had longed for the easy intimacy they mostly, if not always, conveyed.

This address of each other had always intrigued him, and it set him apart from his companions. The memory of this episode, of her shy but firm permission to call her 'Nonnie', now coloured the present, quite hostile silence between them. With his slow smile, he stopped his pacing and turned to her again.

Still, he was reluctant to arrest the debate, however slow and painful its course. He hesitated as yet to ring for Mary, wished desperately to take Nonnie into his confidence. But the glasses shielded her. He could not find the words. He went to the bell, then turned abruptly.

'Nonnie,' he said, almost in a whisper, 'Nonnie, I have to tell you. I've enlisted. I called on my way here from the station yesterday. They said I'd hear in a matter of . . .'

'What! You've enlisted – to join the Army?'

So that was what he had meant by 'out of his hands'.

'Yes. And because of Cambridge and all that, they said I'd probably be offered a commission.' Was that not pitching things a bit high?

That she had not guessed it at all shocked her as much as the fact. William's shoulders slumped apologetically as he watched her take it in. Even as he uttered the words he could see that their effect on Miss Pomfret was like a body blow. She clutched at the edges of her black crocheted shawl and gazed at him in stupor through her glasses.

From a bond of peace and love between them and others, he knew she was grappling frantically with the image of him outside that peace and love, of his carrying arms and leading others in violence against other men. He knew, as she gazed, that what he had just declared was unthinkable to her. The thought of a lethal weapon in his grasp, ready if duty called to strike down, to kill, was unimaginable.

She turned away, still grasping her shawl tightly round her shoulders, as if fending off some evil presence. The debate on peace or war at a time like this was natural – but this act, this precipitate act of his, in the middle of the debate was not only a betrayal of her, of *their* principles, but of the bond between them. How could it have happened so quickly, so easily?

The hurt was too great. She could not look at him. She flung out of the room, and he could hear her ascending the stairs to her bedroom.

William knew that Nonnie was about to descend into one of her rare destructive silences. He was not finished yet. There was the second person to introduce into their lives. He had planned to bring up both issues at once – if 'planned' was the word to describe the drift towards a log-jam of confused feelings between Nonnie and himself.

He had miscalculated. While there had been one or two indiscretions, or deceptions, to confess, he might have got to the end of the matter without alienating Nonnie. But confession is never easy, and the enlistment had occupied the forefront of his mind as they endlessly debated the war.

Once again, Nonnie's departure had prevented it. The shock of one issue between them (of peace or war) was too much. Was he being insensitive? Were there areas of Nonnie's sensibilities he had offended needlessly, not only by what he had just declared, but by his way of saying it? Yet there seemed no other way of doing it. The second matter, therefore, must wait yet again.

For one thing, there was the previous weekend, illicit in its way if otherwise innocent. He would have liked to get it off his chest. He would not wish his conscience about it to drag on indefinitely, not now that he had enlisted.

It was not so much what he—what they—had done, as the manner of its doing. It was simply that the whole thing between Laura and him and Nonnie had started awkwardly and suddenly. At the time, he had not thought it mattered. Even posting a letter had now become a tiny deception each time, to avoid questions he would find it hard to answer.

Now he longed to clear the whole thing up, along with this dreadful business of enlisting. Indeed, in his tormented mind the two issues were inextricably involved. Having declared his decision on the first, he had hoped the second would follow with comparative ease.

Joining what he thought of as the 'moral lump' to free Belgium of her German oppressors was by now a firm conviction with him. It was signed and sealed, out of his hands, beyond argument. So the second issue loomed ever larger now, and as Nonnie swept past him, speechless with what he construed as rare anger, he felt the want of confession even more. Turning to the mantel-shelf again, he covered his eyes with his hand, as though in pain.

When supper was brought in, Cook was appalled that Miss Pomfret had not come down. William ate alone. Mutely, old Sally gazed up at him with great eyes, as though to offer help in a situation clearly out of joint. He brought his hand down to stroke the old grey muzzle in acknowledgement.

The decision was made, disclosed. He would hold fast. He had not made it lightly; it had cost too much inner torment to even think of changing it, whatever Nonnie might think or say. The 'confession' however must wait. Each of us, he mused, is a vessel of life, and there's a limit to how much it will hold at any given time. For the present, Nonnie must be spared further confession; his decision to enlist was almost more than she should be expected to take. Ought he to have broached the two issues the other way round? But the thought of still having to announce his enlistment horrified him. He had been right.

In this mood of vacillation, he went to the door where the dog-lead hung from the knob. With a seductive shuffle, Sally sidled up to him, held her head patiently for the lead, and out they went into the raw November air. He headed, deliberately, towards the main tram route about two hundred yards away, towards the sociably clanging noise of the trams.

The silences with Nonnie, his long delayed announcement of enlistment, and the further delay of the second issue, were all suddenly too much. And he had a letter to post, written hastily before supper and telling Laura that he had enlisted.

Sensing there was no urgency whatsoever on this outing, Sally sniffed every lamp-post, gatepost or shrub in their funereal progress, as if to declare that however inadequate the years may leave one, nevertheless standards must be maintained and rituals even more strictly observed. William was so little anxious to return home that he allowed Sally every indulgence. He had too much to think about. The step had been taken, irrevocably. He knew that he must leave Nonnie awhile, to take the blow.

It was the second issue which concerned William Dobie as he pushed the letter home in the pillar-box. He would talk it over with Nonnie. There was no reason in the world why not. It was just that, as with her, he could not find the words nor imagine the circumstances in which they might begin.

If his joining up had caused a breach, then the news that Laura Venables and he had an 'understanding' was hardly likely to help. As it was, Nonnie did not even know of her existence.

There were areas in Laura's world of which Nonnie would not approve. All this possibility of a distance between Nonnie and himself had arisen in the last term. Now even posting a letter to Laura was a painful business, and he was angry with himself for having started off by making it difficult. Now he could only wait for an opportune moment to introduce the name. That seemed further away than ever after his recent disclosure about joining the army.

Laura's keen involvement in the women's suffrage movement would not worry Nonnie, indeed, would stimulate some pert remarks, for Nonnie was a stout feminist. But Laura's suffragettism went along with a whole lot of uninhibited expressions that Nonnie would abhor with a severity he knew only too well. Perhaps severity was too hard a word. When, he asked himself, had Nonnie been severe? No, it was a silence in her that he feared, a momentary pursing of the lips. And, in any case, was he sure what his relations with Laura were, except that they were definite?

Laura had a powerful effect on him, and it doubled his life, so to speak – there was *he* (whom he thought he understood), and there was this new being whom Laura stimulated. Cambridge had lifted certain veils which allowed him to think in terms of sexual awakening with little inhibition (although he would be lost in trying to discuss it with anyone). No, it was more than that. Hitherto he had been a book waiting to be written. And Laura, at once, from the very first, the very odd meeting, was now writing it.

He had been in London with Litherland, a fellow undergraduate, a few weeks previously at the beginning of term, visiting a 'settlement' that Litherland was in charge of, or was patron of (William never quite knew, except that Litherland's zeal had soon suborned him to the cause of drying out people). It was a house in Stepney that had seen better days and now housed distressed alcoholics.

He could always discuss Litherland's activities with Nonnie, indeed she waited eagerly for news each time he returned home. Litherland's ardent teetotal campaigning answered his own earnestness. Nonnie often laughed at William's accounts of the more bizarre events at the settlement, in spite of their mutual recognition of the need for the cause, with gin all too readily available. Nor did Nonnie flinch when William went into the more sordid details.

What, for the life of him, he could not discuss with her was that first odd meeting, when he and Litherland, on leaving the settlement, had seen a demonstration coming towards them. Whatever it was, the procession of women was provoking anger in the street. Men jostled with the demonstrators, pulling down banners and showing signs of actual violence.

As they got nearer, the young men saw that the demonstration was in the cause of women's suffrage. It was violent indeed; abuse was flying freely from the crowd, banners came down in a flurry of fisticuffs, and they saw women lying on the road in passive resistance to the violence.

They felt they could not help. It was all too evident that the women in their pacifist response were making their point most effectively. But when William saw a burly man go up to one young woman, kicking her as she lay, he suddenly rushed over, grabbed at the man's collar and pulled him away.

The man flung back at him, but William at once exceeded the bounds of merely protecting himself by laying into the man with a passion. He did not quite know what he was doing. Something about a man kicking a defenceless woman made him lash out blindly. It was an uncouth bundling and pushing, rather than actual blows (which William would not know how to deliver in any way that would hurt a man), and when the man saw that his kick had drawn blood from the woman's scalp, he lost nerve rather than gave way. He turned and was lost in the heaving crowd.

William bent over the woman, who seemed to be unconscious. As he turned her gently to see what damage there was, he saw that she was very young. She looked at him with a fearless expression, as though to say that man though he might be, and therefore the stronger, he could do nothing to shake her spirit or her belief in the cause.

But the cut looked bad, possibly requiring stitches. She did not resist when she realised he was not about to deliver another blow. He raised her to her feet and helped her to the pavement. She was not entirely in command of her senses, and in no time, with Litherland's help, William was half dragging, half walking her to the settlement in Stepney near by.

All that: women in the streets, men laying hands on them, the threat of violence towards a cause that would surely appeal to Nonnie . . . It was something entirely alien to their pacific life together; no wonder he had not known how to begin to explain!

Then Laura's "Take your bloody hands off me!" uttered with vehemence as she came round and saw William trying to clean the scalp wound – how would Nonnie have reacted to that as a first utterance?

As she quickly recovered her wits and guessed that they did, in fact, mean to help her in a most disinterested way – that is, in a non-specifically male sense – she allowed them to attend to the wound on her scalp.

It was slighter than they had thought, a wound not unknown at the settlement, and one resident showed the greatest interest with the knowing air of a man who had, in his time, suffered much the same on more than one occasion.

'Anybody got a cigarette?' she asked.

Since neither Dobie nor Litherland smoked, the resident lovingly moved in on the scene.

'Here, darlin', 'ave one on me.' And he held a match to her that might well have set his breath alight, but which he offered shakily with a practised tenderness which left the two undergraduates speechless.

What next? That was the question. Should she be allowed to return to the demonstration? That was obviously her idea. The cigarette was less an indulgence than a stimulus to recovery and return to the fray. But when she stood, she swayed, and Dobie caught her before she fell.

'Concussion?' he signalled across to Litherland, who knew such cases well, knew when the doctor was needed and when not, knew the cost, and also the impatience of most doctors being called out at weekends on such cases of collision with lamp-posts.

'No need for the doc, I think,' said Litherland, 'but we'd better see her home, just in case ...'

'Fitzroy Square', she said when asked, realising that for the moment she was defeated and had no choice.

The house in Fitzroy Square puzzled Dobie. There seemed to be men, and women, independent of each other, on every floor – as though it were another 'settlement' with the malady not alcohol, rather a high-flown academic euphoria, judging by the badinage. The ease with which they came and went, leaving doors ajar and generally ignoring custom and convention, intrigued Dobie.

Before they left her in her top-floor flat which she shared with her sister (to Dobie's relief, in *this* house, he did not know why), he asked for her name, 'in case it might be necessary ...'

As she looked at him with large, candid eyes, she laughed a little at the silly excuse, in spite of the pain in her scalp wound.

'Laura – Laura Venables ... and yours?' She seemed uninterested in Litherland, but William took it that she meant the one in charge of the settlement.

'He's called Litherland, Bob Litherland', he said.

'No, yours, idiot!'

The sheer directness startled him. Yet the eyes were laughing, unmalicious, perhaps a little rueful from the ache in her head. It was a kind of humour, a directness of approach to people that he would have to get used to.

Dark, slightly waving hair, touched by red, and slightly dishevelled from her adventure; laughing eyes that, he could tell, would enjoy mischief; long, slender nose; an almost Latin colour overall, with lips that were all too ready to talk. He had never quite taken in a woman's face before, but his eyes would not stop gazing. She obviously required a response; her expression brooked no delay.

'Oh, I'm sorry,' he said lamely, 'mine's William Dobie.'

'Nice', she said with a smile that enchanted him. 'Good old English name, simple... Well, thanks for bringing me home, William Dobie.'

'Will you be all right?'

He was reluctant to go, but realised they had done their duty and ought to leave without more fuss.

'I'll be all right if I know you're coming back to see me. You seem to be my self-appointed doctor. Isn't it etiquette for a doctor to come back to see his patient?'

He did not have the nerve to take up her invitation and left it in the air. But he felt sad, and the invitation tormented him.

And so, next time he went home, after chatting with Nonnie over this and that, he went upstairs to his room and wrote to the address in Fitzroy Square, giving Cambridge as his address, and feeling decidedly furtive about the whole operation in relation to Nonnie.

If the issue of peace and war could never be settled between them now, this little matter could hardly be mentioned even – not while the great gulf continued to exist. And Nonnie, displaying every sign of feminine awareness of a letter in his hand, had suggested that Mary should post it. He had resisted the suggestion, and from that first furtive little move he dated the beginning of the rift between them.

The two things, enlistment and Laura, went oddly together. But that was life. It was Laura – or rather the posting of that first tentative letter – that started it off, and since then both issues had accelerated at such an alarming rate that by now he felt Nonnie receding into a distance he had not thought possible. The thought saddened him. Were they about to quarrel?

That he could not believe, but he felt the silence descending even so. He derived no comfort from it at a time when, like every other young man of his age, decisions were having to be made one way or another. With posters on every corner saying 'Your country needs you', it was his generation that was indicated, and one could not stand aside

31

easily. It was no time to quarrel.

White feathers were flying, and if he felt it right to withstand that particular taunt, he would. By now, however, he was convinced that the pacifist position was no longer practicable, or even valid, in the present case of Belgium. He was convinced and had no regrets intellectually. But in other ways he felt clumsy and insensitive in relation to Nonnie.

He might have taken more time, allowed her to debate it further before springing this on her – and at least he might have got the whole business of Laura off his chest first, for that was real enough by now and the last thing he wanted was to go on being furtive about it.

When Laura had promptly answered that first enquiring letter (under his Cambridge address), it was with a positive assurance that caught him off balance. He had told himself – believing himself to be the first man ever to have told himself – that he did not expect a reply. As to writing to her in the first place, he had no doubt: those dark Pre-Raphaelite looks had captured him at first sight, and the directness of her approach had delighted him.

She replied that, yes, she had fully recovered, 'Thank you, William Dobie', but she was deeply hurt that he, her 'medical adviser', had not been back to check. To enable him to give her ' a clean bill of health', therefore, she intended visiting Cambridge that very Saturday.

He had only to confirm – and that he promptly did, with a beating heart. By now, he was not sure about any of it. Had he ventured too far? This girl's assurance bordered on boldness, and that could mean experience, of what kind he could not tell, but experience at any rate. He felt he might not be able to cope with that, since he was himself totally devoid of it. Did not the intimation of experience cancel out that image of pristine innocence he had fondly nurtured since first helping her up off the road? He hated to adjust, preferring to keep that first image fresh till they met again, and then to see.

Nevertheless, she was arriving at Cambridge and that was that. There was something vaguely improper about the apparent absence of a chaperon, though judging by the bold tone of the letter and the confidence with which Laura seemed to make plans, she would probably dismiss that as stuffy. He could not help agreeing and hoped she would stand by her convictions. In short, he had no experience of 'experience' in a woman, did not know what to expect.

32

Of one thing she seemed sure, that William Dobie would be at the station to meet her off the 12.45 and perhaps they could go somewhere to luncheon, 'when you can assess my health, since you ask about it . . .' The round girlish hand but firmness of style and expression brooked no negatives. But supposing she might have a chaperon of some sort, he asked Robert Litherland if he would care to be in attendance. But the redoubtable servant of distressed alcoholics was not to be deflected from his weekend work at the settlement in Stepney, and with a fluttering heart Dobie found himself alone, anxiously scanning the windows of the train as it drew into the platform. At first sight, he was astonished.

She was alone. Away from the dishevelment of the demonstration, Laura was well groomed. The Pre-Raphaelite impression was doubly enhanced by a long chiffon scarf which she had tied round her brow. The scarf trailed gloriously in the draught of the train as the compartment came past him. All his doubts fell away at once. He ran but she had already opened the door and was out before he could do the honours.

Remembering her cause he reflected that she might have views about the conventional honours, for clearly she had views, of all kinds. What should he do? What say?

'William Dobie!' she cried delighted, 'William Dobie, I knew you would come!'

'Miss Venables, how nice of you to come. Are you. . . ?'

'Oh rot! I shall call you Mr Dobie if you insist on that sort of polite nonsense. You know my name. Don't dissemble. I distinctly remember telling you, William Dobie!'

'You look different somehow.'

'I thought today I wouldn't wear sensible clothes', she said, regretting saying it at once. She was conscious that it mattered, might explain something different that she saw reflected in his eyes in their initial response. Yet she fretted over it.

She had spent more time than usual at the mirror – an adjunct of feminine dependence that the women's movement implicitly eschewed. If women were to take their rightful place in society, might not sensible clothes be one external requisite? On this delicate point of attractive clothes she felt anything but confident. It was all so calculated to captivate and, of course, to be captured. Yet here she was in a creation of black-and-gold silk with the chiffon scarf the final touch that had taken quite ten minutes of careful adjustment.

33

Nor was she altogether convinced by her own reasoning concerning footwear. Why was it that up till now she had almost, though not quite, preferred sensible boots to decidedly feminine slippers – and now with William Dobie in the offing would not be seen dead in anything less than a rather dainty pair of shoes picked up in Oxford Street the day before? She only hoped their perambulations through Cambridge would not be too long. That her world of beliefs was set for collision with another might have troubled her had it not been for the extraordinary comfort and pleasure she derived from simply being in his presence.

One had to be ready for so much in life! What education she had enjoyed was addressed to preparing her for life to be sure, but Aunt Venables had been most explicit that that meant preparing for its *dangers*. What had not been done was to prepare her for the delight she felt at the memory of this strange, inscrutable man who had helped her off the Whitechapel Road and at the thought of seeing him again.

She might have been 'brought out' more rather than repressed. Why did no one educate you to expect a William Dobie? She might have been less confused, she thought, as she chattered away, conscious of – well – sweeping him off his feet.

She could see it before her: the sheer male fright before the guile of the female. She could have wished for something better. The last thing she wanted was to be guilty of mere feminine sauce in this masculine sanctum of scholarship.

Yet she could not help herself. If she had been prepared, educated, for the delight as much as for the danger, she might have behaved differently. Yet she also enjoyed the confusion of those first few moments and wondered if he, so patently confused, was aware that she was even more so, despite her gay façade. She saw that he was taking her in all over again, the dishevelled girl he had helped off the road, scalp bleeding, wearing severely sensible clothes and so full of the cause as to virtually spit at him, 'Take your bloody hands off me!'. What had she to do with the girl jumping gaily off a train, dressed to kill, with a scarf trailing feminine chic among the plebeian grey of the passengers rushing to the exit?

He was dumbfounded. Experience. . . ? Altogether, he too was confused. From a contented bachelor existence, disturbed only by cogitations on his personal position as a pacifist in this dreadful, all-embracing war, he was suddenly escorting a young woman he had met but once in accidental circumstances.

He had hardly spoken, much less acted. He was sure of one thing however, that a railway station must be left, one way or another.

'Do you know Cambridge?' he asked as the cab trundled along towards the town. He was enjoying the intimacy of sitting next to this strange girl.

'Of course not.' She turned to look into his eyes, as though to confirm her image of him. 'It's thoroughly male. Cambridge is the sort of place that believes women have no brains. Decoration, that's all we are in Cambridge. Do you like *my* decoration?' she asked playfully, fingering the trailing chiffon.

'It's very nice.'

'Is that all? – and I tried so hard to impress my "doctor"!'

And he smiled, slowly. He was getting her measure. 'It's beautiful', he said. And looking her full in the face, to confirm *his* image, he thought: 'How lovely she is, half wild, half sophisticated . . . I don't know what . . .' He was finding it easier to fall into her ways.

'Laura,' he said. He could see this delighted her, the first use of her name. 'Laura, I thought we would eat at a favourite place of mine and, since it's a lovely day, we might walk along the Backs.'

'William Dobie, that's delightful!' She descended from the cab and looked him full in the eyes as he dared to offer his hand.

He loved the way she closed her hands palm to palm in childish glee. Threading their way along the narrow pavements, he did what every undergraduate feels obliged to do for strangers: he began to describe the University.

'That's Peterhouse, the oldest college. Thirteenth-century, I think', he said, more by way of covering his confusion than of imparting information. But nothing escaped her, it seemed.

'Oh, so that's Peterhouse.' She gave an air of knowing.

'Why, do you know it?'

'No, of course not. But I know of it. I know all about this place. I'd pull it down if I had my way. D'you know a woman can study all she likes, but places like this won't award her a degree?'

'Oh, really? I didn't know that. I must say it just hadn't occurred to me.'

He had learnt already that on the cause of women she was formidable – and in his own tormented debate with himself, he wondered if he had met a modern Lysistrata. On *that* lady's cause, their respective

35

dominant social and political interests met, so there was hope.

Then, earnestly looking at her, he said, 'You wouldn't actually pull it down, would you? It's so historic and beautiful, don't you think?'

'Well, I'll concede you your buildings. But the whole academic structure I mean – not a woman in attendance, never mind in a position of power.'

'Well, there *is* Girton, of course.' But she did not want to hear that apparently. Whatever Providence had arranged in the way of their first meeting, each was intent on gazing at the other, to fill out that first momentary image, she confident in her tone and manner, he diffident at first, but soon warming to her eyes and voice. For she was outrageous occasionally.

He had not had time to digest her views on women's suffrage and would have felt threatened in a way had she not laced them throughout with a humour that forced that slow smile, almost in spite of himself.

'I'll grant you Girton,' she said. Apparently she missed nothing. 'But where is it in all this great wedding cake?' He had to say he did not know.

'You must give me time,' he said, 'I haven't given much thought to women's suffrage. To be honest, they work us so hard here that I haven't given women a thought, I must confess.'

'Except me?'

'Except you, Laura.' And he saw that she was pleased.

But her boldness terrified him. He took it up however.

'And you?' he said, gazing into her eyes and glad of this chance to examine her boldness by counter-attack.

'What? Thought about women? Of course, you know that, surely.'

But he was determined the chance should not slip.

'No, I mean men,' he persisted.

She tossed her head. The chiffon rustled over her shoulders.

'Not a thought, I must confess', she replied, deliberately mimicking his solemn way of putting it.

'Except me?'

How she laughed, cornered by her own boldness.

'Except you, William Dobie.' And their hands met for a brief moment.

Her lightness and his earnestness were two poles of the same magnet as their hands met and parted. 'Except me,' he thought, and still could not work it out, delighted though he was.

Wherefore the boldness, he wondered, if not with other men? That house in Fitzroy Square, for instance, where did that figure, with all those strange characters of both sexes wandering in and out of rooms?

With his most passionate sense of privacy, that was a boldness he found difficult to understand or approve. But, at least, it was not the sort of boldness, or experience, that he had at first conjectured. It was more academic in a way, a freedom rather than boldness, the freedom exercised by his fellow undergraduates wandering in and out of each other's rooms.

'William,' she said as they lingered over coffee, 'you're far away suddenly.'

'I'm sorry', he said, preferring not to explain why.

But Laura was not satisfied. 'You were miles away. I was watching you. I insist on your telling me.'

'Well, since you ask ... I was remembering that strange house in Fitzroy Square where I last saw you.'

'Oh, that. What a funny thing to think about. What's strange about it?'

'All those people, just wandering in and out of one another's rooms. It seemed odd to me, and funny too. Who does it belong to?'

'To me.'

He could not believe his ears. 'To you? That enormous house ... yours?'

'Why not?' Laura looked hard at him before continuing, 'If you want to know, my mother's been dead for many years, my father's a rotter, far too interested in a woman he wants to marry to have any time for my sister and me. So we rebelled. We don't live with him any more.'

William was appalled.

'Don't gape so', she chided him. 'I suppose he's not that bad really. It's just that he's selfish, and it's true, he never gave much time to us. Aunt Venables, his sister that is, saw to it all and helped us get out. There was a flaming row between Aunt Venables and Papa about this other woman, about us and all that ... He's stinking rich, and as Aunt Venables is an emancipated woman with more brains than the whole of Cambridge, she made him buy the house next door to hers. It just happened to be up on the market. Wasn't that lucky? A bit of Fitzroy Square as an investment for Caroline and me. She declared me quite fit to look after myself and Caroline. She's a marvellous woman, Aunt Venables. She may be old but she's still game. A great suffragette!'

37

But before she could extend recklessly into the women's movement again, he prompted her hastily, 'Go on – about the house, I mean.'

'I was coming to that. I was already active in the great campaign. Father hates that! Women should be draped in feather boas, seen but never heard as far as he's concerned. Anyway, Aunt Venables was so incensed with him that night, and he with me for campaigning . . . I was still only nineteen, still a child in his eyes . . . When Aunt Venables said it would be healthier to move us two girls to Fitzroy Square, where she could keep an eye on us in our own house, he was glad to give in. That other bitch – his paramour, I mean – moved in with father next day!'

William was shocked. As always, his dark brows gave him away.

'Don't look so disapproving', she said pertly. 'She *is* a bitch. She runs Papa round her little finger. She doesn't give a damn about us. All she cares about is clothes. She goes about like a peach melba.'

Again the slow smile. But he did not care to pursue the subject. It was all outside his experience. That people could be so *extreme* was beyond him, and he preferred to take his time to learn, if at all.

Being with a girl of his own age was quite enough to be going on with, and even that uninhibited expression was something he had to get used to. They had stretched luncheon as far as decency allowed.

'Now what shall we do?' Laura asked, hands held palm to palm again in anticipation. 'What about *your* college? You've seen my place. Are you going to show me yours?'

Did she by any chance mean his rooms? What would she make of old 'Emma'? William went scarlet. It had not occurred to him. It was not so much the proctor – chaps did have sisters, after all, though all 'sisters' were screened with a jaundiced eye – nor even his colleagues in hall. But in his haste to complete an essay, and then clean up and rush out, just in time, he had left the most unholy mess in his room, probably a dirty shirt or two and a pair of unwashed socks flung into a chair. Hurrying to get out, he could hardly remember, except that he knew it was in an appalling mess.

The waitress saved them. She presented William with the bill, and in the ensuing altercation they forgot about the visit to his rooms. For Laura firmly insisted that one half of the bill was hers, and that was that – or nearly that, for Laura found ammunition too in the business of a tip which, she declared, was condescension to the waitress and undignified. When William pointed out that the waitress was probably receiving only ten shillings a week and would count on tips to make out, she gave in, but added a rider that had it been a waiter, they would not dare pay him only ten shillings a week.

He sensed that there was much they might quarrel about. She took a moral stand on each point that, on reflection, he could only approve. She, all too obviously, did not like 'the system', but then neither did he. While the great debate raged within him, whether or not he ever enlisted, he too detested 'the system' which made war possible and denied 'that of God in every man', as Nonnie constantly pointed out.

As they emerged, William and Laura both a trifle shaken, he by her language, she by her feeling that for once she might have gone too far, he knew that in contrast to the widening rift with Nonnie, this girl invited every confidence.

They strolled along the Backs, but despite his half-hearted attempts as guide they were too engaged in gazing at each other to be much interested in dates and styles of architecture.

He had not quite looked a girl in the face before – and Laura, from being interested, had eschewed the whole 'charade' of flirting as her political feminism asserted itself. Without being really aware of it, each had a lot of ground to make up in relation to the other sex.

He was aware that she had been the more forthcoming of the two but was curious to hear yet more. But as they strolled idly along the river-bank Laura was quick to assert her rights.

'You know all about my sordid family now. May we hear something of yours?'

'I didn't suggest it was sordid, did I?' he replied, anxious not to offend.

'What? Yours or mine?'

'Oh . . . I thought we were talking about yours – when you used the word "sordid". I wouldn't call it that – only sort of odd . . .'

'All right. It doesn't matter. What about yours? I take it it's distinctly not sordid!'

He was unsure about that. Did she hope it would be? Would she be disappointed at the picture of his spinster guardian and their silences?

'Well,' he said, 'my mother died when I was a small child, my father died when I was fourteen, and I've been brought up since then by a Quaker lady called Miss Pomfret. Does that fill the bill? That's all there is to it – not as exciting as your life!'

She looked at him as he spoke, smiling at the very revelation of it all – he an orphan, and the ward of a Quaker woman.

'You may think so, but it sounds intriguing to me all the same,' she said softly. 'Miss Pomfret', she repeated the name, wrinkling her nose slightly at the formality of it. She decided against prying further however. It was, she sensed, a very private world of his, withdrawn, hardly to be discussed, not in the least like her own more dubious history.

But he seemed ready to continue, without prompting.

'Actually,' he said slowly, as though finding difficulty in formulating his thoughts, 'Miss Pomfret and I have been at odds lately.'

'Yes...?' She found the slowness rather attractive. He would never be thoughtless; perhaps tedious at times, never thoughtless. She tried to help him: 'Go on.'

But he was not sure. What would a girl like Laura make of a debate about pacifism, about peace and war?

He stopped and faced her.

'Do you have any views about the war?' he asked bluntly.

'Views? No. I've never thought about it, not being a man. I suppose I ought though...' She looked at him searchingly.

'I mean, do you believe in war, in general, not just this one?'

'Of course I don't, silly. Who does, except a few unemployed generals?'

But he was not satisfied. 'Do you believe in *this* war?'

'I suppose I do ... yes, I do. After all, we can't leave Belgium in the lurch, can we?'

'That's what I think. Miss Pomfret doesn't. She's an out-and-out pacifist; as far as she's concerned all wars are wrong. That's why she and I are at loggerheads. I believe we can't stand aside any longer on Belgium although I've been brought up to believe that war is always wrong... I can't see any way out. Can you?'

She was startled. 'Are you asking me? Nobody asks women, do they? Men make decisions about war without consulting women. They just go, locking their women up in chastity belts!'

But that was beyond him.

'Perhaps some other time we can talk about it. It's a bad time.'

'Between this lady and you?' she asked shrewdly.

'Yes, that – and also the war. It's not easy, you see, being accustomed to resist all wars and then to find yourself, at my age, facing decisions about poor little Belgium.'

She wondered at his age. To look at, he seemed so mature. Yet he was still an undergraduate, barely over twenty probably, uncertain about so much. He was concerned about the war and Belgium in a way

40

she had not encountered before. Most men just went, if they felt like it. If they did not, they would never discuss it. The only man in her life, her father, was probably above service age and was too content with his lady-love to think of volunteering.

'So what have you decided?' she asked, pleased to be in on a family debate.

'Nothing, yet. But we do talk about it at home.'

'Home. Where's that? The post-mark on your letter was not Cambridge, I noticed.'

But he did not appear to hear that, too busy thinking. This girl was free of constraints, could do as she liked. She was a ready listener, eager to respond.

He felt the rift with Nonnie more keenly in Laura's company; Laura Venables, who was more than herself. She was a *woman*, and he needed her, not only to talk it all out with, but simply to be with.

They were nearing the end of their time. Soon he would see her to the station. So absorbed had they been with each other they had missed the glories of Cambridge. Even the Backs had been the venue of a stroll only, and each was determined that it would not end there. He found himself thinking longingly of Whitechapel Road.

It was the end of their second meeting only, yet he felt he had known her much longer. By now there was an easy familiarity and trust between them. As they passed on to the departure platform both sought a means of extending their acquaintance but short of another bold letter from Laura it was about to slip away, for the train was already in. He knew the next move must come from him.

'I go to London again next weekend – with a friend,' he said limply.

'A friend?'

'Yes, Robert Litherland. He and I – well, he really – work at a hostel for alcoholics in Stepney. You've been there – remember?'

'Yes, I remember your Mr Litherland, of course I do. How could I forget him, or his settlement? Well, then, William Dobie, why don't we meet again?'

Again the boldness. But now he felt more secure about it, for it was so apt in the face of his own shyness and diffidence, his sheer want of experience. He excused these as he remembered her own ample opportunities for free social intercourse in that strange house of hers.

He loved Nonnie dearly, but this girl was showing him what enormous gaps there were in his own social rearing. He smiled down at her. He could not believe his luck, that of all the people he could have helped on the Whitechapel Road, it was this delightful sprite in her chiffon scarf, with her views and her boldness.

'I'll tell you what', he replied, enjoying the conspiratorial note. 'The best place for us both would be about Charing Cross, wouldn't it?'

'Yes, we could both get there easily, you from Stepney, I from Fitzroy Square. What about Lyons Corner House?' She was so delighted with herself; again the hands were gathered together as though in prayer.

'All right, Lyons Corner House, at three o'clock next Saturday?'

Gallantly he handed her on to the train and she did not demur. He lingered to see the last of her chiffon scarf trailing gaily on the wind as the train moved out.

It was almost as though they had set up home together and Lyons Corner House at Charing Cross was their address. There the simple conspiracy would be taken up and advanced: to be together, no more, no less than that, and each to learn what the other was about.

The week between Cambridge and this first meeting at Charing Cross was torment for William Dobie, for by now he was reaching a stage in his inner debate when he felt he must renounce his pacifism and take up arms. Only the inevitable reaction of Nonnie was holding him back. Now he had this added complication of Laura to cope with, for that too would not be easy to discuss with Nonnie, not the way it had come about and developed in so short a time. But by comparison with his pacifist dilemma this new complication was pure delight.

The week seemed endless therefore but when he finally arrived on the pavement outside Lyons at ten to three on the following Saturday, having left a surprised Litherland to cope with his Saturday topers on his own, he saw Laura threading her way through the buses and cabs to reach him.

The atmosphere of the streets, the enthusiasm that was building up about the war effort, the general quickening of the pace affected this couple no less than any other at the time. There was so little time, it seemed, and as they entered the restaurant, they saw it filled with khaki soldiers entertaining their partners with much the same urgency. It affected William, for though he himself was not in khaki, he felt the pressures building up within him. Even the reedy orchestra, wearily threading its way through the afternoon repertoire behind the potted palms, seemed to be saying good-bye rather than welcome.

With some difficulty William found the table he would wish, against a wall.

By now, any little constraints between them had gone and after an hour and a half over tea and muffins, it was with some difficulty that they parted, each wondering why so early, yet unable to find plausible reason for extending it further. But there was no doubt about their arrangement to meet again at 'the same address' a fortnight later.

Again followed two weeks of agonising over Belgium, not unaffected by this new complication, for a decision on the first must affect the second and he wanted to advance things further with Laura first, though how he had no idea as yet. But when they met at the appointed hour at Charing Cross for the second time he had no doubts. This time he was ready as they dawdled over tea and without any spoken agreement they were soon strolling along the Mall and into St James's Park, with the first autumn leaves crackling under their feet. Only the closing of the park brought them back to earth and both suddenly protested they must get back – to what? each wondered. Before they crossed Trafalgar Square prior to parting, William dared to catch at her elbow and arrest her with his eyes.

'Look here, I'm off to Wensleydale in a fortnight for two days', knowing as he said it that it was a lie. He was affecting the air of a man who got about a bit and had a place in the country; if it was not quite a lie, at any rate it was made up on the spur of the moment. Nonnie and he never went near the cottage in October. He felt guilty, conspiratorial, yet delighted.

'Wensleydale? Where's that?'

'It's one of the Yorkshire Dales, North. Where they make the cheese. It's beautiful . . .'

It was like playing a trout. He watched her every move. This was rather more than offering Charing Cross. The whole world met there, yet with her views he was afraid of dictating any action. Her views threw him off stride a little. He was far from sure how to guide whatever course they were taking.

She, in turn, tried to find the balance between freedom and safety. She plunged at the bait.

'I don't suppose I could come too, could I?'

'Of course you may. That's why I mentioned it. I knew you'd like the idea.'

43

'Oh, did you?' she asked, a little put out at having been led down the oldest garden path. 'But where would I stay? Where are you staying?'

He caught her meaning. But he had thought it all out quickly and carefully. It must be proper, quite proper, however illicit otherwise.

'Actually, we have a cottage there.'

'Will Miss Pomfret be there?'

'No. I'll be on my own. You can stay at the pub in the village.'

He knew he was taking immense risks, both with Laura and with Nonnie. He had not consulted Nonnie about the cottage, indeed had not thought of a visit until now.

If this came out, it would drive a further wedge between Nonnie and himself. He had no idea how she might react. Yet he loved the risks Laura entailed as he watched her intently, knowing she was falling for the temptation.

Yet he wished only to be proper, to extend somehow this friendship with a girl who responded so easily to his every feeling, every least mood. The simple enjoyment of being together was not to be wasted, and since by now he was reaching conclusions on enlistment, he was not going to let any opportunity slip. He must see as much of her as possible. Time could run out. Recklessly he went on, 'Be my guest please. It'll be lovely to show you Wensleydale. I think it's the loveliest place on earth!' (Not that he had seen much of the island of Britain, much less the world).

Her smile was all he needed. She was intrigued, gratified at the obvious risk, and though she would rather he had proposed the visit than merely thrown out the bait for her to grab at impulsively, she pushed her arm under his as they negotiated the square. It was his turn to be startled.

'William Dobie, oh William!' she cried, 'it's perfect, perfect. I'm dying to see – where d'you say?'

'Wensleydale – yes?'

'Oh, yes, yes, yes! Wensleydale! And we'll eat lots and lots of cheese, shall we? But how do I get there? Is it a long way? How long will it take?'

He felt severely practical now. All this had to be contained. It threatened to explode. 'Let's meet at King's Cross, Friday week. We can have the whole of Saturday and travel back on Sunday. I can be at King's Cross by four. There's a train at four-thirty. Can you be there?'

'Of course I can. What shall I bring?'

He was stumped at that.

44

'The usual, you know,' he replied, trying to appear casual. 'And don't forget to bring good walking shoes. We'll arrive in the dark, I'll see you into your billet at the pub, then next morning we can be up on the moors with a picnic . . .'

As far as she was concerned, all her footwear was sensible enough for walking, except for the Cambridge shoes and those were special. The opportunity might occur – she would take them too.

He was astonished at the ease of it, though he had to concede that he had forced Laura to make the final plunge.

Yet again the fortnight dragged endlessly as he ploughed through Walter Bagehot and endured a more than usually acid tutorial with old Walker who took him for political history. But on Friday at four, Laura was at King's Cross, sensibly clad in tweeds, he noticed, her smile more radiant than ever.

He rushed up to her, took her hand for the correct handshake between them. But she placed hers with the neatest of movements under his arm as they romped off to the barrier. In the exigencies of war, they found no empty compartment, so the journey was restrained, though even being together, sharing a seat, became a sort of conspiring not to be shared with other passengers.

About the propriety of this little escapade he felt decidedly uncomfortable in relation to Nonnie. But after seeing Laura settled at the inn, he retired dutifully up the hill to the cottage and exulted in the thought of a whole day, alone, with this girl on his favourite moors. He was grateful that, by an unspoken compact, there was no question of Laura entering the cottage. Next morning, at eleven, William led the way through the clinging fronds of the bracken as earnestly as he did all things.

The recent rain of late October had turned the dead bracken a deep copper colour and now a fitful sun dried it out. He walked like one with a sure destination, which Laura did not consider quite necessary. They were simply walking in the dales for the sheer enjoyment of it, of being together at last, alone.

But she knew better than to argue. The few hours together had taught her already that when this man set about something it must be done with due deliberation and no argument would turn him from his purpose.

This seriousness of his half infuriated, half endeared him to her, for

45

she knew by now it was quintessentially he, as earnest over anything to be done as a boy scout tying knots. And since that was William, then she was prepared to put up with it. If only he were not too long in getting them through this beastly bracken ...

'I'm sure there are snakes in this stuff!' she called after him.

'Don't be silly, Laura. They're already asleep somewhere – somewhere you could never reach, in the middle of a great wall probably. Snakes like it warm and comfortable.'

'But you admit they live here, don't you, even if they've gone to bed?'

'Oh yes, they live here, in summer that is. But they're awfully difficult to find.'

'Find!' she exclaimed. 'Avoid, more like ...'

'Oh, they're only grass-snakes, quite harmless.'

'Are you sure?'

'Harmless? Of course I am. You can pick them up, and they won't do a thing to you.'

'I believe you ... But what I mean, do only harmless snakes live here? Or do others also?'

'Well, I *have* seen an adder in this area, but only once.'

'I suppose you killed it at sight, since you're still here, thank God!'

'Now you're being dramatic. No need to thank God this time, Laura – I didn't kill it, why should I? The creature had just as much right to life as I ... We just looked each other in the eye, then it slid off into the bracken. It looked rather beautiful, I thought, with lozenges down its back.'

Laura shuddered at the thought of the adder still there, somewhere in the bracken, unkilled by William and still a menace to her. She ran forward and clutched his arm.

'Silly girl. The adder's asleep too at this time of year. Anyway, he has no reason to be looking for you personally, you little egotist.' He could not bring himself to call her 'idiot' yet in the way he now found so funny when she used it.

Laura was even less reassured by her own behaviour in this little episode than by his answer. The image of the frightened female betrayed her; it was an expected role, which she loathed. She was relieved therefore when the bracken gave way to heather. She enjoyed stepping among the tight tussocks covered with purple blossom.

Even so, he led, still intent on reaching the site he had in mind while the westering sun held. She resented it slightly in spite of herself. There

46

he was in his knickerbockers, woollen stockings and strong fell-boots and she in her skirts and thin buttoned boots with highish heels. What chance did a girl have to keep up?

But she silenced herself. The miracle was their being here at all. She was determined that wherever he was taking her on this wild walk, they would talk. If they were to go on meeting, he must introduce her to Miss Pomfret.

She was touched by the bond between the two. That much was clear to her, that Miss Pomfret, to a great degree, had made him what he was; the innocence, the seriousness, were Miss Pomfret's doing.

But there was something else. Laura thought him just beautiful, and that was not Miss Pomfret's doing. She had been impressed by his unique quality at their very first meeting – and what a meeting it had been – the uncertainty, the slight awkwardness, a shyness when he hung his head just a little as if to ward off a blow. All Laura knew was that he was very special.

She ran up to him.

She tugged at his arm.

'William, stop! You're going much too quickly. I'm tired. Please...'

'There's a place I want to show you, Laura. We must get there, it's only a few more minutes.'

That, she knew, might be anything up to an hour. Over luncheon he had described the rock he wanted to show her: some place at the top, he had said, where the limestone scaur rose sheer out of the heather, and at one particular place an enormous block had loosened without quite detaching itself. That was his destination.

He had shown it to no one before, not a single soul. She was to be the first, the only one with whom he would share it. The rock, he had told her, was hanging loose, and looked from the side like an ancient prophet – a Moses gazing from Nebo...

As they rose over the heather towards the scaur, the dale lay far below them; the village a string of dolls' houses with the old ruined castle and the church dominating it. It was all laid out like Lilliput. The trees clustered like soft cushions of gold near the river which glinted in the late autumn sun. Over the other side of the dale the clouds were clearing off the top in great, dramatic, trailing formations.

'We couldn't have come at a better time', he said, then, 'Shhh!...'

He stood quite still, transfixed, looking straight ahead, but stretching back his left hand to reach her. Motioning her to keep silent, he drew her closer and encircled her shoulder with his arm. There, not eight yards away, a small creature stood equally transfixed across their path.

'A weasel . . .' he whispered.

It seemed to hypnotise them with its tiny beady eyes. They could make out every white whisker, the lithe curve of its sleek brown body, and the small round ears. The weasel stood its ground cheekily, seemingly unafraid, perfectly still except for the barely discernible twitching of the nose, as though needing to confirm their presence by smell as well as by sight.

How marvellously nature reveals herself, thought William, how it draws aside a curtain from time to time to show off something extraordinary. 'A sort of epiphany', he said aloud, as the little creature took off into the heather with a rapid curling movement.

'What?' she asked.

'Epiphany. A sort of showing off. Nature revealing herself.'

Laura had found the weasel's smallness and lowness to the ground slightly sinister. She clung to him, still watching it wriggling through the heather before it disappeared.

'Wasn't it beautiful,. the way he stopped to have a special look at us?'

'I suppose so,' Laura replied doubtfully. 'I don't know whether I liked it or not. How d'you know it's a he?'

'Well, it seemed rather large for a weasel.'

'It looked awfully small to me.'

'But weasels *are* small. That was large for a weasel, so I conclude it's a male, a fairly old one judging by his whiskers and his boldness.'

She had never walked in the country before and knew little about its features. Her wildest walks had not taken her further than Hampstead Heath.

'Oh, everything's male in this world', she said moodily, impatient with her long skirts and inadequate boots and of the whole business of following rather than leading.

Privately however she thanked the weasel – funny, how she had assumed that weasels – or was it walruses? – went with carpenters! She thanked the dear creature since the moment of his 'epiphany' was when first William had put his arm round her shoulder to direct her gaze. At last he had done something she longed for him to do of his own free will!

And now, as though deliberately to drag out the walk, he turned to make a detour.

'Now, what?' she asked, arms akimbo in protest.

'Oh, nothing. We don't want to pass this place. It's where the sheep sleep – I can't stand the smell.'

'I didn't know sheep had any particular smell.'

Tired by now by the unusual exercise, she was at the edge of rebellion. There was too much to take in – even the smell of sheep. But, remembering his arm round her a moment earlier and looking at him striding away from her, she relented. He was in his element in this upland so utterly alien to her. Head high, alert as though in communion with his surroundings, he could put away from his mind all distracting noises in the distance. A Shelley, she thought. Then dismissed it. She could not admit William Dobie into that particular view of the Romantic pantheon. Shelley she imagined as sharp and bird-like, whereas William – for all his communion with nature – lumbered rather, not at all bird-like, as he attacked the last slope. Insects, too small to take in properly, drifted in the wind like so many seeds. It was all so new to her.

'Well,' he was saying, a few paces ahead of her, 'I don't intend that you should learn what sheep smell like. It's not really very far, I promise you.'

But she was not satisfied. The minutes were slipping by. They had not had their talk yet.

'William,' she started, 'I really think you should tell Miss Pomfret about me. I want to meet her. I have a right to, surely. I'm not a whore.' She knew that her vocabulary shocked him on occasion. She now offended deliberately, to make her point the more forcibly.

Why did she have to do all the persuading? *He* should persuade, take her in his arms. They had known each other for a short time, though it seemed longer. It was natural for them to be together. Yet it worried her that it was she who seemed always to take up the running.

William appeared not to hear. She had noticed that men had this faculty for not hearing. He had forgotten his arm round her, so intent was he on getting to his 'Moses'.

The heather gave way to thin wind-blown grass as they approached the scaur towering above them. It ran like a rampart all along this side of the dale. Breathless, she held out her hand to him to help her over the last few yards. As they arrived at the foot of the rock, again he put his arm round her shoulder to direct her gaze at the strange, loose rock formation. He's learning, she thought with satisfaction.

'See?' he spoke gently in her ear, his head near hers as the wind blew wisps of her hair across his eyes. 'Moses, don't you think? Moses looking out over the Promised Land!'

She found it difficult to stop trembling at his nearness. 'I think so', she murmured. 'That's his nose – and below his great beard trailing. Yes, I see what you mean.'

'Don't you find it striking, that great head brooding over the dale?'

'No, leave it there', she said with firmness, for he was about to take away the encircling arm to point away over the dale below.

Persuading again, she thought. But there seemed no other way. It was not that he was shy; he had been plain enough when suggesting this weekend. He lacked the furtiveness which goes with shyness. Rather it was his certainty about the pace at which things should proceed that held him back. Now he obeyed, put his arm round her again. She reflected that he was so intent on showing off 'Moses' to her, he had no room for anything else.

'Yes, it *is* striking', she said, exulting under his arm. But she had to have her say. After that, she would leave the pace to him. 'Did you hear me, William?'

'Yes.'

'You didn't answer. Well?'

'About meeting Miss Pomfret?'

'Yes.'

'I see your point,' he said unhappily, 'but everything has become difficult somehow. This little escapade for example. What if Mr Crowther tells Nonnie I'm here without her knowing?'

'I guessed that much.'

'Funny, isn't it? Me alone at the cottage, you in the inn unchaperoned...'

'I don't think it's funny at all,' she retorted, offended that he should evade the issue yet again. 'Would Nonnie mind so much?' she added after a pause.

'I'm not sure.'

'What am I to call her? Miss Pomfret?'

'That's her name.'

'Why haven't you told your Miss Pomfret about me, William?' Laura moved away a little to turn her gaze from the rock to his face.

'I couldn't – I'm not sure I can now.'

'I don't understand,' she said severely, astonishing him, 'how you can deceive one so dear to you? Here we are, seeing each other every other weekend, and you haven't had the courage to tell her. I don't like the deception. Or isn't it important enough to you to take your courage in your hands...?'

'You know it's important, Laura,' he said sulkily.

'Go on.'

'Well, when I first wrote to you to enquire about your health, I didn't tell Nonnie. I didn't think I'd get an answer, you see. There was a bit of awkwardness about posting the letter. And once you start on the wrong foot...' He did not finish.

'Awkward or not, I think you must tell her without further delay.'

'That's easier said than done. We've been meeting alone; I have an idea Nonnie might find that not quite proper, you see...' (Why was he embarrassed?)

'Don't be stuffy! We've been perfectly "proper". We're not living in the eighteenth century exactly! You haven't even kissed me...'

There she was again, persuading. He was visibly startled.

'I...' he muttered.

'Well, it's true, isn't it...? After all, I'm not your sister!'

He gazed at her in awe. How he gazed, she thought, at everything – and now at her. The idea, quite obviously, had not occurred to him. Perhaps he had not kissed a girl before – nor had she, not a man she liked.

They had touched very little before now. She looked at his troubled face. Was his conscience at work still? She wondered how Héloïse had first seen her Abelard, or Beatrice her Benedick. Despite the accelerating pace created by the War with its mounting casualties, she and William had been reticent and most correct. She longed to gently push back the thick, almost black, hair from his brow. Like Troilus – 'He that will have a cake out of the wheat must needs tarry the grinding,' says Pandarus. And poor Troilus: 'Have I not tarried?'

Well, her Troilus had tarried indeed. Even at the cooling, would he be afraid to burn his lips?

He bent over and kissed her, obeying, full on the lips. He did not linger. Instead, taking away his arms, he led her up a steep gully that marked a gap in the scaur, out on to the very summit. In the gentle sunlight behind them, the dale lay spread out, more gold with every passing minute. Ahead, the broad moorland rolled away with only the butts breaking the level heath until it descended to the next dale hidden from their view. A muffled boom of distant explosions disturbed the light soughing of the wind.

'Do you hear that?' William asked, his hand still in hers.

'What is it?'

'Military manoeuvres in Wharfedale. That, Laura, is the other thing between Nonnie and me. To be brought up as I've been to believe that violence achieves nothing in human affairs, and then to enlist – Nonnie would be . . .'

'What do you mean?'

'Nonnie, as I believe I've hinted more than once, disapproves of war – and until very recently so did I. I still disapprove, of course. After all, I've been reared all my life as a Quaker. Now I know I can't go on clinging to pacifism in the light of what's happening in Europe. Have I the right to stand aside? Can a man of nearly twenty-one stand aside while his contemporaries are dying by their thousands to defend a small country like Belgium. . . ?'

'Yes, you mentioned it. I understand how tormented you must be by all this. I've thought about it. At the end, you must do as your conscience dictates. It's a matter within your own heart, not between you and Nonnie – or even you and me. Why does the dilemma affect your telling Nonnie about you and me? Or am I being insensitive?'

William shook his head.

'You're wrong, Laura. It's more than just my own heart. Nonnie has everything to do with it. I think it would break *her* heart were I to enlist, and I couldn't do a thing like that lightly. It would be setting at nought all that she's brought me up to believe. That is not an easy thing to do.'

'But of course, William. I can quite see that it cannot be done lightly. I don't expect you would rush in regardless. But, really, you must make up your own mind and not allow considerations of Miss Pomfret to affect your decision. I'm sure she'll understand better than you imagine. You're afraid of her, aren't you?'

'No, no!' he answered vehemently, 'I'm not afraid of Nonnie, only of hurting her. I'm just about all there is in her life. And, I must confess, she means everything to me.'

'Everything?' she asked pertly.

He did not have to be persuaded this time. He took her in his arms, as though to protect her against the cold wind that blew over the scaur, and kissed her a second time.

'Everything but you,' he said, releasing her.

'All the same,' she persisted, 'you may not be afraid of Nonnie . . . oh, I mustn't get used to calling her "Nonnie" – Miss Pomfret – but I do think you underestimate her. Have you ever tried her?'

'Tried her?'

'Yes. Presented her with a problem? You can't have been all that angelic to bring up, William Dobie, surely. You make her sound as though she can't be tested without a total breakdown in your relations.'

'I suppose I do. That is a pity, because I happen to know she's well aware of the problems that life can throw up. No, it's just this one particular issue – or rather two – and I'll admit that the second is my own idiocy . . . I praise the day you answered my letter; but I never thought you would, you know . . . On peace and war however, Nonnie is implacable. She's the ultimate Christian, turning the other cheek, loving her enemy, prepared to make the ultimate sacrifice, but never to spill the blood of others. I suppose Nonnie is a sort of ultimate character, like a saint. And they still crop up from time to time. I'm afraid that if my conscience dictated that I should enlist – if I do – it would kill her. But I'll tell Nonnie, I promise you. And I'll tell her about us too. But if I find that she can't take the two together, bless her, I'll write to her about us a little later.'

He seemed to brood on it. She watched him as he paced a little into the heather of the flat moorland top. She could see that the distant gunfire disturbed him, reminding him of that inner problem that he would prefer to put away from his mind while he was with her.

William Dobie, she thought as he paced moodily about, for the moment seemingly unaware of her – and she liked to tease him with the whole plain name, pedantically – William Dobie, you almost reconcile me to the whole world of men which I hate for what it does to women. But you force me to persuade you to do things and like a flirt I engineer that first kiss. She was irritated with herself suddenly, with the unfamiliar silence of tiny insects on the wind, and even with William Dobie. Shall we ever be lovers, William Dobie, or shall I have to wait for ever for the next move from you? For no reason she could think of (except that her one great passion beyond the cause of women was Shakespeare) she began quoting to herself from *Troilus and Cressida* – 'but here's yet in the word *hereafter*, the kneading, the making of the cake, the heating of the oven, and the baking . . .' While he continued his pacing above, she snatched at a sprig of heather. William Dobie, she continued whispering to herself, while he seemed quite oblivious to her musings, I know you like me, more than you're prepared to say, I *know* it. And I like you enormously, in spite of everything. Is that simply because I *can* persuade you, dominate you? How dreadful if it were true. But no, surely . . . and she was just as good at persuading herself . . . there are things you would never be persuaded to do. I'm not 'persuading' you, I'm just impatient at the tarrying. I'm in too much of a hurry. William Dobie, it's this wretched war, oh William, I love you. If up till now 'love' had been reserved for *Troilus and Cressida*, this was new, direct, physical; now she knew what the 'heart' meant, for hers was pounding.

She was firm with herself however and decided not to persuade any more, not to break the precious silence. She had come on this wild breathless walk, he had put his arms round her, he had kissed her, albeit just a little, twice – and was now, she could see, making up his mind about something that was crucial to him in a way that did not arise for most men, who found no difficulty about going to war if the call were there. She decided to wait, just to let the wind blow her hair about, and let him return to her in his own good time.

He turned, wanting to get away from the distant gunfire and to be with her. Hand in hand, they half ran, half tumbled down through the heather and bracken, over Mr Crowther's dry-stone wall as they came to pasture, through the old wooden gates that seemed to have been there since Domesday, and into the pub where high-tea rewarded an appetite Laura had not thought possible from her fastness in Fitzroy Square. For William it went with the thick stockings and fell-boots, part of the reason for ever coming to Wensleydale. And he exulted in her patent enjoyment of it all.

That so much could have happened, that he and Laura could come to know, to recognise each other so well in so short a time, seemed to him incredible. But the times were like that – and his mind was now firm on another matter, and that, heaven knew, left all too little time for the heart's affairs.

The following weekend he went home, as conscience dictated, for a visit to Nonnie was overdue and his studies now counted for very little in his present turmoil. Between the station and home he called at the church hall and enlisted. The Army was to have him, but with a thudding heart he resolved that, Nonnie or no, he would have Laura.

Yes, there was an understanding between them. Now, as he posted the letter and turned back with Sally to face Nonnie again, he exulted in the idea. It was like returning from dream to reality however, and his steps were as slow as Sally dictated by the time he reached the house.

He loved Nonnie as a mother. But the blow had been struck, after weeks of sparring over the issue. He felt the cruelty of it yet again, wishing it could have been done without hurting Nonnie. Was this the fate of all parents, to reach a stage when their children cut loose into the unpredictable?

When he got back she was sitting there, looking thoughtfully out into the hall as, laboriously, he loosened Sally's leash and carefully hung it over the door-knob as was proper, making quite a show of hanging his coat and eventually went to join her as though nothing had transpired between them.

'William,' she said at once, 'you're still only twenty. I wonder if you know what you're doing.'

He had seen her impatient sometimes, but never angry. Yet, when he had announced his enlistment, and she had flung out of the room with such a tightening of the shawl, he knew she was warding off the thought of what she could only construe as treachery. Now, without dining, she was back in the room, calm by now and evidently with much to say, if only this once. It might be her last chance.

He knew she had been sitting, perhaps kneeling, in silence in her room for the past three hours. She would be upset, not only at what he had disclosed – which would be dreadful enough for her in any case – but at her own abrupt departure in the face of it.

She would know – as he did – that even though she had not said much, there was enough impatience, even hostility, in the manner of her departure to speak volumes. She would find that unpardonable in herself. In silence, she could recollect herself, wait on the spirit.

This, he knew, touched on an area of her character verging on intolerance. She would be hard put to keep certain words back – 'treachery', 'stupidity' – which she would not mean and would later regret. She would recognise her own intolerance, and fight it. William knew that she had been engaged in a silent wrestling of the spirit, praying for him and condemning her own want of understanding and sympathy for his struggle over the past few months. With that battle presumably won (for she possessed an uncomfortable self-awareness), none the less she would still stand for her cause with uncompromising vigour. Two wrongs may not make a right, but two rights invariably make a wrong.

If Nonnie and he could divide so in their love for each other, was it any wonder that mankind divided in mutual suspicion and envy and the need for security and empire?

'Nonnie, I've thought and thought, and even prayed in my own way, which I don't suppose is much. And I've weighed the arguments.'

'May I ask,' she said, and he could see her framing the question with a delicacy only she was capable of, 'if you're not denying your conscience?'

He knew what she meant. A few young men of the Meeting had already suffered insults and had white feathers thrust into their button-holes by smart young women who would never have dared otherwise to be so bold as to accost a man in the street. Others had volunteered for the Friends' Ambulance Unit, a mission which the hard-pressed Army in France had gladly accepted, and in one case at least, he knew it had brought death under shell-fire.

'I know the alternative, Nonnie. And I know that conscription could soon force pacifists to face the ultimate sacrifice, by firing squad. I don't know. All I feel is that in the face of what is happening in Europe, I, at any rate, am standing on the sidelines while the rest of my generation is giving its blood in defence of values I share with them. I honestly believe that by standing aside I'm betraying both those men and values, I really do, Nonnie. Can't you understand?'

'No, I'm afraid I can't. I, and your father before me, have tried to teach you a certain truth, a certain credo if you like, which is concerned with that of God in every man – with love. Yes, love . . .'

He sensed in her a reluctance to speak the word, as though to utter it would dissolve it in the air. She would not sully its heartfelt reality by talking it out of herself. It was there, cool and strong, as in a deep well of pure spring-water, hidden from view but the more real for that.

She was still speaking. '. . . and this war, you know, is a denial of all that truth and love. It begets lies and hate and death. And it's the innocent who are suffering. Can we believe half they're telling us? Even the soldiers who fight each other are mostly innocent, like lambs being sent to the slaughter. Somebody has to speak out, somebody . . .'

His heart went out to her as he guessed at her meaning, that if he were that 'somebody' who would speak out and gather moral force by joining other somebodies, she would have been as proud of him in her way as some mothers were reputed to be at sending their sons to the Front. He was denying her, her love for him.

'Nonnie,' he replied, his dark head bent as he tried desperately to collect his arguments, 'Nonnie, I feel it's much bigger than all of us somehow, that some things are a sort of repository of evil – and that is what's happening in Europe. Pacifism will never eradicate it. I believe, in fact, that evil would feed on our pacifism. I really do. I feel it inside me. I don't hate Germans, you know that, I just hate the great evil thing they're engaged in, which makes them do what they're doing in Belgium, and which . . .'

'Until someone stands against this thing of war between men, it will always be there, always. Until we stand, even peace will be used to prepare for war.'

'Yes, Nonnie, you may be right. In an ideal world, war couldn't happen. But it's not an ideal . . .'

'So long as we all talk like that, William, we'll never have an ideal world, shall we? We have to start somewhere. It's no use starting at the end of a war, when millions will have died or suffered for nothing. It'll be too late then. Belgium won't be a scrap better if we win this war. Her suffering will have been too great for her ever to recover. We must fight for peace now, with the weapons of peace.'

'I wish I could still believe that, Nonnie.'

'I hope you won't mind me saying this, but I trust you aren't feeling heroic about this. The world seems to have gone hysterical, any excuse is good enough to go to war. I almost think it's a sort of escape from the boredom of most people's lives.'

He found that hard to forgive. He could honestly confess to cowardice at the thought of enlisting, and if in the face of it he had still enlisted, it was because she had taught him to approach all arguments in a mood of soberness, truth and objectivity.

'No, Nonnie, I don't feel heroic. In fact, the opposite. It is simply that, as I see it, the pacifist position is no longer valid in the face of what has happened to Belgium. How can we stand aside?'

'It is not a matter of standing aside. It is a matter of looking at what war has done in the past as a solution to quarrels between nations. Belgium may be invaded by the Germans, and my heart goes out to poor Belgium. What the Germans have done is evil, I don't deny. They have resorted to war and, what is worse, they glory in it. But will it help if we go to war against them? War will be a greater evil than the invasion itself. So long as the nations go to war against Germany, the more Germany will feel justified in her stance. War justifies a nation like Germany. But passive resistance, moral resistance by the community of nations will put them beyond the pale. You may say that that would be all right if the nations could agree on it. But where are we to start if not at home?'

He recalled an old tradition among Quakers that illustrated this all too clearly. The sect had grown in days when violence on the roads was commonplace. If a Quaker met a footpad, he first showed that he was unarmed except for a walking-cane. With his cane he scored a line on the road between his would-be assailant and himself, and said, 'Come no further, friend, lest thou do thyself harm'.

Yes, Germany had crossed the line – and had done herself harm. That assault on a small nation was evil and the doing of it would harm its perpetrator for years to come, perhaps generations. Who would ever trust the Germans again?

But it was still no help in Belgium's present case.

Nonnie could see him agonising and sought to help, if possible even to retrieve him from the brink of what was to her unthinkable – that this boy, his father's son, her son in all but blood, should take up arms... She thrust the thought, the image, of any weapon away from her – the very thought that his hands should take up anything that could cause offence to any man was too much for her.

'Peace now, with the weapons of peace...'

But she knew she had lost him, that however they argued, he was going, indeed was as good as gone, for it was only a matter of days now between enlistment and call-up. And the difference lay between them like a heavy curtain.

Even Sally, the old golden Labrador, seemed to look up at him with great haunted eyes, as though she knew he would not be taking her for her walks very much longer. The very water-colours and the books on the inner wall of the drawing-room seemed to lower in silent reproach.

Instinctively, he felt that suddenly Nonnie was just a guardian and no longer a loving parent. He wondered if his mother, whom he could not remember, would have argued quite like that had she lived. After all, the same arguments would have held, since it was likely that her Quaker doctrine of peace would have grown deeper with the years.

Possibly both parents would have embraced full membership and would have reared him no less rigorously than Nonnie in the Quaker way of peace and love. Yet he sensed that a mother would accept, would never draw a curtain between them, because there is an extra bond of love that embraces acceptance.

And this loss of Nonnie, the unquestioned focus of his filial affection since boyhood, hurt deeply enough to make him waver. He contemplated returning to the Town Hall and filing his conscientious objection to joining H.M. Forces. His own inborn gentleness and the compassion for suffering humanity that Nonnie had instilled in him, the quiet indwelling and unforced atmosphere of loving instruction at Friends' School, all would carry him through, he felt, if he objected.

Yet he knew it was not so simple. He still felt that, just as a few rare examples, like Nonnie, were natural repositories of goodness, so too there were occasions when a person or a community of people was the repository of evil. Just as with Nonnie it was a matter of grace, a gift bestowed from outside herself and in a way gratuitous and none of her own doing in its final essence, so evil crept and occupied the soul of a person or a people, equally none of their doing; they were victims as much as perpetrators. No amount of passive resistance would dispose of it.

In the event, he was off within a fortnight.

Miss Pomfret could not help herself. She mourned his going. How could she otherwise?

As he stood before her with his small valise and a Gladstone bag, she looked at him intently, desperately trying to reconcile this impending young officer with the boy she had reared in the Quaker tradition. She recognised that he was not enjoying the prospect, that if he was going, it was out of a sense of duty. She wished she had not expressed certain thoughts in their recent exchanges. But it was done.

He had not fallen for the current hysteria and flag-waving. He really did feel he must contribute to that 'moral lump', as he put it, which must free Belgium from the German stranglehold. She could see that. And now there was no more to say, no need even to say how deeply she loved him as a son. He knew that.

'Shall we sit awhile in silence?' she said, hands folded in her lap.

Eager as he was to make the break now that his mind was made up, he observed the silence, the quiet minutes of composure and recollection, and even fell into its spirit as the minutes ticked by on the old grandfather clock in the hall.

She being the elder was the first to break the silence.

He bent over her and kissed her tenderly and reverently on the brow.

Such love, if undemonstrative, was none the less deep and abiding.

As 1916 approached, with the Allied front not one bit advanced despite the Autumn push, the speed with which men were transferred from the street to full Army service became a matter of pride. Pals' regiments enlisted *en bloc*, to keep some native or industrial *esprit-de-corps* intact for Kitchener. Four weeks were often enough to 'make a man of you'.

Four weeks were hardly enough for William Dobie, but well before March of 1916, he had passed successfully out of the OTC at Aldershot. It required a real expertise to fail, so he took no great pride in the single pip on his shoulder. But since his arguments with Nonnie on the present morality of assisting the 'lump' to free Europe of evil had left him with a firm conviction in his service, he looked forward to joining a company – possibly, even probably, to take charge of a platoon.

He had quickly adjusted to the contradictions of the Army which exaggerated 'civvy street's' class barriers to an alarming degree, yet otherwise looked after a man to the last detail, even granting him leave after such and such a programme. The Army was both humane and inhumane.

He had been given a batman, one Roberts F.X., and in six weeks at OTC, they had got so used to each other as to encourage a certain familiarity, or at any rate an ease of working which cut out the system's more irritating corners.

But the drill sergeant-major, who although not holding the King's commission, ruled the cadets with a rod of iron, spotted this easy-going comradeship between cadet and private and had bawled them both out. As Dobie winced under the blast, he felt every sympathy with Roberts whose weekend leave was cancelled for merely talking to him direct while not in cadets' quarters.

As he fastened a single pip to each shoulder of his tunic, he surprised Roberts packing his kit. He had grown so used to having Roberts around that he felt he could at last bridge the social gap and say good-bye on a human note. The drill sergeant-major was not in sight and, anyway, was beneath him in rank now he had received his commission and his pip.

'Well, Roberts, I hope we'll meet again. I'm very grateful for all you've done for me. I trust it hasn't been too hard for you, looking after me and all the other duties to do.'

He was not sure what those other duties were. As soon as Roberts had cleaned both his room and his kit before morning parade, he just disappeared, not to be seen again until five, when he would find Roberts laying out his mess uniform and boots for dinner.

Roberts looked startled. 'Oh, I'm going with you, Sir, to Catterick.'

This in turn startled William, whose last thought was of travelling with anybody, much less his batman, as he was going on weekend leave to see Laura in London before proceeding to Catterick by train on Sunday afternoon.

'Oh, I see. Are you going on leave first?'

'No, Sir. The RSM cancelled my leave if you remember, Sir.'

'I'm sorry about that, Roberts. You must have been looking forward to it.'

Although he himself had been partly responsible for talking to Roberts outside quarters, he could not help being relieved. He was not sure what one did with one's batman when travelling on the same train. But he felt conscious-stricken by the cancellation of the leave.

'Yes, Sir, I was. A bit of trouble at home like. I wanted to sort it out.'

There was indeed a sadness about the man, yet as he said it there was no blame in his expression.

It crossed Dobie's mind to intercede for Roberts, but he felt cautious about it. He had had to learn how impersonal the Army could be, and he did not relish the idea of going to the CO and requesting that the drill sergeant-major's punishment be reversed. In fact, he did not know the procedure, the protocol involved.

The CO, even the adjutant, were distant figures who had addressed him only in the most impersonal terms, even in the informal get-together in the mess after dinner, when cadets tended to keep to themselves and the senior officers, permanently stationed, kept close ranks never far from the head of the table and the port.

Weakly, he decided against interceding and felt badly about it as he picked up his kit.

'I'm so sorry, Roberts. Perhaps we can arrange something when we get to Catterick.'

But the patent disappointment on the private's face clouded his journey to London, and only dispersed when he met Laura, as previously arranged, at the Lyons Corner House at five. He had dropped his kit at Litherland's.

Speculation at their postings had it that this would be their last leave before going to France, where things were supposed to be building up for an Allied push. Laura and he had Saturday evening.

By the time he saw her, Roberts's problem, whatever it was, had completely left his mind. The hours left to Laura and him were all too brief, but he hoped they would be decisive. In what way, he did not know, except that when he jumped off the tram, he ran to her and they met in an uninhibited bear-hug that quite took their breath away. The Army had kept them apart too long.

As they broke, he thought it was decisive enough, but what next? Time was so pressing. Laughing, they went inside, out of the cold February wind.

As he saw it, this was to be the last leave before embarkation for France. *France*, only twenty-three miles across the Channel, did not imply distance as such. It was the connection of the word 'embarkation' rather than the distance that made the impact. The news from France and Belgium was grim.

Tracing her hand restlessly over the damask table-cloth pattern, and sensing that this might be his last leave, Laura thought that she would never again look into eyes that meant so much to her.

'William Dobie, we'll marry one day, shan't we?' she cried impulsively – then blushed scarlet.

Why had it just come out like that? She saw how startled he was. Both tried to cover their confusion in ardent tea-stirring.

Whatever happened to him – and thinking of France, knowing what usually 'happened' – she was glad that she had said what was uppermost in her heart and mind. She met his gaze.

His eyes, dark-brown under the straight black line of the brows, were upon her, gazing hard.

Ever a gazer, he took in every detail: the dark hair with just a hint of bronze as it swept back from the candid eyes and forehead and was gathered up for the occasion in a proud *chignon* on top. Too shy, even now, to reach out and brush aside the errant wisp that fell near her eye, he was lost for words in the face of her frank admission, at last, of what they meant to each other.

He touched her hand to arrest the baroque movement over the cloth, then held it captive as though to still her restlessness.

'Yes, Laura. We will marry, we must. I hadn't thought that far – does that sound unkind? I'm only at the beginning of ... everything...' He swallowed. 'I don't even know – what can I call it? – the procedure, the ritual, whatever one does about such things. I suppose there's a first time for everybody, as though it hadn't ever happened to anyone before...' He spoke quickly, too quickly, trying to cover his confusion.

62

He had to confess to himself that, brief though their acquaintance had been, broken by war and by firm conviction on either side, he had, in fact, just let the word 'marriage' enter his thinking.

'Does one meet a few girls, then choose the best?' he went on in an attempt at banter, 'I can't imagine anyone better than you, you know!'

She laughed, making him smile.

'No,' he went on doggedly, still holding down the small hand as though to steer his course through uncharted territory, 'I mean ... Is this how it happens? Isn't there something like courting, engagement and the rest of it?'

'Oh, rot! That's all nonsense, a ritual rigged up by the male world. It's the oldest market in the world, bartering the bride for the best possible price. You'll be talking about a dowry next!'

Then she laughed to cover what she half realised was ungracious in front of his earnest effort to find words for something he did not know the first thing about.

Still, he persisted:

'I didn't mean that only. I mean, I'm due to leave soon for France. I wonder if it's the right moment for such talk ... we've known each other for such a short time; now I'm about to leave England for ages, goodness knows when I'll be back, certainly not before Easter ...'

'Do you have a conscience about it, William?' Laura held his eyes. 'Do you mind me bringing it up – er, marriage – just like that?'

Here, he lifted her hand to his lips. The gentleness and chasteness of the gesture affected her deeply.

From habit and upbringing, both looked aside to see if they were being observed. The moment broke her feminist self-assertion. He saw her hesitate slightly as he released her hand.

'I love you, Laura.'

She looked again, hard into his eyes, then bending her head, she searched in her pocket for a handkerchief, and failing to find one, brushed away a tear with her forefinger.

'What is it, darling? Does that upset you?'

She turned towards the wall, reaching out a hand to find his. He waited, still as ever. Eventually, eyes brimming, she turned back to him.

'No, no ... it's just the thought, suddenly ... you mentioned France. I can't bear it.'

'I'm sorry.'

'No, you're right of course. I'm always suggesting things. I ought to wait for you.'

'But you will wait, won't you?'

'I didn't mean that . . .' Laura shook her head. 'Of course, I'll wait. What I meant, I'm so afraid of male domination that I always take the lead – even with you. I never wait for you, not once. I was dead set against marriage and now I'm the first to bring it up, with you of all people!'

'Well, then – who else?'

'Nobody, silly. But I might have waited till you brought it up first. *You*, William Dobie. And you're quite right to remind me you're going away – and it's too . . .'

He brought out his own handkerchief and she took it from him without demur, distractedly wiped her eyes.

'But did you hear what I said?' he tried again, feeling at last that he was right in following his instincts rather than some ritual he knew nothing about.

'About France? Of course. That's why I'm crying like a hysterical female. I don't know what's the matter with me. After all, everybody seems to go to France these days, even women.'

'No. I meant the other.'

She tried to focus through her tears.

'Oh, William, I'm sorry . . . I . . .' She could not carry on. She wiped away the tears, as though angry with herself. Then, collecting herself, she turned to him to pass back the handkerchief. She was impatient with herself.

'William Dobie,' she said with clear resolution, tossing her head, 'I'm truly sorry. The women's movement is making me silly. Here you say the most important thing anyone's ever said to me in my whole life and I'm worried who said what first!'

But still, she felt cross with herself – like William, she too felt deficient in the ritual, whatever it was.

He took courage, helped her by reaching across with his hand to brush aside the wisp of hair. Quickly, she took his hand as it tucked the hair behind her ear.

'Thank you, William.' And she bowed her head, as though to declare that her feminist defences were over.

But the waitress came with the bill, and due decorum had to be observed. Delicately, he placed a tip with the rest in case yet another altercation on its propriety should arise, but Laura was too busy pretending to search her left-hand pocket to notice.

She was struggling with herself. The conflict of a cause with an issue so personal was too much for her. Nothing but the cause had occupied her burgeoning years. Aunt Venables had nurtured a feminism first implanted in her by her differences with her father – men had become an abstract force to be combated with all at her command, young though she was.

Nothing had satisfied her measure of the world as she found it so much as the cause. It had been her all, had occupied both her inner thoughts and her outward actions to an extent that took little account of any personal relationship that might arise outside the 'sisterhood'.

William Dobie, a man who quite by accident had been there to help her up off the road during a demonstration, from the beginning, from her first glance into his dark concerned eyes, had occupied the front of her mind and ruffled the chaste absolutism of her fight for women's emancipation. It was not that he was William Dobie, nor that he had no particular thoughts either way about the cause – it was that, simply being *he*, he could deflect her life and thoughts so drastically.

'I can't talk here, William. Shall we go?'

They rounded the square, arm in arm, heading for the Mall as the quietest thoroughfare in a choice of so many, yet not so far that each could not return easily to base in the restricted wartime traffic.

Under the dimmed lamps, the old feeling of Wensleydale returned, of his first putting his arm round her and kissing her. Here, under the royal avenue of plane trees, she felt at last in command of herself – not in command of him, that is, but ready to respond to him.

For he had, at last, taken the lead. And she knew she must respond. Despite the noise of passing cabs and the occasional chugging rattle of an army scout-car, they felt a profound and grateful silence around them. She was reluctant to break the spell.

'William,' she said in a subdued voice, spellbound by the mystery of this still strange experience of being alone with a man, 'William, can you ever forget that I brought all this up in the first place – marriage, I mean? I could bite off my tongue. What I meant was that I ought to wait for you, can you see? I'm so afraid of following a man's lead that I've ruined a precious moment...'

'No, no, no, Laura, you haven't. Please, Laura, don't be afraid, don't chastise yourself. I wouldn't have you otherwise, you know. I know I'm slow, I take my time over things. I like you to be – well – whatever you are. Impulsive. Impetuous?'

'Yes, impetuous. You're right . . . I'm all right now', she went on, nestling closer to him, half frightened of the dark rustlings of tiny creatures in the trees in the park on their left. 'William, what you said in the restaurant – I haven't forgotten. Nobody's ever discussed it with me. I know nothing, absolutely nothing. Aunt Venables is a dear, but she only talks women's suffrage. And all I know about being a woman is that you're the most precious thing that's ever happened to me. And your saying what you said, first, without me leading you on to say it, is something I'll never forget. Is that love, William? Oh William, I do love you so – that's all I know . . .'

At the heart of the British Establishment, nay, in its monarch's front garden, two of its sternest critics, without thought for the passing cabs or a strolling policeman, turned to each other and paused a moment, each waiting for the other to take the lead in what was the most natural thing in the world. Then they laughed as they embraced.

'Suffragette!' he whispered in her ear.

'Male monster!' she replied.

Still unsure, the words eased their way, for neither would wish to be thought following what they believed might be accepted behaviour – if they thought at all, for they certainly knew next to nothing.

Still laughing, they momentarily held apart and looked into each other's eyes. War and the world might not have existed. Neither had anything to learn thereafter – eyes speak volumes. They drew together – nothing could be more natural.

That, he realised, was the real beginning. The world changed then, time changed. Love was not so much a fact, but a futurity. For they had had so little time together, done so little together, seen – of their common land – only a few fleeting hours of foetid London, an afternoon of Cambridge, and a full day of bracing autumnal Wensleydale.

What they had not done, what they might do together, at that moment under the trees of the Mall was a whole futurity, an eternity as far as he was concerned, and – observing one of his customary silences, gazing into her face to see what he could of those eyes – as far as she was concerned too.

There was the whole backbone of England to be explored, his beloved North, rock and grass and heather to be trodden beneath their feet together, and pavements to be covered, doors entered, theatres and museums and pleasure-domes of her London to be explored too, books shared, music heard – and, above all, blessed silences to be observed together.

66

Nonnie, at that moment a matter of conscience for him, had in her own inimitable way opened life up to him. She had nurtured him, faced him towards the light, and if, perversely and against her every instinct, he had temporarily chosen to enter the tunnel of war, still there would be light at the end.

Laura, each hour understanding more, took his arm and, never breaking the silence, turned with him towards the hub of the universe, Charing Cross. Even the taking of his arm in such a way was to enter a new-found land in a slow progress that had been shy and defensive on both sides. Possession here was about giving and not counting the cost.

Next morning at King's Cross, he walked to the far end of the plat-form, to be as near alone as possible and because, in passing the barrier, he noticed one or two men he knew. He had not taken too easily to the ritual of saluting in public and went out of his way to avoid it. He could see the point in camp, but was grateful that Lither-land was not about when he was forced to return a salute.

He saw Roberts, his batman, among the men shuffling towards the barrier, trying desperately to catch his eye. But he read the headlines of a newspaper studiously to avoid contact.

He was glad too that the First Class carriages were at the front of the train. That kept him apart, and he could rely on the few officers travel-ling to observe a proper British reticence on the journey. For he had much to think about and preferred not to talk. The last thing he wanted after the precious hours with Laura was male camaraderie of any kind. The contrast between being with Laura and settling back into the masculine world of the Army was too great. He settled down to read, but his mind was elsewhere.

With France in the offing, he had too much on his mind. There were matters to reconcile within himself and they would not be reconciled. But then so too would Laura have the irreconcilable to consider. She too had principles that made life difficult. The wicked thought that he was courting a virago crossed his mind, but he had no difficulty in dis-missing it.

Of course Laura was intent on her movement. Emancipation from her father, and Aunt Venables with her preaching, had fanned the flames. Living in her own house with young academics from the Uni-versity, one painter and easily the most unsuccessful writer ever (if rent for his room were any indication), all had confirmed her freedom. She obviously believed in it positively, with joy and messianic fervour, and longed to share it with her sisters – and never to concede an inch of it to male domination.

Then, again, it had to be considered – no man would ever possess her. She would never consent to being a mere chattel. But did this preclude him from loving her? He had no doubt that she would be putting the question to herself.

Why should his loving her involve or even imply possessing her?

He did not understand the women's movement, and certainly not the fervour that they brought to it; but of being with Laura, of taking her in his arms, he was absolutely certain of the rightness, not to say the mutual pleasure of it.

Yet he knew, even as he kissed her and felt her slight form against him, that she would have views better left unsaid at that moment as far as he was concerned. Since possession of the wife was more than ninetenths of marriage in society as it persisted, then they must explore together the no-man's-land of loving without possession, a no-man's-land that only a few emancipated women were interested in examining.

It had been delicate, he realised, from that first moment of raising her up off the Whitechapel Road. Her preoccupation with emancipation of women; his with reconciling his latent pacifism with the recognition that Belgium's plight cried to heaven for help, if not for vengeance; all this, and their very natures, had held them away from what both would have regarded as the shallow rituals and hypocrisy of flirtation. However gaily she laughed, she too could be earnest. No, she was not to be possessed.

So, they had an understanding, no more than that; but remembering her eyes, he was content with that – for the present. The rest they would work out along the way. They had kissed, not as friends but as lovers, albeit with a due reticence, for the no-man's-land of loving/ possession had to be trodden with care.

If at twenty-one he could formally propose marriage, it would have to be understood that possession must be no part of it. The thought suddenly terrified him. They had gone this far, and Nonnie did not even know of Laura's existence. That was unthinkable, yet he could not think of how it might have been done, not while debating the problems of war and peace. Nor did he know the ways of courting a girl. It was just that there seemed no pattern, no precedent that either knew, no elder brother or sister to guide them.

He felt frightfully young. But he was determined about it, however long it took – and Nonnie would be told soon enough. He had, after all, recognised the impediments to happiness, as Laura saw them, and would act accordingly as far as in him lay. She had already infected him with horror of what marriage could do to two people who loved each other and fell into the possessive constraints of the laws of society and their demands, so that the woman could never contract a debt on her own, while the man had the freedom to gamble their entire fortune at a bookmaker's or the stock-market if he felt so inclined. Nor could a woman enter into a contract – or even vote.

All this he had not known or considered before. Who had, except a few concerned women whose own sisters misunderstood and disowned them?

By the time he arrived at Catterick and threaded his way through the mass of khaki to find Movement Control, he was very confused. Suddenly, he realised that, though he had gone through the 'naming of parts' at OTC, had lain flat on his belly and aimed a .303 Royal Enfield rifle at a target in the vast gymnasium at Aldershot, he had not actually pulled a trigger. He had been issued with a revolver after the passing-out parade, and Roberts no doubt had carefully packed it somewhere in his kit. At no time had he shot at anything! In the haste of passing cadets through the machine, it had been assumed that his allotted regiment would see to it in good time. At least he knew what a rifle was and the way to hold it. As an officer, he wouldn't have to carry a rifle now. Would they realise at his new battalion that he had not fired a revolver either?

He boarded a scout-car with three other officers. They drove without a single word up to the windswept camp. Catterick seemed a city to him: vast, desolate, hostile.

Once again, the world turned over for William Dobie.

PART TWO

PART TWO

Major Dean-Forbes watched the new lieutenant, assessing him in military terms, personal terms. Military – not bad considering. A year in the trenches in France, and then a few months here in camp, had lowered the major's standards somewhat. If this was Kitchener's New Army, then God help the British Empire.

For a start, the old Territorial spirit was absent. Nobody knew anybody. The only man he knew was the sergeant-major who had been promoted and posted along with Major Dean-Forbes to help lick a battalion into shape.

The commanding officer too had come from France, but why or from which unit no one knew – these were always questions that required an answer.

So, all things being less equal than one might have hoped, the major granted a certain military bearing in the new lieutenant – if nothing else. But personally? No, he was too earnest, didn't mix enough.

In the mess, the lieutenant swallowed a drink like filthy medicine; he would never make a drinker. Whatever the lieutenant uttered required attention. Such earnestness was hard to live with, and for the major that was the supreme test in a life where men were flung together twenty-four hours a day. The major required a certain warmth from people. Dobie, as far as he was concerned, positively chilled the place. To Major Dean-Forbes, Dobie looked a whisky or two below par.

There were days here on this northern moorland of England when you felt that if you looked hard enough to the east, you might see the Urals. Certainly, nothing of any consequence intervened between the camp and Russia. If the wind were in that arc of east to north-east, as it had been for most of February and March, it swept uninterrupted across the north of Europe, picking up even more chill over the North Sea and settling down to freeze this Pennine flank with a conviction based in Siberia. If the temperature was anything to go by, then the coming of Easter held little promise. As far as the major was concerned, the lieutenant did not help. He mooned about too much, was

73

forever gazing at things. You never knew what was in his mind. He stood apart somehow, with his gazing and his earnestness.

It was true, the gazing. Even now, as the lieutenant waited for the sergeant-major to muster the Company on the square, he watched the early morning tumbling of rooks lower down the hill over a group of stunted sycamores and pines. They wheeled high over the trees, tossed about by the rough March wind, then would fall about the sky like clowns, as though competing over which could suspend flight the longest. Then, just as they were about to plunge into the tree-tops, they would veer sharply aside and up into the sky again, intelligent idiots entertaining each other. What surplus capacity did they have that allowed them to make something of the churlish wind and to positively enjoy its waywardness? Their staccato chatter mocked the men assembled on the square. There was not a man who did not wish fervently to get the parade over and be back in the hut over the stove.

The lieutenant walked up to the mark in the square, turned correctly at right-angles towards the assembled Company and stood to attention.

The company sergeant-major, as though with eyes in the back of his head and never less than straight as a ram-rod, turned about, stepped smartly towards the lieutenant to within a yard of him and saluted smartly.

The lieutenant, too stiffly the major thought, returned the salute. The major itched to demonstrate an officer's more relaxed and slow reach of the arm to a salute – but it was no good; Dobie's sheer bloody earnestness defeated him.

'Company all present and correct, Sir.'

'Thank you, Sergeant-Major.'

But however confident the sergeant-major sounded, it had not been a cakewalk. The Company had had a rigorous two months, the CSM's first with the crown on his arm. Most of that time had been spent in freezing winds on the moors above the camp. They had charged sacks with fixed bayonets, shouting their heads off to *kill* with conviction: they had occupied trenches against 'Germans', filled sandbags to make parapets, learnt about firesteps and saps, and in spare moments had polished brasses so that the enemy, they declared, might see them better.

Then the men's money from civvy street had soon run out and their first pay would not be settled until Friday. So, at best, only one or two had attained the sparse night life of Richmond – among them Moffat, already known as Moff, and the only man the sergeant-major could remember, and with reason.

Moffat had taken off a quarter of an hour early the previous evening with his two bosom pals, Pearson and 'Spider' Simpson. The two returned just before lights out and reported that Private Moffat had fallen into the river.

Corporal Dinsdale, who was local and knew how treacherous the River Swale could be on its great bend round Richmond, was so terrified by this complication that he forgot to put Pearson and Simpson on a charge for leaving camp early. Scared out of his wits by the prospect of hauling Sergeant-Major Green out of the sergeants' mess at that hour, he had questioned them closely.

Where had Moffat fallen? When? Corporal Dinsdale had volunteered only three months earlier, and only his knowledge of the locality had pushed him forward sufficiently to warrant two stripes. But three months' experience was enough to know how quickly you were returned to the bottom of the pile if you slipped.

He grabbed at Pearson and Simpson in an effort to get some sense out of them. Where had Moffat fallen? When . . .?

But the two were more or less inarticulate by then, only fit to be put roughly to bed. They did not seem unduly worried about Moffat. He had left them, they said tipsily, to go walking by the river with a girl. They giggled inanely as they tried to tell the story.

Having relied on Moffat all along as a leader, they had transgressed by leaving camp early at his behest. They had tried desperately to keep up with him. Moffat was always one for being a move ahead.

The corporal gathered that Moffat had not so much fallen into the river as been pushed in by the girl when his hands strayed too far. They had fished him out somehow, then lost him again. Finally they had lurched through the camp gates and into the hut, where Corporal Dinsdale now worried over it all.

Weakly, he decided to haunt the path outside the sergeants' mess and wait till they came out. At eleven, the door opened, the light flared in his face, and the sergeants tumbled out.

The corporal, pretending to be just passing, fulfilled his duties as night-picket and slammed the door shut after them. After all, Zeppelins had bombed Hull the week before, and sergeants or no, it was no time to show lights. He quickened pace, reached the group in which Sergeant-Major Green was grumbling away good-naturedly.

'Sergeant-Major,' murmured the corporal nervously.

No response. There was a certain dignity to be maintained in the purlieus of the sergeants' mess.

'Sergeant-Major!'

'Yes, what is it Corporal, eh?'

'It's Moff, Sir – Private Moffat.'

'Well, what about it, eh, what about it then?'

'Private Moffat's missing, Sir.'

'Missin', what d'you mean missin'? You're a bloody fool, Corporal, what are you?'

'What's that, Sir?'

'You're a bloody fool, that's what you are. Missin'?'

'Yes, Sir.'

'So you say, Moffat's missin' ... Bloody marvellous! And tomorrow morning, nine sharp, Colonel's inspection. Missin'?! How missin', eh? Gone? Scarpered? Gone for his bleedin' 'olidays to Clee-thorpes, I suppose, eh, Corporal, missin'? How?'

'Fell in the river, Sir. Pearson and Simpson fished him out, but then lost him again. They turned up all right, Sir. But Moff – Private Moffat still isn't back.'

'Bleedin' marvellous, eh, marvellous!'

By now his cronies, anxious to avoid any sort of regimental trouble, had left him behind in their slow procession to sergeants' quarters.

'Look, Corporal, what time is it, eh?'

The corporal pulled out his fob, shone his lantern on it and answered. The sergeant-major cogitated a moment, thumb and forefinger rubbing the voluble lower lip.

'Ten past eleven, eh? Fell in the river, eh? Fine bloody mess his uniform'll be in, I bet. Look, Corporal – go back to the hut. I'll bet he's back if I know Moffat. Probably crawled under the wire to get back into camp for a start. Sly young bugger is our Moff. Just go back and see if he ain't in his bunk. And look, Corporal. If his uniform's got as much as one tear, mark or crease on it, I'll have your bollocks on a hook. All right? Now, get on with it! All right?'

And sure enough, when Corporal Dinsdale got back to the hut, Moffat was slumped on his bunk. His tunic, soaking wet and still bearing evidence of a crawl under the wire, was flung over his boots on the floor. For the rest, he had given up and dropped off on top of his blankets in shirt, trousers and puttees.

Corporal Dinsdale roughly pulled the braces off Moffat's shoulders, unwound his puttees, pulled off the trousers and tumbled the blankets over the unconscious figure.

He then rushed to the guard-room, where with an iron he steamed out, dried and creased the tunic, trousers and puttees. By half-past midnight he had returned them neatly folded to Moffat's bedside.

At six next morning, the night-picket wakened the corporal. He had managed less than four hours' sleep all told and felt rough. But unless somebody had crawled out through the wire, he knew the Company was intact – and if Moffat, Pearson and Simpson had sobered up sufficiently, the Company would parade in full-strength 'fit and free from infection' for the colonel's inspection at nine.

That was all that would matter as far as the sergeant-major was concerned. And the sergeant-major's concern was the corporal's guiding light in all things, military and personal. After that, all that remained was to keep them out of trouble for another two days. On Friday the whole Brigade (assuming there *was* a Brigade – the corporal rather doubted it) would parade for the brigadier-general's inspection. Then, all being well, they would entrain for France. After a month or two with this bunch in this hole, Dinsdale almost felt relief at the prospect of service abroad, however bad the rumours flying about might be.

'All right', he mumbled to the private. 'Blow Reveille.'

At seven-thirty, with everybody back from ablutions and breakfast, he inspected every bed-space in the hut, every kit and every man from cap-badge down to boot-toes, and was satisfied. The three doubtfuls were all tidy, standing straight though looking grey and anything but fit for France.

'All right, stand by your beds', he shouted from the door of his cubicle, the only refuge of a corporal from the crowding of beds in the hut.

Sergeant Forster appeared at the door a few minutes later. With a very conscious eagle-eye the sergeant passed down the hut, the corporal at his heels. The sergeant seemed satisfied, paused a moment at Moffat, looked him in the eye, then moved on. He ordered the men to fall out, not to move anything and to wait for further orders.

By half-past eight they were lined up in the square. It was then that the sergeant-major had nearly lost them. He was calling the roll. All went well until he came to the Ms.

'Mitchell!'

'Present, Sir!'

'Moffat!'

77

No reply.

'Moffat!'

'Present.'

'MOFFAT!!'

'Present – SIR!'

'Take that man's name, Sergeant . . . Neale!'

'Present, Sir!'

'Roberts, J. H.!'

'Present, Sir!'

'Roberts, F. X.!'

'Present, Sir!'

'F. X. Hellfire! F. X.! What's that?'

'Francis Xavier, Sir.'

'Francis what?'

'Francis Xavier, Sir.'

'Whatever was your muvver finkin' of, Francis Saviour?' But CSM Green could have bitten off his tongue, not only for the lapse into doubtful language, but for being personal. The Company tittered, amazed at their own noise and started to laugh out loud.

'Attention there! Attention, you shower!'

But they did not quite come together. He lost them for a moment – and with this lot, a moment was too long. He carried on down to Yudkin – now, there was a rum one, but this time he held his tongue – glaring at them, then stood them at ease to await the arrival of Lieutenant Dobie, Orderly Officer for the day.

Now, as he turned about to march up to the lieutenant, Sergeant-Major Green was conscious of releasing them from his hypnotic stare and thought that even now the whole parade might collapse. Letting his eyes shift momentarily over the lieutenant's shoulder, the CSM could see Major Dean-Forbes on the Orderly Room steps and sensed his irritation, the unmistakable tweak of the moustache before mouthing some blistering sarcasm.

The sergeant-major found the lieutenant easy to keep in his place, but the major – that was another matter.

As a sergeant under Captain Dean-Forbes (as he then was) in Flanders, he had both suffered and enjoyed enough to know every move of the moustache. He returned his eyes to the approaching lieutenant.

There were things about him where he might agree with the major. He could not work the young lieutenant out. Not that it mattered much. While the CSM knew he had to take what came his way from the major, he knew he could cope with the lieutenant, whatever the difference in rank.

The lieutenant's easy 'Thank you' had hardly been said when the sergeant-major saw the major slowly descend the three steps from the Orderly Room verandah. Now what? As the major briskly accelerated over the thirty yards towards the lieutenant and the assembled Company, he gave every sign of being about to swallow the young man whole.

CSM Green braced himself to correct somehow the slackness he was conscious of in the ranks behind him. The lieutenant, surprised, incorrectly turned his head right to see why the major was making this unexpected move, then quickly reasserting himself, set his gaze on the sergeant-major's cap-badge and waited. Still the rooks wheeled and clowned over the woods below.

'Mr Dobie', said the major, amiably enough it seemed.

'Sir?'

'Dismiss the men for an hour, keep them confined to barracks and ready as they are till further notice – oh, and come to the Orderly Room at once, will you?'

Most unusual, quite out of order. But CSM Green was relieved. The parade might well have been a shambles – and his own fault at that. He dismissed the men.

In the Orderly Room, Major Dean-Forbes sat at his desk, ordering Dobie to sit down. He plunged in at once:

'Dobie, when you salute, don't yank your arm around like a bloody railway signal. Leave that to other ranks.'

'Sir, I was upbraided at OTC by the drill sergeant-major for waggling my arm like a flipper.'

'"Upbraided"?' It was not a word in the Major's vocabulary. 'I don't give a damn about OTC. You're here now. There's little enough privilege being an officer, but at least we don't have to polish our own boots and brasses, nor salute as though we had haemorrhoids or something.'

'Well, Sir, the men have to.'

'Have to what?'

'Salute as though they had haemorrhoids, Sir.'

'Dobie,' the major replied with infinite patience, 'men are men. They don't have responsibilities, they don't have to lead as we have to. Salute like an officer, relax. You've done your training at your blessed OTC – pah! This isn't what I wanted to see you about... We're off

79

tonight, at midnight. Understand?'

'Tonight, Sir? What about the colonel's inspection this morning – and the Brigade on Friday?'

'All off. Emergency. We're off tonight.'

'Abroad, Sir?'

'Maybe. Dobie, you don't ask questions in the Army. I said we were off tonight. Is that understood?'

And that was that. If volunteering and training had gradually stripped him naked, the Major's words now plunged him into the deep end. 'Off' – it made all the difference. But the major had no time for the lieutenant's blank stare. The last thing he wanted was another earnest exchange.

Brusquely, he dismissed Dobie. Slowly, the lieutenant turned, abstracted, and forgot to salute, then remembering too late, half tripped over the threshold as he left. But no blast came as he proceeded to walk towards his billets.

There, the sudden air of urgency prompted him to write to Nonnie. Contrary to the rather cool letters he had received since enlisting, her latest amounted to a plea for forgiveness, with messages that wherever he might be, her thoughts and prayers went with him. No return to the argument, but rather to that loving understanding that had made their mutual dependence so dear to both.

Now, the interview with the major over, back in his tiny room – no more than a cubicle in the officers' lines – he wrote:

'Dearest Nonnie,

I was happy to have your latest letter. I hated the way we parted, didn't you? We need each other so much. All this nonsense is merely an interlude. They say it will be over by Christmas – it's always Christmas, you notice; they've been saying it for the past two years – I'll be back in no time.

'Look, Nonnie. We've had news. We're off, abroad, tomorrow morning. I'm in a frightful hurry. I must rush off to Darlington to buy a compass. I'll write the moment we get some peace. Everything, suddenly, is awfully harassing. That's just like the army. Don't worry about me, Nonnie. I'll be all right. Love and remembrances, William.'

He felt it was casual enough, however painful.

As he gazed through the inadequate window of his room, his brow darkened slightly – he could just see, round the corner of a barrack hut, the light in the sky rising beyond the camp.

It was this slow gaze that Major Dean-Forbes had observed from time to time and regretted in an officer. It was as though he were in a trance. Whereas Miss Pomfret respected, and even loved it in him as one more echo of his father, the major wanted to kick him.

In his gaze he would pick up the slightest detail, the flight of a buzzard on the skyline or the rustle of a vole in the foreground. Now he was watching a newborn lamb not fifty yards away, just beyond the camp perimeter, staggering on its feeble legs in its attempt to reach the bulging udder of the ewe grazing indifferently two yards away.

Then, quite deliberately, he turned and, taking up the letter to Miss Pomfret, slit the envelope and took out the sheet again. Under the signature he added: 'There is something I'd like to talk to you about. It can wait till I get home.'

He sealed the letter in a new envelope and left it where Roberts would see and post it. Then, remembering that the men would be confined to their huts, he took it and strolled over to the Orderly Room and thrust it with an air of finality into the post-box.

At least, things would be tidy now. He would talk it over with Nonnie – there was no reason in the world why not.

Reluctant as yet to turn up at the mess, he returned to his room and, looking through the window, his gaze fell again on the sheep and her lamb.

Remembering the day in Wensleydale, he thought that the great drawback with sheep was their smell. There were certain places on the fells out of the wind where they scraped, shuffled and scratched hollows for themselves. Strewn with their droppings and wisps of wool, those were places to avoid, for the smell, ammoniac and sheepish in the extreme, seemed to cling to you long after you had passed the place.

Even now that sheep was settling, shuffling her burden of wool round her and already dozing in that intense and cud-chewing way of sheep, creating the smell. Suddenly, as though aware of his gaze, the lamb looked up sharply in his direction. It held his gaze, as if to make contact, but Dobie knew the lamb could not possibly see him in the semi-darkness of his room. Yet the gaze held, compelling in its steadiness. There was that other day when just such an animal gaze had held him, some five months ago – was it? The day would remain with him all his life, a Saturday afternoon in October up on the heights above Wensleydale, not so many miles from this place of preparation for France.

William continued to gaze until the lamb finally settled, conceding defeat, flicked its tail as lambs do and strolled step by slow step to snuggle down, its small head over the ewe's shank. The lamb looked neat and dainty against its mother's rump, making itself comfortable. But the smell of their sleeping quarters too he recalled, not unlike the smell of the other ranks' barrack-room. For however much he disliked it, as orderly officer he sometimes had to inspect the men's quarters – and beyond the occasional whiff in Litherland's settlement, he had never thought humanity could smell so.

He longed to help the poor. Why, he wondered now, did he identify the poor with smell? Be that as it may, he longed to help – for, truly, they must inherit the kingdom of heaven. Nonnie had not merely taught him compassion, she had spelt it out: behind the simple, almost austere purity of their shared home, there were 'good works'. In time, no doubt, she would introduce him to hers once France and 'all that' was over and done with. One thing however would never be easy to bear – the smell of the poor, almost as bad as the smell of sheep.

He wanted to be in the open, and although he realised that officers were confined to barracks too, he left his room. The letter had detained him.

Saxton, Harwood and the junior officers would be in the mess, pumping the CO for information. The Old Man would love it – and Major Dean-Forbes would not be far behind him with tales of nights out in no-man's-land negotiating the wire, hugging the ground and diving into the nearest shell-hole as a Very light flared overhead.

Even William Dobie had got the picture and knew the vocabulary, though like as not his eyes would be held by the antics of a spider negotiating the cornice as he half listened.

Yet, fearful though it all was, he hoped the present build-up would not result in the Germans being cleared out of Belgium before he got there. He must be part of that, to justify his breach with Nonnie.

As he closed the door behind him and saw the deserted spaces of the camp in the reluctant morning light, he drew in deeply the keen moorland air and shivered. The prospect of France, of shell-holes, saps, German mines and the wire oppressed him. He would not make the King's best soldier.

One hand held loosely in his Sam Browne, he continued to shiver. It was decidedly chilly in the open. He must pull himself together and enter the mess. They would miss him, and the major would find something acid to say again; that would bring all eyes round on him.

Yet thinking of Wensleydale, he ambled slowly. The burden of having to tell Nonnie about Laura weighed heavily on him. Why had he not been frank from the very beginning? He could just see the copse of sycamores and pines, now a dark profile in the eastern light. Not a sign, not a glimpse, of the rooks that had tumbled so playfully at dawn.

Yes, he would be missed. As he made his way to the mess, he tried desperately, as always, to prepare himself for its mood.

The parade over, back in the barracks, Moffat sidled up to Roberts F.X.'s bed-space, picked up one of his neatly folded blankets and draped it round his own head and shoulders, monk-like. He shouted down the hut:

'Hi, boys! How about Francis Bloody Saviour?'

They roared. Roberts went scarlet, but waited patiently at his bedside.

'D'you hear the sergeant-major?' Moffat rattled on, imitating the voice on the parade square: 'Whatever was your mamma finkin' of, Francis Saviour? Where'd you get a monicker like that, mate?'

The men followed the rollicking humour. It thawed the frost of lingering fear. Roberts just glowered, standing his ground. Sergeant Forster, at the door having just entered, let them have their laugh, whatever it was about.

'All right, you lot. Cut it!' The sergeant's voice carried across the hut.

If the men had found a chink in the CSM's armour on occasion, there was none in Sergeant Forster's. They found him scrupulous if mean – a combination not easy to fathom. And the sergeant had shown every sign of intending to keep it so.

As soon as he saw the sergeant, Moffat dropped the blanket in the aisle between the beds and skipped back to his own bed-space.

'Whose is this?' the sergeant shouted, toeing the blanket gingerly.

'Mine, Sergeant,' replied Roberts F.X.

'Pick it up and fold it properly, or I'll have you on a charge.'

'I didn't put it there, Sergeant.'

'Don't back answer, boy, just pick it up and fold it correctly. Do I have to show you?'

Roberts did not move.

'Boy, you're trying my patience.' The sergeant went up to Roberts, took hold of his ear and dragged the still protesting man towards the blanket, lowering him over it and seemingly enjoying the sadistic necessity of it all.

'If I didn't have news for you, boy, I'd have you in the guard-room like a shot. That's right, pick it up, my lad, and get back to your place... Now, listen everybody. The brigadier-general's inspection's off on Friday. And today's too. We're off at midnight tonight instead. So – on parade, full marching orders at half-past ten tonight. We march to the station with the whole Battalion. Is that understood?'

There was a murmur of excitement across the barrack-room.

'France, Sarj?' a voice daringly piped up.

'Quiet, all of you,' the sergeant went on. 'I've no idea what's on. Whatever it is, take my tip and write a letter home, all of you. Might be some time before you get another chance. Just say you're changing address. Understood? Anybody stupid enough to mention France will have his letter destroyed by the censor. All right?'

As soon as the sergeant closed the door behind him, Roberts F.X. sauntered slowly through the noisy hubbub of excited speculation, up to Moffat's bed. He took the top blanket from Moffat's kit and delicately threw it into the aisle. In two seconds, the chatter gave way to the ring of boots over the floor as they flocked round the figures of Moffat and Roberts wrestling and clawing aimlessly at each other on the floor. The noise brought Corporal Dinsdale at the double. He scattered them, lifted the two antagonists by the collar and glared at them each in turn.

'One more bloody murmur from either of you, and I'll report the whole hut. Now, all of you, keep this place spick and span. Watch your uniforms and your kit. You're not leaving this place like a pig-sty when we leave tonight. Now, get back to your places, you two – go on, get on – any more trouble from you, Moffat, and you're for it. I pressed that bloody uniform of yours with my own fair hands last night, so watch it!'

Something of the passion of F.X.'s attack quietened even the ebullient Moffat. For the rest of the day they repolished brasses and boots, cleaned rifles, or just dozed between meals.

Except for F.X. who had first seen to Lieutenant Dobie's packing as far as he was allowed, then returned to the hut. The lieutenant seemed too far away, too remote to approach once again about his own problem. Yet he felt the urgency of it more than ever. What Sergeant Forster had said could mean a long absence, and he had already been away from home for four months without leave. He had missed that last leave because he and Officer-Cadet Dobie had been observed talking. After that, F.X. was cautious.

Doing what he could for the lieutenant, he was soon made to feel redundant and curtly dismissed with the usual absent-minded 'That's all right, Roberts. I'll manage the rest myself. You'll need to pack your own things, so you may go now. Thank you.'

He had not wanted that. He had plucked up courage to talk once again to Lieutenant Dobie – and the dismissal came too early. He was back in the barrack-room barely twenty minutes after leaving it, brooding on his problem once again. Now they were confined to their quarters and he could find no excuse for leaving again, not even to attend to his officer's needs.

As for polishing, he merely went through the motions. Just before midday, he rose from his bunk, walked quickly down the aisle, and asked Corporal Dinsdale if he could see Lieutenant Dobie.

Irritated by this breach of routine and by the possible evidence of cowardice at the prospect of active service in France, the corporal tried to send F.X. packing. But the private was so doggedly persistent, he had no recourse but to refer it higher.

'All right. But you'll have to see Sergeant Forster first. I warn you, if it's France that's worrying you, Roberts, then you'll soon get your marching orders.'

'I've got to see Lieutenant Dobie.'

It was worse with the sergeant, who took no pains to conceal his contempt for a man who urgently required to see his Platoon officer at the first whiff of danger. By the time F.X. was escorted to Lieutenant Dobie's room by the sergeant, he was visibly shaking.

'What is it, Sergeant?' Dobie asked in a voice that offered some re-assurance to F.X. compared with the corporal and the sergeant.

'Private Roberts requests an interview, Sir.'

'Bring him in then.'

The lieutenant kept his seat at the camp-table near the window and, since he was hatless, the two visitors did not salute, but stood stiffly to attention and took off their caps, tucking them under their left arms with the deference due to an officer.

'Yes?' The lieutenant's tone indicated an informality for which the sergeant was ill prepared.

'Well, Sir,' he blustered in the absence of any utterance from the bewildered private, 'it's highly irregular at this stage with the Battalion preparing to be off tonight, but Private Roberts won't be put off, try as I might – he says he's got to see you, Sir . . .'

'That's all right, Sergeant. What's the trouble, Roberts?'

F.X. looked from the lieutenant to the sergeant, and back again. 'Can I see you alone, Sir?' he said.

'Not really, Roberts. It's perfectly proper for an NCO to be present at an interview like this. So fire away.' As he said it, Dobie gazed at Roberts's patently unhappy face, ashamed. How readily the silly Army phrase tripped off his tongue! Was the little power he possessed corrupting him just a little?

'I'm sorry, Sir, I can't. Can't I see you alone?'

'Well, not really – it's quite irregular. You know King's Regulations. In fact, if I cared to insist, you could be ordered to address me through the sergeant. Do you understand?'

He realised that all this was for the benefit of the sergeant only. He was quite willing to talk directly and privately to Roberts if the man needed it. He and Roberts had been together long enough for it to register that he was a man with something on his mind.

'I'm sorry, Sir. I have to see you alone.'

'Is it about going on active service?'

'Not exactly, Sir.'

'Because if it is, there's nothing we can do about it. We're off tonight – and that's that.'

But something about F.X.'s face worried Dobie. He thought there was no more than a month or two between them in age – and here was Private Roberts coming to *him*, an officer, with something on his mind as a son might approach his father, or a student a tutor.

His whole instinct was to hear this man, urgently, privately, and see if he could help. Nor could he forget the reason why F.X. had missed his leave between Aldershot and Catterick. He felt responsible therefore. Still, according to King's Regulations, an NCO had to be present.

The conflict between personal and army requirements was fierce in the lieutenant as he ignored the sergeant and looked into Roberts's unhappy eyes, seeing a man, not the other rank and batman.

The sergeant retained his stiff, aloof stance through the momentary silence, eyes fixed ahead, almost insolently impersonal, willing the lieutenant to hardness. Dobie was not unaware of it.

'All right, Sergeant,' said Dobie, having resolved to pull rank and waive the regulation – after all the sergeant knew that Roberts was his batman. 'I'll handle this myself.'

The sergeant's stiff left turn, stamp and march out of the room spoke volumes of contempt.

'Now, Roberts, what's troubling you?'

'I've got to get home, Sir, it's urgent.'

'Wait a minute, Roberts. We all want to get home.'

But he saw the man was near breakdown. The head turned right, then left, as though to quell tears in that ridiculous 'attention' position.

William Dobie, instinctively, put out a hand – a token gesture of comfort. At once he corrected himself, held back. He had not realised things were quite as bad with Roberts.

'Look here, won't you sit down? Bring that chair over here and start at the beginning.'

But it was not going to be as easy as that. In the first place, despite the officer-servant relationship, the division between officer and private was unbridgeable. This was not going to be anything like Nonnie comforting one of her 'fallen women' and trying to elicit a few facts.

Roberts fumbled with the chair which was awkwardly wedged between the wall and chest-of-drawers – once he had extricated the chair, he did not know where to put it, as if afraid lest he trespass on the almost palpable aura that surrounded his officer.

Dobie realised the man's difficulty in shaking off the inherited burden of workmen touching forelock to the master. The Army, far from abolishing it, exaggerated it with elaborate procedures of rank.

'Put the chair there,' he said quietly, trying to calm this very agitated man.

The CSM's public play on his name and Moffat's subsequent mimicry had upset F.X. and served to increase his deeply seated unhappiness. Dobie knew nothing about the parade and its aftermath – all he saw before him was a man brooding over something, about to lose control and clearly in need of help or counsel.

Roberts sat on the edge of the chair, trying – and failing – to find words. His head, involuntarily, kept turning from side to side.

Then Dobie remembered Miss Pomfret's way – silence. He realised that positive silence, sitting unmoving, would not be possible or even wise. There was silence – and silence.

He rose and took out the little compass he had bought from his valise. He had purchased the compass from Lieutenant Saxton who was as always hard up and short of funds. It had not been possible to find transport to Darlington as Dobie had intended.

Over each small movement of opening the compass and examining it, he imposed calm: scrutinising, testing. It was like stalking a very shy animal, familiarising it with one's presence in order to establish trust. Dobie packed the compass.

'Now, Roberts...' Looking him in the eye, Dobie tried to engage F.X.'s confidence. 'We've been together for quite a few months – and I still don't know what the F.X. stands for.'

Roberts flushed. 'Francis Xavier, Sir.'

'A good saintly name – *he* wasn't afraid of active service abroad, was he? You're sure you're not afraid of France, are you?'

'Well, Sir, no, not particularly. I mean we're all a bit afraid, Sir, aren't we?'

'Yes, I suppose we are. So you didn't want to see me about that.'

William Dobie was relieved. He had not been quite sure. Now he continued to compel F.X.'s gaze, to keep contact. 'So what is it?'

Roberts, more comfortable now under the officer's quiet gaze, almost jumped at the question, as though merely to ask it would achieve his aim.

'I've got to get home, Sir, I must.'

'Yes, I quite see that now. But you realise that just as we're about to go on active service, we'd have to have a jolly good reason for getting leave, wouldn't we? Can't you give me a reason?'

'I've just got to get home, Sir.'

'Is there a death in your family, or something?'

'No, Sir.'

'Anybody seriously ill? Are your parents all right? Are you married?'

'No, Sir,' said F.X., having considered all these for a second or two.

'Then what is it? If you want compassionate leave, you'll have to supply a reason and a good one at that. You do understand, Roberts, don't you?'

But that only brought another silence – and a renewal of the head-turning. How agonised he is, thought William Dobie, how deeply lonely he looks... And he reflected on his own solitariness and how rich it was with inward memories of Miss Pomfret and Laura and with absorption with all that is in all landscapes, even in the camp. Again, on this black site, his eyes searched out the lamb that staggered about in its brave new world. This man's loneliness was of emptiness – of loss of some sort. Yet there seemed no way to develop their brief contact.

'Listen, Roberts', he said gently. 'You can tell me anything you care to tell me, however private. I give you my word I won't discuss it with another soul . . .' That this verged on an oath, forbidden to Quakers, disturbed him slightly, but he knew he had to speak in a language Roberts would understand. How far from Army protocol they were getting! Yet he knew from the man's face that only calm and confidence between them would achieve anything if F.X. were to be helped.

'I've got to sort something out, Sir. And I've got to get home.'

'Can't you tell me what it is?'

'Oh no, Sir . . . I don't think I understand myself.'

'Perhaps I can help you to? I think you'd best tell me, you know. Then, whatever it is, I'll be able to judge whether or not I can petition the colonel for you.'

But, again, the dogged silence. Dobie returned to his valise. Roberts just sat. One last attempt, thought the lieutenant.

'Well, Roberts. Can't you say? Give me a good reason and I'll go to the CO at once. I promise you.'

Roberts rose, fumbled with his cap, tried to find some formula for dismissing himself correctly, then reached for the door-knob and was out before the startled lieutenant could speak.

Sad – sad – I've failed him somehow, Dobie thought. Sad, that we put up such barriers, that a man as unhappy as that can't express his feelings in a way that I might understand and help. Sad – sad . . .

At once, thinking of Roberts and his problem, he remembered Laura's letters. He had written to her to say the Battalion was on the move and he would let her have the new address the moment he had it. But all her letters to him – there were over twenty, for she was as ardent a writer as talker – they were all there, still in their envelopes.

He felt they should not go into his valise – he had heard what happened to kit in France sometimes – and he was desperate not to lose these letters. Nor could he send them to Nonnie. So he got them all into one package and decided to ask Laura to keep them safely for him.

'My dear Laura,

I'm packing frantically. These are too precious to push into my valise – will you look after them till I return, my dear? They have sustained me during this army spell when I've been allowed to see you only once. Bless you, my dear Laura – see you soon, William Dobie.'

He could hear her saying it over, as she loved to – William Dobie! – and smiled, then returned again to the thought of poor Roberts and his problem, whatever it was.

Were men all over Britain, in strange bleak camps like this one at Catterick, also doing this, packing for France and the rumoured big offensive, also remembering and returning precious letters for safe-keeping?

Again, he walked to the Orderly Room and posted the package, then mooned through the rest of the day till ten-thirty at night and the parade.

This time, with the whole Battalion on parade in the dimmed lights of the square, CSM Green made quite sure of his Company. He did not hesitate to bawl out any individual who gave trouble of any kind, however trivial.

There were officers swarming like flies, he noted, and 'A' Company would not be the one to hold up the train if he could help it. As he marched at their side on the way to the railway station, he ruminated and resolved and reached a determination to hang on to his crown of rank, knowing that only one more promotion would be his ultimate in a soldier's life.

The entraining was their last link with Blighty. The very act bestowed upon them at once the right for the first time to use the word, for they all knew that, once locked in their compartments, they would not be released until they were paraded below the side of some troop-ship that would carry them overseas to foreign shores and the battle-field.

Beyond an occasional train journey, there was hardly a man who had travelled more than twenty miles from home, and the prospect both excited and alarmed them.

As the train picked up speed in a flurry of steam and falling smuts, they speculated wildly until the night enfolded them in drowsiness to the soporific click of the wheels over the rails.

They were on the train for six hours, dozing the night hours away, till dawn broke over a sleeping town where they stopped. Unwashed, they fell in on the platform and were marched to a quayside where a ship loomed over them. They embarked in single file. Privates and junior NCOs were on the open decks, while officers and senior NCOs disappeared into the bowels of the ship.

'I know this station,' said Roberts J.H., a swarthy little South Walian, 'it's Holyhead.'

'That's Wales, isn't it, Taffy?' Moffat asked him.

'Yes, Anglesey. North Wales it is.'

'As usual,' said Moffat, 'can't even face the right bloody way with a ship! France is over to the other side of England, ain't it?'

But Roberts was not as sure about that as about their present location. Nor did he care which way they faced, so long as it was away from home.

When he had decided to enlist, he was coal-hewing in Penrhiwceibr in the Rhondda and earning good money. The money was good, yes, but the life was horrible. He had first gone down the pit when he was twelve, and if he had ever known which side of England France was, he had forgotten in the press of life. In any case, since he was inclined to agree with nothing Moffat said, but did not know why, he was prepared to argue, but knowing Moffat's power of speech, thought first.

Whatever he said, surely they could sail from anywhere and still get there. With a miner's logic of moving coal to where the pit-tub is in order to get it out of the mine, he thought the reason for embarking at Holyhead was simply that that was where the ship happened to be. Easier to move them than the ship. But he was too tired to argue and was almost glad to get aboard, however long it took to get to wherever they were going.

Life in the Rhondda had been horrible enough – and the least the ship could do was to sail away from it. Married at twenty to Rhiannon: their first child came well within a year and the second the year after that. Remembering the honeymoon in Anglesey, he thought it possible that Evan had been conceived here on the island.

Evan had not allowed them more than an hour's consecutive sleep. If ever a child was meant to torment parents, Evan was champion. Life with Rhiannon had declined so sharply that when a second boy, Ceri, was born out of their sleepless nights together, Kitchener's finger became ever more compelling.

More than a quarter of the colliery strength had already gone. The call was strong, and when he told Rhiannon her allowance would arrive automatically and he would also send her what he could of his own shilling a day, she too was so worn out in spirit as to show little more than the vaguest interest.

Brought up 'strict Chapel' and remembering those halcyon and holy days in Anglesey, it was Moffat's language that offended Roberts J.H. even more than his opinions. Although at the colliery he heard certain words at a distance sometimes, and could not always avoid them, he would seldom have to endure the daily propinquity of a man like Moffat.

'Do you have to swear all the time?'

'The buggers make you swear, Taff. Trust them to start arse-first on the way to France!' retorted Moffat.

He neither understood nor liked Moffat and his crew – and the not understanding went as far as actual language. It was not just the cursing and swearing, it was their use of English. Moffat did not seem to be speaking the same language at all. It was like understanding the northern Welsh spoken in Anglesey – he and Rhiannon had grasped every second word only. But at least it was Welsh.

What Moffat spoke was alien not only in what he said or how he pronounced it, but in the aggressive manner of address. Although Moffat, Pearson and Simpson all spoke in the same aggressive way to one another till John Henry thought a fight must break out every five minutes, he noticed that nothing in fact happened remotely like violence between the three Londoners.

Yet when Moffat addressed him, John Henry bridled at the sheer frontal attack of the language: quick, clipped, unconsonantal, and mostly incomprehensible, with every other word a curse. The three Londoners, moreover, somehow implied in their manner of speech a breadth of experience he knew he could never claim. They even seemed to have travelled further, met more people outside their own 'tribe', whereas his own experience had been confined to his own folk in the Valley.

One night, back in Catterick, he and F.X. had found themselves together in the recreation-room and come upon a battered old atlas among the cast-off volumes donated by charity. Trying first to establish where each came from and how they had travelled there from Catterick, they were surprised to discover that otherwise neither had previously travelled further than a few miles outside his immediate orbit (except for the annual holiday at the seaside – and that never more than a day in length), in F.X.'s case the fields and woods round Nottingham, in J.H.'s to the tops with the whippets, or a few miles down the Valley to Cardiff once in a while. The Anglesey honeymoon had put him one up on F.X., and they had laughed.

As the ship eased out past the harbour mouth and turned west, Roberts J.H. saw South Stack Lighthouse and could make out the delicate bridge that connected it to Holy Island. Rhiannon and he had both spat from that bridge and watched their respective gobs swerve in the gusts that swept through the narrow channel between precipitous rocks. They had laughed, gambolled on to the lighthouse, explored the stout white-washed outworks with a childish glee – then returned late for supper at their lodgings in Holyhead and tumbled, happy and tired, into bed.

Were children born of such happiness meant to turn out such miserable destroyers of sleep as Evan? Remembering the day at the lighthouse, he half grudged Evan his life for having destroyed Rhiannon and him. Coal-hewing was just about bearable if you enjoyed peace at home. He knew he ought to glow with love at the thought of the two babes, but lack of sleep deadens a man. And the two years of anguished parenthood had killed something that had been precious to him. He felt dead in his heart – France held no dread for him.

As with Lieutenant Dobie, the Army had meant a tremendous upheaval for John Henry Roberts. But it had also meant release, from Rhiannon, the small boys, Taid and Nain his parents, and the street at Penrhiwceibr with its three Chapels: Methodist, Presbyterian and Baptist.

He had not given it much thought – and been glad to leave it all and enfold his dismal nocturnal misery in the routine and banality of camp life. He had kept both past and future at bay. Now with the future suddenly flung at him, the past came rushing in – not Rhiannon however, but the only release he had enjoyed at the time: his whippets.

When he was on a day-shift, from six in the morning to two in the afternoon, he was home by three. Rhiannon had the zinc bath ready near the kitchen fire, washed his back and laid out his meal between attending to Evan's constant needs. He would dress hastily and wolf down the meal. Tying a muffler round his neck, he then went out into the yard where Sian and Lowri curled their sleek bodies in eager anticipation of the evening run. They were highly strung, lithe springs of energy, ready like primed guns to explode into speed when released on the hills above the coal-tips.

He always took Sian first – and Lowri hung back, knowing her place since Sian was her mother.

'Sian *fach, hogen dda*,' he murmured to her caressingly, '*Da iawn*,' as he put the wide collar round her long neck and attached the lead. 'Lowri *nawr, dere nawr*.'

It was always Welsh with the dogs, a secret language between them.

And if they climbed westwards and met other whippet-fanciers on the tops, it would remain Welsh. But if they went east, he would lapse into English, for the Valley was beginning to mark the division. On that side he would meet men from the Rhymney Valley, where Welsh was slipping away already as a sort of archaism.

At once they climbed the hills behind the house, and up and up, to the tops over a thousand feet above. Once there, he would pause, quieten the two quivering creatures below his scarred hand, and point them up-wind. He would release them from the lead and then walk them forward stealthily. They were obedient to his least command, keeping to his heels, treading through the thin blown grass with a fastidious, articulate air, sharp noses sniffing the wind. He knew the minute they picked up a scent. Sian would step just ahead of him, small head down, alert as a coiled spring. Then Lowri would fall in beside her. '*Cwningen*', he whispered, and off they would fly, great hind legs biting the ground in twelve-foot leaps. Sometimes they would disappear from sight, into a dip, but he knew they would only wait, either too late at a burrow, or as often as not astride a dead rabbit unscathed but for a broken neck. Most evenings they would catch a pair, one for the family or a neighbour, the other for the dogs. If the evening were warm, John Henry would sit on a stone, gazing over the valleys at the smoking collieries and the row after row of houses.

He was in no hurry to return home, felt no guilt about Rhiannon slaving away with the two babies and the washing. It was mostly of the whippets that he spoke to F.X. – his only crony in this alien unit – and he had not mentioned either Rhiannon or the boys, not once.

His namesake F.X. was not far away, easing his pack against the hard plates of the ship's superstructure and feeling the cold. Pearson and Simpson, ever inseparable since the day of enlistment, lit Woodbines, and the westerly wind flung smoke at F.X. The smoke, a slight queasiness, and the increasing chill as they sailed further out into the open sea, all contributed to what he could only describe as 'spiritual discomfort'.

The phrase came from Father McNally's perennial instruction on Sin. Whatever he meant by sin, which covered most human activities, you always knew what the priest meant when he came to its consequences – 'spiritual discomfort'. F.X. felt that just now.

Parental vigilance and the jealous guardianship of Mother Church had steered Marian and him safely through the shoals of adolescence and early manhood. Even their walks into the woods round

94

Nottingham brought no harm. They had to come home by nine, at his or hers by turn, for a supper of what delicacies the day had left. Enlistment for a single man was becoming compulsive – and F.X. had felt the urge after the recruiting-sergeant had addressed them in the toolshed at lunch-break.

He told his parents first. He was twenty-one and free to choose therefore. The factory provided sufficient excuse to leave then rather than later.

'You must do as you think best, lad', his father had said.

After supper on his last day at home, his father, ever the devout Catholic, had suggested they say family Rosary together while Marian was with them still. On the way home to Marian's, his arm round her waist, his hand had lifted just the little till it caressed the softness of her breast. Turning, she kissed him so passionately on this, their last night, that before he knew what he was doing, his hands were all over hitherto forbidden areas. They had been so good, so careful. Suddenly, as they lay together in the dark of the parkland, frantically snapping at strange clothes and elastic, the unbelievable happened.

Passionately kissing him, she was crying bitterly. Shocked, they clung together, shyly adjusting ruffled clothes. While she cried on his neck, he hid his head in the grass, his pulse thundering to breaking-point. The intense physical love of that moment he hardly remembered. He remembered only the long and innocent love of years together as children and companions. There seemed no possible connection in his mind between the Francis Xavier of then and the F.X. of now. He remembered helping Marian up, wiping her tears, frantically trying to get her into a fit shape to go home.

'We'll be late, Frank – oh, what can I do? Tell me, Frank, what'll I do?'

He remembered only the dreadful remorse – and helplessness, the 'spiritual discomfort'. It came in great bouts of pain now in the smoke and the cold of the deck of the gently rolling ship. F.X. tucked his great-coat over putteed calves and felt quietly desperate.

As Moffat passed again, calling for 'volunteers' at a game of 'Crown and Anchor', F.X. wondered what Father McNally would have to say had he been able to consult him – or rather, confess to him; surely nothing for comfort. He wondered how Marian was. Curled uneasily against the cabin wall and now far removed from the sights of the harbour, he could only see Marian's face, crying bitterly. Again, the guilt – the 'spiritual discomfort' – as he recalled evading going in

95

to see her parents on the last night to bid them good-bye. In the porch they had whispered frantically as she renewed her efforts to repair her ravaged face and rearrange the bun of rich gold hair that she gathered up at the nape of her neck. Finally, sensing that he was unable to face them, remembering his ordeal on the morrow, she said she would tell her parents that he had to pack and had no time to come in.

'They'll never forgive you, Frank, but I'll tell them.'

'Please, give them my love.'

'I'll remember . . . Oh, Frank . . . What am I going to do?'

As she was about to break down again, he had pecked her on the cheek for the last time.

'So long, love. I'll come to see you the first leave I get – I won't be long. God bless you. Look after yourself . . .'

'You was a long time, lad', said his father. 'I thought you was never coming back. You'll have to keep better time in the Army. Now, get to bed and have a good night's sleep while you can . . .'

He and Marian had been 'all right' – elderly female relations nodded knowingly to his mother when they saw them together: 'Those two are all right . . .' Fixed, if not signed and sealed. It was certainly 'all right' by Francis Xavier. He had known Marian since school days. They were of the same age. They had waited till the age of eighteen before leaving the flock in which they had first met, and taken to themselves. That they were 'all right' was an opinion that meant not only that they were suited and looked right together, but also that they could look after themselves and would not get 'into trouble'. Though elderly female relations, if pressed, would have been hard put to find the proper words. 'Trouble' was enough – 'least said soonest mended' . . . 'Trouble', in fact, was unthinkable. If 'trouble' threatened, relations would somehow conspire to have the couple parted by organised exile for ostensible reasons that puzzled and enraged the victims, farmed out to conniving relations to be parted by as much as five miles. But the miles were enough to separate people whose tribal pattern had been confined from birth to a village or a single quarter – even a street. If 'trouble' showed any sign of threatening a family group, then elderly female relations would close ranks and the offenders be treated like the cat or bitch in season: they were locked in till things blew over. Still, on all counts, F.X. and Marian were pronounced 'all right'. They were closely observed, though they were unaware of it. Reared on the Penny Catechism, duly baptised and confirmed by the One True Church, they were adjudged 'all right'.

Now, F.X. puzzled over what had happened. It was no comfort that he could half guess. He realised that their being 'all right' consisted of being together, and that his enlistment had wounded them mortally with its threat of separation. As the days slipped by and call-up approached, they were hurtled rapidly through the last mysterious ritual of love with a speed for which they were not prepared.

The impending separation gave them only days for what, in the normal course of events, would have taken years. They were no longer 'all right' from the moment the recruiting-sergeant had appealed to F.X. in the tool-shed at the factory.

Why he had enlisted F.X. did not know, except that his instinct had told him if it were not now, it would be later, not so very much later either. The threat of conscription in the recruiting-sergeant's message was clear – the prospects for volunteers would be so much better. The line had worked, so Francis Xavier was one of several who had enlisted that day.

It was only when he met Marian afterward that he knew that, though the action was not unusual, its effects on their lives was very unusual indeed. Marian's elderly relations seemed to disappear suddenly. He and Marian were left more to their own devices – things were less 'arranged'. The impending separation changed them too. From being mere playmates, 'all right', they had become lovers. Hitherto they had linked arms, walked out together, but they had never kissed. That they belonged together no one had questioned – there was no apparent threat in their togetherness. Now the separation imposed a threat, they too had changed. As in all things, they were together. It was not she – or he – who made the first shy advance into forbidden territory. They simply fell into it, rapidly and increasingly, as soon as call-up had become known. They had nothing to learn – it came as naturally as their long companionship. They had helped each other, not talked about it; in the ever-decreasing days, they had embraced, kissed and caressed with increasing delight in each other.

Suddenly F.X. knew things he had been content to ignore and wait for. They no longer linked arms – now it was arms round each other's waist. It was not merely the loveliness of her waist under his arm, but the extraordinary feeling of her arm round his. From flank to flank, the progress to a full embrace was rapid, and if elderly female relations detected various signs and portents in their behaviour, they gave no hint of it. Normally, they would have interfered long before.

Indeed, by their various presences, it could not have happened in respectable working-class circles – and there was all the difference in the world between respectable and unrespectable. In the strata that society carefully bedded itself into, the gulf separating the two in the working class was probably the greatest of any in the scale.

It was within that sacred rule of respectability, rather than of religious scruples (though they counted), that Francis Xavier and Marian had been nurtured in an acceptable constraint – and so long as they were together, they had accepted and enjoyed it without questioning the rules.

Now events in Flanders, the scale and horror of the passing months, had changed people's inner lives completely. And when the young people were caught in a whirlpool of changed circumstances – interior and exterior alike – for which they were ill-prepared in moral terms. Nature, ever ready, took over.

It was as though all society, horrified at its own death-wish in Europe, were conniving at providing for the future of the human race. It was neither discussed nor thought of particularly. It was assumed however that things being as they were in France, where chances of survival were slim, subsequent marriage would soon mend matters in the case of those who came back – in the other case, all loving care would be lavished by patriotic relations on another war-widow and orphan. It was not so much a case of Gadarene swine, though France seemed mostly that, as of Nature asserting her rights and loosening the bonds which peacetime society had woven round her sheer excesses.

Neither F.X. nor Marian were aware of this complaisance. Their last few days had been tender and loving, a crescendo of physical caresses of a kind they had not dreamt of and which made their last evening inevitable in its outcome. Once over, and the separation enacted in an agony of guilt on both sides, the letters betrayed fears and scruples which terrified them both.

If the elderly female relations had kept out of sight, neither had they said anything to assuage guilt. Just now guilt and spiritual discomfort outweighed Francis Xavier's love, aching though it was.

Now, against the throb of the ship's engines and the chatter of the 'Crown and Anchor' game a few yards away, where Moffat was in his own element, F.X. puzzled fitfully as what he had not dared imagine began to seem probable.

*

Two things could always be assured where Moffat was present: money and 'Crown and Anchor'. He never went without either, and though he had been forced to leave the board behind at camp, having judiciously sold it the evening before they left to a man remaining behind in the home party, he still had his portable kit ready for just such an occasion as this: a cloth with the familiar insignia printed over its surface, and a set of small dice and a box to match. It took no room in his pack, and as far as Moffat was concerned was worth its weight in gold.

The CSM spotted it at once and was immediately afflicted with the same unease of command that had marked the morning parade. For he knew he ought to suppress the game at once, but was unable to. The game was forbidden – and he knew that Moffat knew it. They all knew it was rife in the Army, the cause of considerable marital distress in cases where married men gambled their way into debt. The authorities tried to stamp it out, and even the Home Office, taking its life in its hands, had approached the War Ministry about it.

They did not go far, since the War Ministry knew too well that it was more important to keep men happy if the Army were to be effective at all. A good game of 'Crown and Anchor' did much to that end. Gambling, even more than drinking (for men could be easily confined to barracks where that showed signs of getting out of control), was the one great relief from the inevitable boredom of camp life. Of all the games devised, however – and no amount of surveillance could be effective all the time – 'Crown and Anchor' was by far the most popular, the working man's roulette, so to speak.

Moffat, with an insatiable appetite for life, had early suborned CSM Green. They had been at camp two weeks when they were awarded twenty-four hours' leave. It was little enough, and most had not known what to do with it, or were without funds to make use of it. They had walked out of camp in small groups, returning hungry for each meal, having gone a mile or two to sniff the air and feel what freedom there was outside the camp perimeter – and no more.

Not so Moffat. He knew there was a steeple-chase meeting at Catterick and, patiently lounging through the morning (not for him the pointless exercise of walking without an objective), had marked with a stubby pencil various horses in *The Sporting Man*.

After the midday meal, he walked smartly out of camp with Pearson and Simpson towards the outskirts of the little garrison town. Carefully doling out four half-crowns to each of his henchmen, knowing without asking the state of their pockets, he advised them briefly and comprehensively on form, favourites and possible outsiders.

'And don't ask another question, the two of you! Put your money on what you fancies and pay me back if it comes up. If it don't, I'll chalk it up, right? But don't ask me any more stupid bloody questions – I ain't got the time. Just leave me alone. I don't want another bloody word out of the pair of you. Right? Now, scarper!'

They took the hint. Moffat left them and paid to get into the main stand. He was a solitary private among officers and the local gentry. He knew too well the permissible limits of equality of a race meeting – and it did not bother him that he was alone among the quality. Here, a certain amount of money and a hard-won knowledge of form were sufficient. Any member of the lower orders without either, he knew, would soon be frozen out. Moffat had sufficient of both to outstare anybody who might try to suggest he was not welcome.

Bringing out his purse, he placed a sovereign to win the first race at a booth under the stands, then sauntered up the steps to watch the horses parading in the paddock. It did not surprise him when he saw Sergeant-Major Green below him. Every man had his weakness – and he had noticed the CSM buying *The Sporting Man* each morning from the camp newsvendor. And as the buffer between officers and other ranks, money or no, Green would just qualify for a place in the grandstand.

Moffat's horse came fourth, which was good enough for him. It pointed to conditions – heavy after some March showers. He carefully revised his estimate of the various handicaps on each horse he fancied – and noticed at the same time that the CSM did not rush to claim any winnings.

He waited, watching every move of the sergeant-major and saw him finally make a decision and proceed to the bookmaker's booth, obviously to place a second bet. He waited until Green returned, then rushed down to place his own bet. He dashed back, checked that the CSM was still there below him, then set his attention on the race.

Moffat's horse came first, but he did not rush to claim his winnings. He knew that the bookmakers under the stand were reliable. Rather, he watched the sergeant-major again. The head was down to the race-card. Loser again, thought Moffat.

He waited. Slowly, the CSM turned and made to descend the steps.

Moffat followed. Green was going through his pockets. Broke? Probably. Moffat quickened a little. Brushing past an officer or two, he contrived to arrive at the booth just in front of the sergeant-major.

He made sure he was seen, collected five sovereigns, placed two of them each way on the third race, and turned – face to face with the sergeant-major.

'Well, Moffat, so we like a flutter, do we? In the stands, heh? Flush, are we?'

'Oh, hello, Sir. Fancy meetin' you!'

'Any luck?'

'Two winners so far, Sir. Can't grumble. And you, Sir?'

'Damn it, no luck at all . . . I prefer the flat. I think I'll make this my last and call it a day, heh? What have you backed, eh?'

But Moffat had been too long in the game to fall for that one. If he gave a loser, he would be in the dog-house for ever – and he was not prepared to share winners with any man.

'Ah, that would be tellin', Sir.'

'Quite right, Moffat, quite right. Mustn't spoil a good run.'

Moffat watched as the sergeant-major changed his mind and placed a bet with half-a-sovereign. Then, with a sure instinct, he took up his stand near by, but sufficiently removed to preserve the delicacies of rank.

His horse came third, but at each way, he was well satisfied with a third of the odds. As the horses passed the post, he turned to descend the steps at once, to make sure his win was observed. As he claimed the winnings, he turned and saw the CSM preparing to leave, then turning hesitantly towards him.

'Come up again, heh?' he asked.

'Yes, Sir. Ten to one', Moffat lied, ostentatiously stuffing seven sovereigns into his purse. The sergeant-major recognised a master when he saw one.

'Time you left, boy, while the going's good.'

'Oh, no, Sir. You'll never catch me leavin' a meetin' in the middle, win or lose.'

Green was trapped. He was broke, and he sensed that Moffat knew it. But to leave in the face of a confident assertion like that was more than a CSM could do in front of a man like Moffat.

'Are you off, Sir?'

'Well, er, no . . . I think I'll try one more time. My only trouble is that I've left my purse in the Orderly Room safe. You know how you have to look after everything in camp, eh? I'll tell you what, boy, could you lend me a fiver?'

Thus they achieved equality. That was as Moffat had calculated. He was a bit thunderstruck at the amount, but a sergeant-major must be presumed to have the cheek. He counted out five sovereigns with alacrity and reckoned it was well worth it.

He kept his distance – and watched. The CSM did not speak to him again. For the rest of the meeting, Moffat both won and lost – Green did much the same. He reckoned that the CSM left with more or less the £5 he had borrowed. He knew he would not see it again, but was satisfied.

Back in camp, he had no fears for his 'Crown and Anchor' board. The corporal was one of themselves, and therefore easy. The sergeant, no doubt, had been primed by the sergeant-major whom to pick up and whom not. Now Moffat's game proceeded with impunity on board the ship, while the CSM kept a weather eye for any NCO who might feel like interfering.

But of 'Crown and Anchor', of ships and men, Robert F.X. was soon oblivious as he dozed off in the warmth of his curled position, grasping his pack to his belly with his back against the ship's plates. At last, he had succumbed to tiredness. He knew no more till he heard shouting all round him and Corporal Dinsdale rousing him with: 'Land ahead!'

F.X. eased stiffly out of his cramped position. He saw his companions crowding at the rail and gazing right. As he rose, he saw the ship was passing a lighthouse on their left, marking an isolated rock some way from land. They were going quite fast. He could hear the gentle swish of the water beneath. The ship was steady. His queasiness had gone.

As he struggled to find a place at the crowded rail, his 'spiritual discomfort' had passed too.

Over the men's heads, he saw a gracious cone-shaped mountain some miles ahead and slightly left. No signs of battle. He had imagined this moment so often in the last month: troops, transport, the gun smoke and distant rumble of explosions.

He saw only a green land, as peaceful as home, with hills along the skyline. The war, the battle – he could not picture the scale or location of it, however hard they had tried to simulate its conditions way back on the moors above Catterick – must be away beyond those hills, and some distance too, since there was not the faintest sound of artillery.

He had heard that people in Dover could hear the sound of the guns over the Channel, but here all might have been peace were it not for their own presence.

Three officers strolled past with an air of unconcern. The nearest, Lieutenant Dobie, smiled awkwardly.

'France, Sir?' Roberts ventured, but the non-committal 'Mm' left him no wiser and he wondered if he ought to have spoken to the lieutenant. But they were too absorbed to take notice.

He found his namesake, J.H., and edged in to the rail beside him.

'Didn't take long, did it?' said J.H.

'I don't know. I fell asleep.'

J.H. took a fob out of his pocket. 'Just over three hours', he said.

So Moffat had been wrong. A voyage three hours from Holyhead to France could hardly be described as starting 'arse-first'.

A grey town with tall steeples lay ahead, sharp in the morning light. They were entering a harbour with a lighthouse at the end of each of two long piers. They could clearly see men and boys fishing off the nearest pier, trying to eke out wartime rations.

'No sign of anything going on', said J.H.

'No, looks as though the war is miles away', replied F.X.

Tiny Liddell, another private, joined them, small and neat as a jockey.

'If you're right about that being Holyhead, then we can't be abroad, can we? We left at six, and it's half-past nine now. So how could we be abroad, tell me?'

'Well, we sailed across the sea, didn't we,' said J.H., 'and here we're landing. So we're bound to be abroad, isn't it?'

'Wrong,' replied Tiny Liddell, speaking sharply, 'we might be pulling into another British port, couldn't we? Anyway, it doesn't look like France to me.'

'How d'you know?' said a fourth, from Liverpool. 'You've never been to bloody France, Tiny, have you now?'

Even Tiny had no answer to this. J.H. tried again.

'Well...' he speculated, 'this could be Liverpool.'

'Don't talk bloody daft,' said the Scouse, 'Liverpool! If that's Liverpool, I'm a bloody elephant. Liverpool! Where's Bairken'ead? Jesus Christ, mate, you've got the wrong bloody pier!'

F.X., like J.H., had had to get used to the language. It had been bad enough at the toolshop at times, but nothing compared with the Army. But you got used to it – you had to.

What he could not accept was the constant use of the Lord's name in vain, as the commandment put it. Father McNally did not have any priority about the ten commandments – they were all obligatory and fearful, and if the sixth was the latest and weightiest in instruction, the second had been drummed in long since at childhood, and was ingrained.

'I suppose you *have* to swear all the time,' he said to the Scouse, 'but why do you have to use the Lord's name in vain?'

'All right, Saviour,' scoffed Moffat. 'You give him what for, Saviour. Watch your bleedin' language, Scouse. Saviour's watchin' you...'

F.X. braced, then shrugged his shoulders. He knew that the company sergeant-major's outburst on parade would stick as long as he remained with them.

Lieutenant Dobie sensed the men's mood. They longed to ask questions. But he returned to his colleagues.

'The men are restless', he said to Lieutenant Saxton. 'When will we be allowed to tell them, d'you think?'

'Don't know. While you were out, the old man said we weren't to say a word until we have the order. Can't think why. They're bound to rumble. Surely, there's no Irishman among them anyway. Doesn't make sense.'

'Ah, but don't you remember? We left a few behind at the home party, didn't we? They were probably all Irishmen now I come to think: O'Neill, yes? McElroy, Walsh, Devine... Of course, all Irishmen!'

'You're right,' said Saxton. 'By Jove, they're clever, aren't they! No fear of Irishmen being sent back to Ireland.'

On deck, the NCOs were mustering the men. Gangways were hoisted aboard by men on the quay, looking not a bit different from those at Holyhead. The soldiers listened to every word of theirs.

'Paddies, the lot of them', said Moffat, alert as ever.

'Quiet there, all of you!' shouted Sergeant Forster. 'Get your packs on and be ready to move. Davis, Mellor, Roberts J.H., and *you*...' pointing to Pearson, 'follow me. You're baggage party.'

Pearson nodded to Simpson and winked. Simpson followed them. The sergeant would not notice one extra in the party. They went below.

With Corporal Dinsdale in charge, the Company shuffled off down the gangway. The quayside was soon a mass of troops. They were ordered to fall in and were marched thirty yards down the quay to clear the area round the two gangways, then were stood at ease. Looking back, they saw 'B' Company, then 'C' Company coming down, until the whole Battalion was on the quay. Ordinarily, there should have been a fourth Company to swell their numbers, but the losses in France and the delay to conscription had kept this new Battalion to three Companies. Even worse, each Company was short of officers. Each should have had a captain in command, with one lieutenant or subaltern to each of the four Platoons. In fact there was only one captain in the entire Battalion – and only seven lieutenants. Where a Platoon was without an officer, a sergeant was in charge.

'A' Company was without a captain, so Lieutenant Dobie was its commander, if only because his Platoon came numerically before Saxton's. Dobie considered it odd, since Saxton was senior both in age and service. He knew however that one must expect neither mind nor logic in the Army. He was in charge of No. One Platoon – Saxton of No. Two – while Sergeant Forster had command of the third Platoon and 'Chief', a mild sergeant by name of Kerfoot, of the fourth.

No one had any illusions about this thinness of officers – they were all just cannon fodder anyway; more or fewer officers made little difference, so long as they could muster a Company. More worrying to the men was the fact that some of the Platoons were below the normal strength of sixty men. So, depleted as they were, they jostled to their places on the quay.

Finally, they saw the baggage party carrying officers' kit ashore, followed by the junior officers. Only then were they allowed to file into the adjoining railway station where a field kitchen steamed away on the platform.

Hunger and lack of sleep had made them sullen. There was no means of frying bacon for so many, so it had been boiled in the usual dixies. CSM Green strolled behind the cooks, his pacing stick under his arm, as if to indicate that while complaints were not out of order, they were inadvisable.

Having enjoyed breakfast aboard with his fellow officers, Lieutenant Dobie watched them, wondering at the structure that had created such divisions between people. Boiled bacon for the men after standing for half an hour, then filing past the steaming dixies – bacon, a slice of bread in one half of the billy-can, cocoa in the other half. Thinking of his own breakfast daintily served by the ship's steward, he had a conscience about it.

Yet the men were wolfing the awful stuff as though they were used to no better. One more indication that building bridges would not always be the answer, he thought. Those men, some of them looking around for more, would not change places with him any more than he would with them. That however was not the only division.

Just as the men did not know where they were, he himself had no idea what lay ahead. All he knew was the fact that he was in Ireland and the Battalion would not entrain but march. But where to?

To that he had no answer yet. Some senior officers were still aboard in solemn conclave, communicating nothing. He did not even know if 'something was up'. He was sure that, by now, the men had surmised where they were.

Had all Irishmen been culled back at Catterick because of their reputation for drinking and the possibility of desertion on their home ground? But why Ireland? Remembering the vaguest newspaper reports, there might be signs of trouble in Ireland again and it was unlikely that the Battalion was there for further field training.

Yet with the Western Front clamouring for reinforcements, it made little sense to send a Battalion to deal with whatever trouble there might brew in Ireland. Indeed, however ill-trained they might be, the pattern these days was to send entire regiments raw and untried into the trenches in France, so urgent was the need.

The gap in communication offended Dobie's sensibilities more than the class division just now. He had carried out his orders – that is, had transmitted to CSM Green to have the Company mustered in marching order at the landward end of the station platform just as soon as they had finished their dreary breakfast.

The long journey, virtually without a halt and with only fitful sleep on train and ship, had left them weary. The breakfast had not helped. Nevertheless, there was no let-up. They formed fours, sloped arms, turned left, and with Lieutenant Dobie and Sergeant Forster at their head marched off, up towards the town. A train puffing idly in the station showed no signs of moving. In any case, it was not for them. With frequent haranguing from CSM Green to keep their heads up and show the town a smart turn-out, they tried their best to keep a good step. The local citizenry looked at them as they passed, as any

106

spectators will look at a passing parade – from time to time they shouted something, sometimes with marked hostility, but for the most part they showed a studied indifference.

Up they climbed, colliding disastrously with a horde of people pouring out of a large church, then turned right at a sign saying 'Dublin' with some relief, since it seemed to leave the people behind and led slightly downhill.

Yet, oddly, it was the turn downhill, more than the road-sign, that impressed their minds – or, rather, their bodies. The night journey had tired them, and the change from marching uphill into town was all that mattered. The body on occasion blinds the eye – and only a few noticed the unexpected Dublin sign. They simply fell into rhythm and the inevitability of the march without another thought, except for the next bunk where they might stretch their legs in comfort.

When Lieutenant Dobie saw the sign, he wondered why it was so necessary not to tell the men they were in Ireland. Why compound their customary distrust with silly rules of non-communication when every signpost and advertisement clearly proclaimed Ireland? It was such a perverse way of going about things. The perverseness bothered him.

Dublin, yes. He knew that once they had left Holyhead – surely, now the men shared the knowledge. Although he was no less ignorant of the reason: training, rest, duties of some sort – perhaps even action? Remembering the urgent need for reinforcements in France, he found it difficult to imagine what sort of action Ireland might require.

As the Company settled into a steady rhythm down the long road out of Kingstown and towards Dublin, he thought the most likely reason was to guard property, installations, Government establishments and so on.

If so, Miss Pomfret would not be too discomfited. For her, sabre-rattling was abhorrent bullying, but there was still all the difference in the world between rattling and actually using the sabre.

Guarding property, most likely, he thought. Though why a whole Battalion? Although he had not given it much thought, he knew that there was an 'Irish Question'. But that, surely, was nineteenth-century history. Gladstone had devoted some of his tremendous political flair to it, but then he had applied it to many other matters. Ireland was just one of them.

In the drowsy seminars of summer afternoons in Cambridge, the conflict between Gladstone and Disraeli had occupied more of their attention than anything between Ireland and England. The name of Parnell had arisen of course, shrouded in a certain mystery – and in the mystery the promise of Home Rule had never been kept.

Among several things that had distinguished his school from others was the instruction from the English master to read the first leader in *The Manchester Guardian*, more for its style than its content. It was reckoned to be a model of English usage – the plain, objective language suited the Quaker conscience more than other national dailies could. It also served to keep the boys *au fait* with political opinion.

William Dobie had kept the habit. He recalled that the approach of war and the affairs of the Habsburg Empire had supervened and post-poned the revival of the idea of Home Rule for Ireland. Later, examin-ations and the war itself had removed any thought of it from his mind.

Now, as he stepped on the soil of Ireland for the first time, William realised how little he knew – and conversely, how sudden and start-ling the reality was: IRELAND!

At once, he began to rationalise, to keep at arm's length a nagging premonition of the reality. Once out of the town, he felt that their pres-ence – a military presence – was due to some political unrest. Their sheer presence would deal with it. If so, it put off the day when he must go into action and finally deny Nonnie.

He was relieved, because in spite of a degree of knowledge of the Irish Question and its political impact at Westminster he suspected, without acknowledging the suspicion, that there was more there than politics – perhaps violence of a kind? He could not quite pinpoint it, but it disturbed him.

Of his commitment to Belgium – and France – he now had little doubt. He had agonised for months, debated it with Nonnie (and with no one else except Laura), and had come down on the side of the argu-ment of the 'moral lump'. He had gone over the case in detail, and could do no other, however much it might hurt Nonnie.

Now the argument was wide open once again, even while he marched with the men towards he knew not what. He only hoped they were there to prevent rather than to cure. A descent into violence, here, on this island, was unthinkable, so unthinkable that he resolved to keep his thoughts to the Battalion and its actual movement. That was his job now. Thinking was not only a luxury, it was dangerous. This was his first movement in charge of a Platoon. Raw though he was, he was beginning to catch the feeling of *esprit-de-corps*, to know the men, their faces and the surnames that went with them. He even felt a certain pride in them. The Army, at best, was a motley gang. Why was it not possible to help the deserving, like Francis Xavier Roberts, without transgressing the rules?

Major Dean-Forbes, he knew, was critical of his approach. To the major, the men were a recalcitrant anonymous mass to be licked into shape. The major would prefer him to join more in the manly *bonhomie* of the officers' mess to the exclusion of all else.

But the very stubbornness that had resisted even Miss Pomfret also confounded the Major. Dobie had resisted the major's taunts – and given the chance, would gladly have broken the barriers down in Roberts F.X.'s case.

The young man was deeply troubled. Dobie had watched him and seen the depth of unhappiness in the eyes. Alas, the machinery to talk things over with his batman simply did not exist. Even the interview prior to embarkation, irregular as it was, had failed. The CSM represented the barrier between him and his men. To pick up one man for a private talk would be misconstrued. It seemed, in fact, that just then, in the ranks, F.X. was causing trouble.

'Get into step, Roberts!' shouted the CSM. 'Left – right – left – right . . .'

F.X. was far away, and entirely out of step. He shuffled clumsily, and only with difficulty resumed the steady left-right-left-right of the march. Its hypnotic rhythm brought him no comfort. Foremost and ever-present in his mind, over and above the sergeant-major's voice, was Marian. He failed to understand her letters – they were cryptic in a woman's way which he could not fathom. To the steady *tramp-tramp-tramp*, he went over it all again and found no comfort, it was all somehow just beyond his understanding. He should have skipped home before coming abroad, but he had been without money.

The major came up briskly to Lieutenant Dobie, who at once slackened pace to allow the CSM to reach him. He passed on the order. The CSM broke step, walked to the side of the road and waited there till the Company's mid-rank reached him.

'Com – pany – Halt!'

They all knew how bad it was – how far from parade square precision they came to a halt. They were too tired, and CSM Green knew it. He let them settle a moment, then ordered them to fall out and rest by the roadside.

They sagged against their packs, their rifles stacked in tripods at the edge of the road. For a few minutes no one spoke. Then they stirred uneasily, searching for items in their pockets, not knowing quite for what.

'Blimey, this lot never stops', said Moffat. 'First train, then boat, now this bleedin' march. Jesus, they must think we're bloody machines!'

'What d'you think they're after?' Pearson asked.

'Oh – just givin' us the air, I s'pose.'

'No. But what d'you think it is? Another camp at the end, same as last, or what? The chaps think we're in Ireland. What the hell are we doing in Ireland? Tell me that, mate. If it is Ireland...'

'It's bloody Ireland all right,' replied Moffat with a knowing air. 'Just take a butcher's at that lot over there... Listen to 'em – paddies, the lot of 'em, you mark my words!'

A gang of plate-layers on the nearby railway line had rested on their shovels as the men halted. They were now conjecturing on the presence of so strong a contingent of the British Army at the roadside. Although the troops could not catch every word, there was no mistaking the lilt of their voices.

'The bloody officers'll tell you nuffin', don't you worry, mate', Moffat grumbled on. 'Yours not to reason why, yours but to do and die.'

It was all vaguely worrying.

But the officers were moving about, nodding to one another, no more certain what was required of them.

Major Dean-Forbes came up again to Lieutenant Dobie and directed him to the rear. Craning their necks, the men saw the officers foregather and then walk smartly to the low school building, empty of children for the Easter holidays.

A few drays and floats went by in either direction: fish, market produce, milk, bread and the occasional private traveller. Even a few pedestrians threaded a way past their feet.

The sun was warm on their backs. Out in the bay they could see a naval gun-boat hurrying ashore, a great black plume of smoke trailing after it. What had it to do with them? It was all like watching the horses rushing along, pulling the fire-engine to a jangling of bells. Always worth watching – but what else? It was their fire-engine to be sure, but always, thank God, someone else's fire.

But the halt gave time for the feeling of their new surroundings to sink in. It was not merely that they had moved from the moorland of northern England – it was also very different, foreign in a way that did not fit. It did not seem like France – hardly a man had not heard by now the stories of men back on leave from France, of *estaminets*, of the famous statue of the Virgin of Albert, of the odd ways of the French with their garlic and onions and strong cigarettes. But, above all, of the roads crowded with transport and troops marching between base and front-lines and the endless chaos of it.

They had not known what to expect. The emptiness, now that they were well out of the port, was certainly not what they had imagined. And there was something familiar about the tram route – they were both abroad and at home. The grey stone of walls, the sharp green of new grass of spring, the predominance of donkeys in the shafts of the little carts, the low cottages now they were in open country, most of them whitewashed and a few thatched – all were different, spartan, spare.

Yet the port had been very ordinary, an extension of an English tram route, except that they had passed large Catholic churches with elaborately carved marble crucifixes outside, and crowds of people swarming round their porches as though fearing to venture out. That was different. But Woodbines would be obtainable at the tobacconist's . . . It was different – yet the same. And with it all, a vague, undeclared threat.

In the school, the eight junior officers of the Battalion shuffled into the largest classroom, which only just held them.

Lieutenant Dobie, feeling the effects of the journey and the march along hard roads, eased his back against a wall alongside Lieutenant Saxton. Such meetings were rare – quite without precedent in the middle of what was ostensibly a route march of some sort.

'Any idea what it's all about, Saxton?'

'This halt, you mean? Rum ration, I hope, Dobie. I could certainly do with it, couldn't you? It would slip down very nicely in my present state. But why ask me? You're the one who should know; you're reading History, aren't you?'

'True. But you'd hardly call it history – yet. Would you?' Dobie, slightly younger than Saxton, rather doubted the implied drinking prowess, but was not sure.

'All the same, things build up, don't they?' Saxton persisted.

'True too, but I'd hardly like to pronounce on the Irish Question, if that's what you mean – not from my sparse reading of nineteenth-century British history.'

'Oh, come off it, Dobie. Nobody's asking you to pronounce – or even to express opinions. But, surely, Ireland must have figured somewhere in your reading of history.'

Even the normally equable Saxton was giving way to the irritation that was building up in the stuffy classroom. Dobie, ever cautious and unwilling to expose any possible weakness in his scholarship, refused to rise. But Captain Harwood came forward – and rank was not easily denied. Furthermore, at thirty-three, the captain was much the senior of the group whose age ranged from about twenty to twenty-three or four.

'Yes, Dobie,' the captain said rather sharply, for once pulling rank, 'You might be able to help. My own history is rather sketchy, but even I have read enough about English politics to know that Gladstone devoted some of his career to the Irish Question . . . And what about Parnell? Come on, Dobie; anything that might throw light on what we're doing here instead of in France!'

'Well, Sir, it's always been a delicate situation – Ireland and England. That's why I wouldn't like to say anything about it.'

'Oh, hogwash, Dobie,' said Saxton, 'Come on, tell us about Gladstone and what's-his-name!'

Dobie shrank from that. It offended what scholarship he aspired to. But now he was surrounded, a rare event. They were not to be denied. He could almost enjoy it.

'Well, yes,' he began. 'Gladstone and Parnell are key figures all right. That's common knowledge.' He paused, diffidently, measuring how far to go with them. One great mess rule was not to bore people.

'Go on, then', Saxton broke in again testily. 'What about Gladstone and Parnell?'

Satisfied that at least he had educated Saxton thus far to remember the Irish leader's name, Dobie went on: 'Well, I'll try. But I warn you, it's idiotic to render history and politics into a nutshell. The Irish Question's just about as long as British history itself. If you take modern history – I mean as distinct from mediaeval – as beginning with the Reformation, when the Church in England turned away from Rome, then the differences began in earnest, because Ireland didn't – turn away from Rome, I mean. I'd say that was the crux. England, suspicious of any possible threat to her religious independence from Rome and all that Rome stood for, took jolly good care not to let

Ireland become an open back-door for her enemies in Europe – Spain, for example, or France, or Bonnie Prince Charlie, or whoever it might be at any given time. So what England did was to plant a Protestant establishment in Ireland.' Dobie took a deep breath before plunging further:

'Elizabeth founded Trinity College in Dublin so that Protestant gentlemen could be educated and so perpetuate the establishment. Then Cromwell, who dealt personally and harshly with Irish rebellion, actually planted a whole colony, mostly Scottish Presbyterians, in the north to bolster James the First's first Scottish colony there. That, you could say, confirmed a second nation on the island. And that's the trouble, you see: there *are* two nations here, sharply divided by religion – native Irish Catholic on one side, and English and Scottish Protestant establishment on the other. And now they too are native... There's never been any peace really – there's always been an Irish Question; it's the sore thumb of British politics...'

'Not bad, Dobie, not bad,' Captain Harwood said. 'That's all jolly interesting. I've never been able to understand the squabbling myself, but put like that, it begins to make sense.'

'Thank you, Sir', said Dobie, who was content to leave it at that.

Still, the captain persisted: 'Suppose we're here, too, to see that Ireland isn't a back-door for England's present enemy? D'you suppose the Germans could be in Ireland? After all, they're not defeated at sea by a long chalk. They could sail ships round the north of Scotland and get here with troops, couldn't they? It would provide a pretty distraction from the Western Front!'

'It could be. Who's to know except the High Command? And they're hardly likely to tell us anything...' Dobie was eager to clutch at any straw to reinforce his moral stance. He found himself wishing the Germans were in Ireland. If the supposition were true not only little Belgium, but little Ireland too, would further justify him in enlisting.

'But go on,' said the captain, 'you still haven't expanded on the Gladstone-Parnell business. As you say, it's only a generation ago, so it's bound to be around still. These things don't just go away.'

The idea that, assuming they were to face anything, it might be the Germans rather than the Irish, eased Dobie's mind with every passing minute. He felt more confident of conveying his knowledge, such as it was.

'Well, my reading of the Gladstone-Parnell era is that Parnell, though a Protestant landlord, represented Irish feeling at Westminster to such an extent that Gladstone and the Liberal party more or less accepted the Irish case and got as far as drafting a Home Rule for Ireland Bill. For a start, Parnell had united the Irish party in the House, and that represented quite a balancing power between Tory and Liberal in Parliament ... Gladstone represented the great Nonconformist conscience – and after the Irish potato famine we certainly had a conscience. And, remember, things like absentee landlords are an explosive issue for a suppressed peasantry. It only wanted a leader to gather the various strands of Irish rebellion – and there were, there are, plenty of those. The Fenians, the Irish Republican Brotherhood, the Gaelic League, the Citizen Army. There's any amount of them, and they keep changing names and roles – but all for the same end: Irish independence of British rule. They're all supported by their American brethren in the way of funds and moral support in the international field. Anyway, Parnell had the capacity to unite all the various elements – and given the Irish character, that's quite a feat. Parnell was accepted by Irishmen and by Westminster as the Irish leader. His methods were constitutional – at least till the very end, when it's extremely doubtful if he maintained his constitutional principles.'

He waited for reactions, then went on: 'Gladstone went a long way with the Home Rule Bill. The opposition came mostly from the Tories protecting the Protestant interest in the North. No Catholic hegemony for them. It's bitter stuff, I can tell you, and I'd say there's no solution – except, perhaps, an imposed one, and that sometimes makes more problems than it solves. The Irish *are* a different people after all, and if they are, it's understandable for them to expect nationhood in some form or other. One can see they would have aspirations to independence, especially after the famine in the 'forties, when evictions rather than welfare was the attitude of the landlords. And, remember, there had been an Irish Parliament in the late 18th century. Grattan's Parliament, it's usually called. But it got too independent for the British and they abolished it.'

'Go on', Captain Harwood prompted him.

Dobie was in his stride by now. 'Never forget that on the other side you have the Protestants in the North – the second nation. "No surrender" is their motto. They're absolutely loyal to England and Protestantism, fiercely loyal. They'll never consent to being governed by the Irish. Two nations, you see. You can't be fair to one without being unfair to the other.'

Lieutenant Dobie turned slightly, as though to look out of the window and terminate what had become a lecture. But they were too interested to drop it.

In truth, he had started explaining the Irish Question as rationally and as simply as he could for his colleagues, and he felt more and more that they were in Ireland for something sinister. It could not be as simple as a German presence. It did not fit somehow. Ironically, it would be too good to be true as far as his own position was concerned – and no one, British, Irish or German, would give a damn about that. As to the 'back-door' argument, it was surprising how little it had been used, perhaps because of the Protestant establishment.

Deep inside him, he was not convinced that the Battalion was in Ireland to deal with Germans, but rather with some element within the argument he had presented. The other officers wanted to know, to talk about it in the claustrophobic atmosphere of the primary school classroom halfway between Kingstown and Dublin.

Hitherto Dobie had not dared face it. Since the first knowledge that Ireland was to be their destination, he had put the thought away from him, had willed his mind towards the logistics of movement, of disembarking and marching his Company as best possible. But now, by their insistence, his fellow officers were forcing him to focus on the real reason for their presence in Ireland.

'And that's that?' asked Saxton.

'Well, no. Parnell led the most confused private life and . . .'

'You mean, the Kitty O'Shea episode?' Captain Harwood interrupted.

'Exactly', Dobie continued, a little surprised at the captain's obvious knowledge of the salient points of the case – and possibly more than that, for Harwood was usually uncommunicative among the youngsters around him and there was no way of knowing how much he knew.

'Parnell was a brilliant constitutional politician,' Dobie continued, 'but he went off with the wife of another Irish member of the House. Not the sort of thing you can get away with indefinitely, as you can imagine. Not that Captain O'Shea seemed to mind – in fact, he connived, at the beginning anyway. It helped his political career. But it couldn't last. O'Shea turned sour, things reached a head at a by-election in Galway and everything caught up with Parnell at the Divorce Court. The English papers were more than ready to discredit him. They'd already lost a case against him when they used forged papers to associate his name with the violent element in Irish politics. The divorce was just what they'd been wanting. They hounded him. He lost the leadership of the Irish Party, and if the Home Rulers had not been defeated already, that put paid to their hopes. The Irish cause was lost for the time being. But Home Rule keeps popping up like a cork, as you know. It came up again a year or two before the war started. Now, while the war goes on, I'd guess it'll be shelved indefinitely. Anyway, the Irish haven't had a leader of the calibre of Parnell since then. He's become a hero, a political martyr. I'm pretty sure a lot of Irishmen revere his name, scandal or no.'

'Could it be that sort of Irishmen we've been sent to deal with?' Captain Harwood asked. 'There's still trouble around, even if we don't altogether understand. What I find difficult to grasp, if that's the case, is how so many Irishmen come to be fighting in the British Army.'

'Oh, make no mistake,' said Dobie, 'the Irish themselves can be at loggerheads over Home Rule. I reckon a lot of them would prefer to remain in the British Empire, even to stay British. Even if that weren't a correct assumption, we must remember that Home Rulers are divided. There are those who follow Parnell's constitutional approach – and there's always been an element who believed that would get them nowhere, that only violence would achieve independence. Even Parnell in his last desperate days talked of the "hillside men", trying to attract support when constitutionalism was slipping away from him.'

'My God, Dobie, you *are* putting it into a nutshell all right!' said Saxton.

The historian in Dobie warmed to the response to his 'lecture' – for what historian is not, at heart, an exegetist? 'There have always been Irishmen who held with the Union with Britain – and others who'd fight to the death to break it. And, as always, a lot of Irishmen between the two. I have no idea how many would opt for Home Rule at the moment, but I'd guess most of them would want it by constitutional means, the original Parnell line. But though the issue is shelved for the present, the argument won't stop, naturally. What has stopped, for the moment anyway, is any constitutional settlement of the Irish Question – Home Rule, Irish independence, whatever you care to call it.'

'I see', said Saxton, apparently satisfied, for he would have readily admitted to a greater knowledge of Irish horses than of Irish politics.

'You reckon the argument's still going on between Irishmen. What you're saying is that if there are umpteen Irishmen fighting with us against the Germans, there are still some prepared to have a go at us now, to get Home Rule for Ireland.'

'I didn't say that. I said I reckoned the argument between Irishmen wouldn't stop.'

'All right. But if those against the Union decided to take action right now, we'd be in a right pickle, wouldn't we, with a war in Europe on our hands?'

'We might. I've always suspected the back-door argument. Any enemy of England who used Ireland as a back-door would still have a wider stretch of water than the English Channel to cross.'

'That's the German argument. I'm talking about Irishmen. Regardless of Germans, if the Irish opposition wanted to embarrass us, wouldn't *now* be the best moment – or the worst, depending which way you look at it? Honestly, Dobie, d'you reckon they would?'

'I return to my original point, that the Irish Question is too delicate to predict. It's too tricky altogether, don't you see?'

Saxton shook his head. 'No, old man, I don't. Because we're not here for nothing. I gather enough from what you're saying to make my own guess. I reckon we're here because those Irishmen who want to break with England are at it again. They probably think they can get more that way than by Parnell's constitutionalism.'

'Well, actually Parnell's long since dead.' Dobie could not resist a jibe at Saxton's history. 'A chap called Redmond, I think, now. But Asquith and Redmond aren't nearly the same vintage as Gladstone and Parnell. A Home Rule Bill passed the Commons in 1912, but Carson and his Ulstermen managed to hold it off. And that's about it – unless there's something I haven't heard.'

And since they were there as a Battalion and their presence alone would be sufficient to deal with any trouble there might be, the officers broke from the circle. Problem solved, the collective military mind seemed to say.

But Captain Harwood detached himself from the group and returned to Dobie.

'Look here, Dobie, you put it very clearly. I'm not sure we can dismiss the problem so easily. There could be trouble, it wouldn't be the first time. Why is it Englishmen give it so little thought? Saxton here is typical – intelligent enough and all that. But he's more interested in the cricket averages than in the Irish Question. Doesn't give a damn about it. Can't say it's my concern either, to tell you the truth. But listen, Dobie, whatever all this is about, not a word to the men. The Old Man wouldn't like that, you understand.'

'I wouldn't dream of it, Sir. But if it is trouble ahead, the men's lives are as much at stake as ours. So why keep them in ignorance? Why, they don't even know we're in Ireland! There's something dreadful about risking a man's life when he doesn't even know he's not in France...'

'Oh, I shouldn't go all dramatic. Who's talking about risking their lives? France is a certain risk – but here we'd most likely be on stand-by only, guard duties of some sort. Prevention rather than cure... So just keep quiet – that'll be the best policy. Don't you agree?'

'As you say, Sir', Dobie replied, as Captain Harwood turned towards the others who were at the windows of the classroom by now, trying to glean what they could from an outside world that consisted of little more than the walled playground and its diminutive outside toilets.

As so often, he was returned bluntly to his own thoughts. The ordered years at school, the two years at Cambridge – above all, the gentle exchanges and withdrawn silences with Nonnie – had not prepared him for the manly nonchalance of the officers' mess.

Major Dean-Forbes had given him most trouble – only twenty-four hours before he had stood in front of his shaving mirror rehearsing a relaxed salute according to the major's book.

Of Colonel Marsh, the Battalion commander, he had no more opinion than his colleagues. They had all found the colonel inscrutable, irritable, impatient and taciturn. Dobie thought it a very odd society which could put people like Dean-Forbes, Marsh and himself together, expecting unified action from them. In normal circumstances each would shield from the other behind a newspaper should they by some misfortune find themselves in the same railway compartment.

The officers eased their limbs in small groups, speculating on the next move. As time went by they began to show slight impatience. One or two went out of the door but the adjutant hauled them back.

A half-hour went by. After the poor night's dozing aboard and the four miles of marching, they would have been glad to sit down. But in the small classroom no one dared make the first move towards using the children's desks. That would have been construed as clowning, and it was hardly the moment.

So they grumbled among themselves in a quiet voice about the Army in general – and about the senior officers who had told them so little. The tedium was unbearable in the stuffy classroom. They fell silent.

The adjutant had not given permission to smoke. It was all a worrying anti-climax after the hurried departure from Catterick with its implication of action. The little classroom represented a doldrums.

It was the same with the men. In their weariness this halt had become almost an encapsulated norm. The immediate past of journeying and marching was forgotten by the roadside. There appeared to be no future either; just this, a pause somewhere in Ireland – of all places!

Men gambled with pennies and even sixpences while others watched. Some just chatted idly or exchanged Woodbines for, beyond the embargo on wandering, all sense of discipline seemed to have lapsed since the officers had entered the school.

The sun was getting stronger. A pleasant lassitude descended on the Battalion along the roadside. By now, the occasional passer-by was no longer noticed, and the donkey and horse traffic was too sparse to cause interest. The men were intent only on themselves, anxious not to be disturbed.

The plate-layers on the railway were munching sandwiches and drinking what might be porter or cold tea. It was the midday break. No trains passed. It all had a feeling of Sunday. Had it not been for the presence of the workers, the line might have been a disused one. Seagulls banked, swooped and fought for the scraps the men flung at them from their sandwiches. Despite the straggle of khaki along the road and the tripods of arms, it was very peaceful in the sun.

Then, a mighty explosion split the air asunder. It was a sharp, deafening crack followed by great shock-waves which swept over them at once. Every man stood up, startled, as though on a spring.

'Down, stupid, down!' yelled the CSM.

They fell as a body, clinging to the ground as the shock waves seemed to wear themselves out against distant heights, then died like thunder into a dreadful silence. Cautiously, some lifted their heads.

'God almighty – what the hell was that?' Pearson muttered to Moffat.

'Buggered if I know. Some bloody route march is this! That's bleedin' war, that is, mate. Bleedin' war.'

'War?'

'Yeah, war. See that?'

It had taken them a few seconds to realise the source of the explosion was quite distant. At the head of the bay, a few miles away among the buildings of the city, they could see smoke rising. Then another great crack of thunder in the sky – and wave after wave of shock reverberated over the bay.

The gulls tossed madly in the sky, uncertain of direction now. The plate-layers were running in the Kingstown direction.

As the plume of smoke rose ever higher in the sky and got thicker after the second explosion, the men began to register the distance. Taking courage, they rose one by one to peer towards the city. The sergeant-major was afraid of losing them. Along with other NCOs all along the Battalion, he began whipping them into some semblance of order.

'All right, lads, pick up your rifles and stand to.'

But it was no use trying to end their speculative hubbub of conversation. CSM Green knew they were disturbed – it was better to let them talk. They had all heard artillery in training – mostly eighteen-pounders – but this was something altogether mightier, something that cracked the ear-drums and sent shock waves through you.

Yet another crump, and the birds scattered out of pattern yet again. Any sign of local inhabitants had disappeared.

The men felt exposed out on this open stretch of road between the port and the city inland. There was no cover of any kind should they need it. Nobody doubted that it was the sound of war. Artillery blasting into the lonely moors of the practice range was one thing, that great pall of smoke rising over a city quite another.

At about three-minute intervals the explosions continued, and from the relative calm and peace of what they had considered some sort of route march, every man was flung at once into the unknown of real war, wherever and whatever it was. Each man speculated on this new and threatening reality. Would they turn back now? Had the guns dealt with the trouble? Would they be needed? Was there some awful bungle going on? The absence of the officers now filled them with dread. What were they cooking up in that school?

Now, as Roberts J.H. sought out F.X., it was of his family that he thought. The gunfire had flung the future at him at once. He had not properly considered the violence of war, only the opportunity of escape; he had lived in a dull present tinged with dull memories of the past at rare intervals. The great shock waves, quite unlike any sound he had heard in training, spelt death, maiming.

He found F.X. standing alone with head bowed, lost in thought, hands clasped over his rifle.

'What d'you make of it, Frank?'

'Don't know, Jack. Gunfire of some sort. But I've never heard a crack like that, have you?'

'Never, boy, never. Enough to put the fear of God into you, isn't it?'

F.X. looked up and into J.H.'s eyes. 'I'm frightened, Jack, are you? It's the smoke piling up there. Something's up, and they won't tell us. This isn't manoeuvres. They're marching us right towards trouble, I'm sure.'

Yet a part of F.X. was already heading for the trouble, like a moth to a lamp. He needed it, to escape from the dark.

'Oh, I'm frightened too, Frank', confessed John Henry. 'What's getting me is not knowing nothing. Why don't they tell us something? This isn't France, is it? So how could it be a war? They're saying we're in Ireland... Do you know you can see Ireland from some parts of Wales on a clear day? So how can it be a war? Tell me that!'

'Well, anybody can tell you buggers can't read,' said Moffat, who appeared to be everywhere and never missed a trick.

'Why?' asked J.H., stung.

'There's trouble in Ireland. I read it in the papers before I joined up. Some of the buggers here want Ireland for themselves. Bleedin' cheek, an' us at war with the Jerries. Ireland's ours. Always was, always will be.'

Nobody bothered even to contradict Moffat. He usually knew, could work things out.

Indeed, if they needed reassurance, the nearby pillar-box bearing the cypher VR ought to have provided it. There rested Empire, central to whatever education they might have had, the newspapers they read, to their work, whatever it was.

Not to have presumed on Empire would have been not to be British – in a way, not to be fully alive. It was part of the blood, not to be thought about, simply to be lived, however humble one's station in the imperial order of things.

However much enlistment might have offered escape from this or that insoluble domestic problem or simple boredom, the added incentive was always there, in those inborn and inbred assumptions of Empire, of a patriotism that extended to all climes and to all colours of

121

men, leading them in their tens of thousands to volunteer to defend the threatened English Channel from the depredations of the advancing Germans, their only likely rivals for military and commercial empire.

The very sight of the pillar-box and its strident red was a reminder of the latent patriotism that Kitchener had tapped for his New Army.

'Anyway, that ship that sailed over there was one of ours', Moffat continued. 'That was a bloody battleship, and them there guns was 'ers, you mark my words. And if there's any trouble, them guns will have seen it off.'

'No, they won't need us,' Pearson echoed the master, 'not after that bleedin' lot. I reckon there's nobody alive where them shots landed. 'eap of ruins, that's all there'll be.'

'But what sort of trouble could it be,' John Henry asked doggedly, 'that needed guns like that? They would wake the dead, they would.'

'Naval guns, mate', said Moffat. 'In the black countries, when these 'ere niggers gives a bit of trouble like, they send one of these ships up the river, just like that one this morning, and they blast the livin' day-lights out o' the poor sods.'

As the guns went silent and they chatted away their fears, the CSM allowed them to relax again on their packs or to stand in small groups. There was still no sign of life from the school, where the officers continued to fume and fret at their confinement.

Just then, however, a motor-cyclist approached from the Dublin direction. The men whistled as he negotiated the cobbles and the tram-lines with a rattle, but he ignored them and proceeded up to the school, where he dismounted. At the door, he saluted the adjutant and followed him into the building. They walked down the high corridor of glass dividing the classrooms.

The dispatch-rider glimpsed the officers crowded into the little classroom on the left, but the adjutant took him on, to an inner room which was probably the headmaster's. He was so young, it could not have been too many years since he had walked into just such a room for punishment or for advice on leaving school. The officer knocked, opened the door, ushered the dispatch-rider in, then closed the door behind him and returned to fuss over his juniors fuming in the class-room.

The officers were aware of the change, of something happening. They too had suffered the shock waves of the explosion, the dust settling on their shoulders from the pinewood beams overhead. They too had speculated and even allowed themselves to show some excitement over it. Otherwise they had not moved, had not sought cover. Indeed, they had hardly flinched, so afraid were they of betraying a tacit code of conduct.

Lieutenant Dobie stuck to Saxton. His eyes widened, he glanced around at the first crash of sound. His whole instinct was to duck. If Saxton flinched, Dobie was unaware of it. The fair head turned slowly towards the tall windows, then came back towards Dobie. He was the first to break the tense silence.

'That, Dobie, is the first shot in anger I've heard in this whole bloody war.'

The words sent them off again into a crescendo of chatter which the adjutant thought fit not to interrupt.

'So much for the flesh-pots of Dublin,' Saxton went on while Dobie tried to gather his wits, 'I suppose that lot confirms Dobie's story about Ireland. That'll be the Irish stirring it up, I suppose.'

'Now, wait a minute,' Dobie answered with what calm he could muster, 'Let's not jump to conclusions. We're in Ireland. That much we know for sure. But whether that gunfire is from Irishmen or from Germans has yet to be established – or by Englishmen firing at either. We don't know a thing. Do we? Anyway, I very much doubt if Parnell's "hillside men" would work in Dublin. They could hardly capture a city, could they?'

'No. But you don't have to capture a place to be a bloody nuisance.'

'True,' said Dobie, 'but it's difficult to imagine anything less rewarding. Where would it get them? It's not the sort of thing the "hill-side men" would be good at. They're countrymen. I'd have thought they'd find Dublin too well established a place for comfort.'

'Oh, it's well established all right. I've never been there myself, but I've heard good reports of life there. If you're in the right class, it's second to none. If you're not, then you're either having your face ground into the bog or causing trouble by conspiring against the Government. I should think they've been conspiring a bit too much for comfort lately and that gunfire was sorting the blighters out a bit.'

'Wouldn't that be a bit excessive though? After all, it's part of Britain. It would be like shooting at ourselves.'

'Don't you kid yourself, old man. It's just what you were telling us earlier. It all comes back. You're right. There are plenty of Irishmen who would like to shove us off this island. What about the Citizen Army? They won't get very far, but they can cause quite a lot of trouble

123

trying. It wouldn't be the first time they tried either.'

'No, it wouldn't. I agree. But gunfire of that nature! It sounded like naval guns. Surely, that can't be against the Irish – it must be more serious than that. It could be Captain Harwood's theory that the Germans are here...'

'You're refuting your own theory, Dobie', Captain Harwood interjected. 'We agree there could be trouble, even if we don't know what kind.'

'I still can't see what the Irish would get out of causing trouble in the city. It's too well secured, surely. And the Irish, they're too divided for any group to get the citizens behind them. It's hardly the Paris *commune* – not with the British Army half full of Irishmen.'

'Wait a minute,' Harwood replied, 'what about the Phoenix Park murders? That was way back in the 'eighties, but it's not that long ago. That's in Dublin...'

This seemed an irritating irrelevance to Dobie. 'That was cold-blooded assassination in the dead of night,' he said patiently, 'and well outside the city proper. You'd hardly fire naval guns at that sort of thing.'

But Saxton had had enough of Dobie's soul-searching. He saw it as merely a refusal to face facts. Irishmen or Germans – what did it matter?

'The trouble with you, Dobie,' he said with a well put-on world-weariness, 'is you've always played stand-off half to life. I don't understand you. It's time you got stuck in with the forwards and had your nose rubbed in it a bit, you know. You wouldn't know what to do if you had your pants torn off in a real scrummage, if you see what I mean.'

'Oh, I think I see what you mean.' William Dobie was a bit needled. Saxton never had problems, it seemed. The Irish Question would never ruffle his steady view of life and its opportunities; no more than getting his pants torn off in a scrummage. If that was what mucking in with the forwards meant then clearly he would always be a stand-off half, for better or for worse.

'And what would you do?' he asked Saxton.

'Who? I? Oh, look here, old man, you've just got to look at my track record...'

'No, that doesn't answer my question. What would you do?'

'But I'm telling you. I always get stuck into it, I...'

'No. What would you do if you lost your pants in a scrummage?

That's what you claimed I'd not know what to do about. So what about you?'

'Oh, balls, Dobie! You know very well what I mean . . .'

But he did not. It was as far as he dared go however. How would Saxton react to a confrontation with Irishmen? Did anything ever ruffle that easy-going mind?

Dobie was feeling steadily worse about his own position, conscious as he was that, at a moment's notice, he was being flung into something nasty concerning Irishmen. Though acknowledged different in some ways, in so many others they were like himself, backing the same cause in the war against the German war-mongers. If having a conscience about having to kill Irishmen meant playing stand-off half to life, then so be it.

He felt that he was exaggerating, as always, exasperating Saxton in the process, wanting answers and never finding them. He and Saxton worked on different time scales. For Saxton there was never time enough – for Dobie a whole world of time. Youth, he reflected, with so much future at stake, could not afford to risk too much. He had neither the temperament nor the inclination to clinch life in a mauling scrummage – not yet.

But Saxton's easy assurance unsettled him and sent him turning things over, regretting certain retreats into innocence when experience might have – well, to quote Saxton – 'torn the pants off him'. The question, as with the Magna Carta, was whether or not it was 'a good thing'.

As the gun continued to rumble, bringing down dust and scales of whitewash, Dobie tried to recollect anything he might know about Ireland. His was an academic, historic view. No more.

When, on the ship, Ireland had been announced as their destination, he had felt relief that the day when he would have to finally deny his pacifism had been put off. By volunteering, he had sworn allegiance to be ready to kill if need be. But he had fended off the actual image. Balancing his argument of the 'moral lump' against the doctrine of passive resistance he felt he had made the right compromise, having lost faith in the efficacy of passive resistance in the face of brute force.

Had he enlisted because of the wrong done to Belgium? Or was enlistment his way out of an impossible dilemma? What if, after all, Nonnie had been right and he wrong? Or right for the wrong reasons? He was no longer certain.

125

'Are you all right, Dobie?' Saxton asked. 'It's damned stuffy in here.'

'Yes, yes,' Dobie replied absently, 'I was just wondering what that gun could be firing at. Will there be casualties, do you think?'

'I should think it's the Royal Navy picking them off like partridges', Saxton said airily.

Saxton never gave a damn about anything – about the men, about the possibilities of a future at war, about casualties. Perhaps it was the right attitude. The battles in Flanders had taken such a toll already that to care too much might lead to insanity.

Dobie was never far from worrying about life, about the gratuitous and the inevitable; but, most of all, about the difficulty, even the impossibility, of reconciling ideals with the corrosive realities and practicalities of life. The ideals were as much inborn as cultivated in him. But whereas at first the ideals had seemed easy to hold to – what more natural, more logical and rational than that men should live at peace? – as time went by and manhood presented new responsibilities and new choices hitherto curtained off from him, ideals became not only greater, more worthy and sacrosanct, but also more difficult to sustain.

He saw that what was logical might not necessarily be natural – or what was rational might not be logical. So much depended. At twenty, life was very much a jungle of dependencies each of whose nuances had to be felt and learnt before the next move into unknown territory. The clinging persistence of realities slowed him down. It was always a conflict of the why and how with the when and where.

Saxton was right, the classroom was stuffy. Dobie felt irritated beyond words and deliberately moved away from Saxton, from anybody. And they knew that mood of his, when the black brows knitted into a frown and he seemed unapproachable. Looking out of the window, he realised he had miscalculated somewhere. Nor was there only Nonnie to consider – if indeed it ever came to killing or maiming an Irishman the irony of his position would be unbearable when next he faced her – but Laura too, for beneath the laughing, insouciant manner, he had found an answering earnestness, a searching not unlike his own and a dissatisfaction with the way things were.

'William,' she had once said, 'you go on and on about Belgium, you know, and I begin to wonder if you could ever live with yourself if you didn't go.'

He did not think in quite that future way, but she was right, he

126

would find it difficult to live with himself should he deny his present feeling about German occupation of Belgium. But he would also find it difficult to live with Nonnie.

'You mustn't think I'm trying to persuade you', Laura went on, anxious not to contribute further to his present agonising. 'You must remember that women can only watch their men folk go away, realising they might never return. It must be awful. William, I don't want you to go, not in the least – you do understand that, don't you? – but if you feel as you do about Belgium, then I do think you'll find it difficult to live with yourself if you deny that feeling. At least that's my impression.'

'Yes, Laura, I hadn't thought of it in quite that way. To be honest,' he dared to continue, for he would hate to lose her even for a moment, 'I think Belgium's plight is more important than how I feel, now or in the future.'

And even Laura had felt his irritation. But she knew it was with himself and not with her, so she let it pass. There was so much yet to learn about him.

The sight of the approaching dispatch-rider returned Dobie to the present. There was something ominous about the motor-cyclist advancing towards the school. Saxton could so easily wound, because he could thrust near the bone. It was too true that life with Miss Pomfret had not fitted him for life's scrummage. Here was a case in point. The very purpose and urgency of the dispatch-rider sickened Lieutenant Dobie in a way he had never experienced. It was almost physical; he wanted to retch.

But one thing Miss Pomfret had always enjoined – and school had reinforced it – he must pull himself together. Turning away from Saxton once more, he tried to collect himself, to recollect, as though to prepare himself for a painful confrontation with his own uncomfortable moral position, or want of one.

Even the few miles of marching on Irish soil had changed him. What we are depends so much on where we are. While sensing that what citizens he had seen spoke the same language, he felt different. Ireland was different: the sky, the houses, the grey of the stone and the sharp green of budding trees – all were different. And while they had marched, they were cut off from it all. They had marched as a Battalion. They could only merge by breaking rank and going native – and that was unpardonable, because un-British.

As the gunfire died away and the officers in turn were left to reflect on what appeared to be a daunting change in the day's proceedings, William Dobie realised that his inner struggle was far from over.

Over the green dado, he saw the adjutant ushering in the dispatch-rider. A few minutes later, Colonel Marsh and Major Dean-Forbes came down the corridor with the adjutant, who opened the classroom door.

'Attention, gentlemen, please.' Mildly said, no sign of crisis. The gun might never have fired, the dispatch-rider never have arrived. Captain Forsyth's face was neutral, impassive. He conducted the two senior officers past the file of junior ones among the little desks to the teacher's podium where, presumably, 'the Old Man' would address them.

The colonel was getting on in years. He had, so they understood, seen action in Afghanistan and South Africa. But in Europe something had happened at Loos – or was it Mons? – when his Regiment had been decimated.

Nobody quite knew, indeed, nobody could quite confirm if it were even true that 'something' had happened, or even if he was truly one of their own and had not been 'rusticated' to them. The turnover was so rapid these days, it was hard to tell. It was unusual for an officer to be returned uninjured from France. Unusual, too, to have a colonel thrust upon a Battalion as Marsh had been. More usual for one of the Company commanders to be moved up. Rumour had it that Major Dean-Forbes, now promoted to Second-in-Command, had been put out by the move. Colonel Marsh had yet to make his mark.

If the colonel's presence in the mess had been unobtrusive, his inspections had been rigorous; his daily orders inconsistent, even cranky. 'Hellfire!' the CSM had exploded on reading them one day to discover that the Battalion had been ordered to take the stiffening wire out of their caps. Green knew, as every old sweat knew, that the soft effect of caps without wire was the privilege only of those who had seen action on the Western Front.

The colonel liked his little drama. As he took up his position in the middle of the teacher's podium, he held his head aloft, peering over their heads and waiting for them to stop breathing before he would open his mouth to convey whatever it was the dispatch-rider had brought – if that were to be the burden of his address. The silence was palpable.

'Gentlemen', he said at last, moving his head stiffly from side to side like a praying mantis, reminding Dobie of F.X.'s head movements during their brief interview at Catterick. The manner was well known to the officers by now. 'Gentlemen, I have good news for you. As you know already, the Battalion is in Ireland. It has not been possible till now, due to the exigencies of war, to tell you why. I gather, in fact, that the situation is very confused, so there was no point in telling you. All I can say with certainty is that the Battalion has been called in to assist in a rather explosive situation which, if allowed to succeed, would strike at the heart of the British Empire at the moment of its greatest peril. What I have to tell you may surprise you. But it has caused no surprise to the Government, from whence these orders came direct to Corps HQ.'

He waved a dispatch with a flourish. They were alert by now, but not for the reasons Colonel Marsh had calculated. Rather, they were assessing his performance. If he had anything real to tell them, why not come down off the podium and stop preaching? There was something slightly un-British about his histrionics, his thigh-slapping with swagger-stick, and his voice.

The officers, mostly very young men, did not move. The colonel's tone, never less than dramatic even when briefing a mere field-exercise at home, was now stentorian. His moment had come, and if they had never been greatly impressed by him, according him no more than the respect due to rank, they were prepared to be impressed by his message, now that it concerned something real and not an imaginary battle over the Yorkshire moors.

'Briefly, insurgent elements have this week occupied strategic positions in the City of Dublin, and though Government forces have already hemmed them in, the situation is serious enough to warrant this call on our Battalion. Let me outline in detail the present position.' With a casual glance at Major Dean-Forbes, the colonel ordered him to unfold a map of the city. With some difficulty, the major fixed it over the blackboard.

'Gather round, gentlemen.' They had kept a respectful distance. Now they leant forward to take in the details of the map.

The colonel pointed with his swagger-stick. 'Here, in Sackville Street, the main street running north and south from this bridge, the rebels have occupied the main Post Office and are still there. At this large flour-mill, here, nearer to us, another force is still in occupation. The latest dispatch, just arrived as you know, informs me that other areas, like Dublin Castle, here, have now been cleared... Our instructions are to march on Dublin over this canal which seems to

129

fairly enclose the centre of the city, to isolate the two rebel strongholds at the Post Office and the mill, then to flush out the devils with all the firepower we can muster. Just before the canal, we enter the permanent barracks, which will be our H.Q. for the duration of the operation. There the men will be fed. Immediately afterwards, I believe we ought to march over the canal and into the city. How we deploy the Companies after that is a matter we shall discuss over the meal at the barracks . . . I shan't hold you any longer. I want the Battalion to be on the move in ten minutes – is that understood? The corporal dispatch-rider has instructions to wait for you at this important road junction here, just short of the barracks, so keep a look-out for him. In the meantime, gentlemen, just follow the tram-lines. Any questions?'

There were none.

As he trotted off with the major and adjutant, they stood stiffly to attention. As soon as he was outside the door, the hubbub broke out again as they rushed outside to muster their respective Companies. This was it – action.

Gunfire was unconfirmed rumour. What the colonel had spoken of was action, siege, attack. They knew the senior officers would promptly disappear, not to be seen until the next H.Q. was established. That was one divide they were increasingly conscious of and did not dare resist openly. They would return to the men, transmit orders to the sergeant-major and get things on the move again.

The CSM, alert for any move from the school, shouted:

'All right, on your feet!'

The men were hungry and thirsty by now, but they knew their allotted places and shuffled stiffly on to the road. In well under ten minutes, they were marching again at the old slack rhythm, feeling a rising grudge as their guts rumbled to the sound of their *tramp-tramp-tramp* – left-right-left-right. Rifle-slings chafed their shoulders, packs rode uneasily on their backs, and the boredom of it all sent their spirits low. The two inner files fought a constant battle with the tram-lines.

A few began to limp as blisters developed. Hitherto their longest route marches had been over the soft surfaces of the moors above Catterick. Otherwise, the sight of a tram route was balm to Moffat, who sniffed the increasing smells of town air.

It was clear and sunny, still freshened by the neighbouring sea. But the smell of horse droppings became stronger as they approached.

130

Compared with the pure air of the Yorkshire moors, there were whiffs of this and that which spelt urban development. Moffat looked about expectantly. The occasional whiff of peat-smoke was unfamiliar, but it was smoke all the same. The gaps between houses and terraces decreased, and Moffat sank into the familiarity of town, of huddled streets, even if they seemed well-heeled compared with Stepney, with the houses getting taller all the time. The streets were quiet, except for knots of men and youths at the corners, watching sullenly.

The CSM drove them on relentlessly, gathering the ragged step together every few hundred yards with an impatient 'Left-right-left-right – pick it up there . . .' – and occasionally picking out the more errant individual with a blistering tirade. It all seemed endless, with no rest from the iron-hard cobbles and tram-lines, and as they covered about three miles more from their halt, they began to hear a distant rattle of rifle and machine-gun bursts from the city-centre, still far ahead. The gunboat must have withdrawn after its allotted task, for the rolls of naval gunfire had not recurred.

But every so often, the less ear-splitting but more sombre rumble of field-gun fire came across the noise of their tramping rhythm.

Lieutenant Dobie and Sergeant Forster marched with unflagging zeal, making a show of not having heard a thing. In the ranks however heads occasionally turned, as though to ask a question but not daring.

The unreality of it, of marching on a city to the sound of gunfire, of not waging war in the open, of not 'going over the top' out of trenches as they had been taught, of possibly fighting in streets – all this was something they were unable to understand.

And the deadness of it all! The march with its nothingness except the *tramp-tramp-tramp* on granite and tram-lines, the sheer downward drag, the sweat, and the half-heard staccato of small-arms fire and the occasional boom of a field-gun . . . It all consumed the men, sapping their spirits.

They were marching past parkland and pleasant houses among trees and gardens. But it meant nothing to them. It was the distant noise ahead that occupied their attention. War . . . ? Surely, not in a city. All their training had taught them that what must be attacked and occupied had to be pulverised by artillery first till it was rubble, ready for their charge with rifle and bayonet. They would either rush an objective in file or sweep over it in waves, rather like the infantry charge of old. Nothing much had changed since Waterloo or the Crimea. And if the war of attrition in France had settled down

131

into the stalemate of trench warfare that, too, was an extension of the old redoubt, the field strong-point.

So nothing was calculated to disturb the men more than the thought of street-fighting; nothing in precedent or textbook had prepared them for what was going on ahead. Not a man, be he a junior officer or other rank, cared to face what he could not understand. Worse still, their speculations on the possibility of fighting Irishmen had brought neither enlightenment nor comfort. They remembered comrades back in camp, Irish to the core. The prospect of facing them after this operation was one they did not care to dwell upon.

They had been lectured on German atrocities – babies spitted on bayonets and the flower of Belgian maidenhood raped – but the present situation had something of the air of a prize-fighter all trained and primed for his fight then finding it cancelled in the last minute, or with a dwarf substitute. As, gradually, they digested the truth, they felt helpless protest rising up in them.

When, at the junction of four roads with tramlines bifurcating along the two ahead of them, the advance Company met the promised dispatch-rider, they were relieved beyond words. Without halting them, he faced his machine forward, raised his left arm to guide them on, and with his machine chugging at an easy pace, he moved forward with their *tramp-tramp-tramp* behind him.

They moved slackly along the tram-lines with pleasant houses set back in well-tended gardens. The palatial air was set off by the front-doors, each some ten feet or so above street level, reached by a flight of stone steps. The streets were deserted, blinds were drawn, there was an eerie lifelessness all round them. Except for an occasional wisp of smoke from a chimney, the houses might have been unoccupied. A pigeon or a jackdaw would flap around them, or a cat would scatter at the approach of their *tramp-tramp-tramp*. Otherwise, for them, it seemed a deserted city. So weary were they of the whole business, they felt that their entire lives had been occupied marching on this bright, sad city of silence and undeclared threat.

The small arms rattle did not seem to get nearer. Whatever was going on was still well ahead. They were still in the suburbs.

The dispatch-rider ahead wheeled right, and they followed him disconsolately down a side street, wheeled round again through a wide gate, past sentries into a high-walled compound, and came to a ragged halt in a parade square all too familiar with its quadrangle of stone and dark brick buildings.

132

Without delay they snaked in a single file through the cookhouse where a mess of cooked bully-beef (only just less nauseating than cold), mashed potatoes and cabbage was served sullenly by the cooks. With sheer relief they slumped over the food and were glad to just empty their minds of all thought.

By now their home and family was the Battalion. When the Battalion moved, they would be disorientated, even starved, until it could re-establish itself and reorganise proper services: Orderly Room, cookhouse, medical services, latrines and quartermaster's stores. Their dependence on the Battalion, on its integrity and organisation, was complete; it was their guarantee against chaos. Outside were the barbarians; the Battalion was their unique and inevitable unit of civilisation.

The boiled bacon at Kingstown station had displayed a weakness in the system that alarmed them. Away from barracks, on the move, they were disorganised unless the move was a predictable one that could be planned and provisioned ahead. Now they understood the boiled bacon, the grease and scum of their unplanned breakfast. The naval gunfire and later intimations of small-arms fire in the city had put all that into context. The march was not a planned exercise, but an unforeseen emergency. They were being pitched into something facing right away from France; compared with France, it was inscrutable and not a little frightening. It did not conform.

And so, sitting at last at proper mess-room tables, they devoured their bully-beef, potato and cabbage from plates, were encouraged to accept second helpings, and then were doled out rice-pudding and tea.

As their shoulders relaxed from the absence of rifle-sling and pack, they were momentarily almost content. The walls immured them against the alien noises of street violence in a strange city. They felt secure in the barracks.

They might, indeed, have remained secure and known no harm in Ireland had it not been for something that had happened to their commandant at Loos.

For the ultimate decision on the next move was the colonel's.

Free from the constraints of Corps H.Q., he was here alone with his own Battalion, detached from Corps, Regiment and Division, free to act as he thought best, so long as he combined with the various Government forces operating in the City of Dublin. Unexpectedly,

Colonel Marsh had the freedom normally accorded only to brigadier-general's rank upwards. The deployment of the Battalion – his Battalion – was now practically his alone, so long as he could find some working arrangement with local forces. Of these he had hitherto known nothing, not even who they were, what numbers, how deployed, nor what precisely they were facing.

What the Battalion did not know was that he did not know. Detached as they were, they did not know that all he had in the way of orders was a dispatch in an envelope in his pocket which was no more than a transcript of an urgent message to Division HQ at Catterick, direct from the War Office, to move one Battalion to Ireland and march from the landing at Kingstown vaguely on to Dublin. That they had almost done.

The only further information the colonel had was the dispatch from Dublin carried by the solitary dispatch-rider, that they were to meet him at the road junction and then follow him to the barracks where they were expected and a meal would be ready for all ranks. It was little enough.

Riding in behind the marching Battalion with the major and adjutant in the scout-car generously provided at Kingstown, Colonel Marsh gave every sign of knowing everything as he alighted and was saluted by the ubiquitous motor-cyclist.

'This way, Sir.'

'Thank you, Corporal,' said the colonel; 'I think you'd better come along too', he added, addressing his senior companions.

The dispatch-rider led them past the noise of cutlery and conversation in the mess-room to an inner room which was obviously an Operations Room. Here the party was greeted by two officers, a colonel and a captain, hatless and showing signs of weariness.

While the junior officers were being entertained in the mess by two local officers, they were unaware of this latest move of the three senior officers. Were they less exhausted they might question the perpetual division between themselves and their senior colleagues, just as the men might question the divide that separated them from themselves. But it was part of a chain of command, and there was nothing any of them could do about it.

All the links in the chain were kept strictly apart until an order from above was transmitted through the system. Everything came down – nothing went back – and what came down was beyond discussion. Each rank below was strictly for transmitting of orders, never for consultation.

Any energy released by the system in the form of friction was expressed in the junior officers' case by mild puzzlement among themselves, and in the men's case by plain 'grousing'. It was expected and therefore allowed; what was not allowed was that any of it should pass upwards.

So while Colonel Marsh accepted a glass of Irish whiskey, neat, from his hosts before repairing to luncheon and whatever briefing there was, the men sprawled at the mess-tables and either dozed or talked.

'Did you hear that noise while we were marching?' Roberts J.H. asked his namesake.

'In the town ahead?'

'Yes, rifle fire or something – machine-guns, you know – the real stuff, you must have heard it.'

'Oh, I heard it all right', said Francis Xavier. 'But this barracks – where is it? Is this really Dublin?'

'Well ay, man. Where else could it be, tell me that, man?'

'Don't ask me. They tell us nothing, so we don't know. I suppose it's Dublin. Who knows? Couldn't that be the locals on exercise?'

'Exercise? What, in the middle of a town? Never!'

'I suppose you're right. But there's no war in Ireland, so what can it be?' said F.X.

'Who said there's no war in Ireland?' Moffat shouted across the table. 'The buggers never tell us anything. What about Jerry landing here and having a go at England's back-door? They ain't getting nowhere in France by all accounts, so who's to say the bleeders ain't here, eh?'

'Go on, Moff,' shouted Pearson above the general din. 'Bloody Jerry 'ere, in Ireland? Go on, mate, 'ave a 'eart. Never get across the sea, 'e wouldn't. Rule Britannia, mate, mark my words... Remember that destroyer we 'eard afirin'? No bloody Jerry ship would be allowed out of port. The bleeders is well looked after in France, see?'

'Right lot you bloody know,' said Moffat with contempt, 'what about all them German submarines? What about the *Lusitania*? Eh? It's the other way round, more like. Come to think, we're bleedin' lucky to be here, the way them subs is lurkin' around. What about last night when we was at sea, eh? Judgin' by what I've 'eard, we could all a bin drowned by now!'

The argument bore logic. Nothing else could explain what was ob-

135

viously trouble ahead. They knew that nobody above them in rank would explain it. But because it was Moffat who led the argument, J.H. questioned him still.

'You know everything, don't you Moffat?'

'I know as much as you do, Robso!'

'So what do you know? We're in Ireland, isn't it, and that's about all. But you've got all the answers, haven't you? You said before it was Irishmen we was going to fight.'

'Oh, fuck off, Roberts. You're like all bloody Taffies, all wind!'

'Don't you start calling the Welsh names, I warn you, boyo. They're as good as anybody and maybe twice as good as the like of you.'

'Bad as the bleedin' Irish, Robso, just as bad. Can't trust the buggers an inch, you can't.'

'Maybe that's what's up in the town over there', replied John Henry. 'Maybe the English has been calling the Irish names too long. And maybe they're not standing any more of it, boy.'

'So we call them names,' mimicked Moffat, roused by now, 'and so out comes their little pop-guns, eh? So where does that leave you, Taffy, eh? Where d'you stand if that's what the little bang-bang is about?'

'I'll do what I'm asked to do', replied J.H. 'Will you?'

'What d'you mean, mate? Are you implyin' I won't do my bit when I'm asked?'

'If the cap fits, wear it.'

At this Moffat reached across the table, grabbed John Henry's right epaulette, and fists were about to fly when Corporal Dinsdale, already aware of the argument, rushed over and broke it up.

'Just stop this bloke here saying things about the Welsh, will you, Corp?' J.H. said mildly.

'Ay, leave him alone, Moffat. What's wrong wi' a Welshman, anyway?' said Willie McAllister, the Company's Glaswegian.

'No man's goin' to call me a coward', said Moffat.

'He didna call ye a coward.'

'He's no bloody good.'

'Ach away wi'ye. There's nought wrong wi' the man that a couple of fights and a fuck wouldna put right overnight.'

Corporal Dinsdale sensed the irritation and stayed with them.

F.X. watched it all with intense misery. That so much energy over nothing could be raised so quickly was a mark of their irritation with the march and with one another. Men queued at the latrines, or fumbled in their pockets for cigarettes and matches. The noise and heat in the mess-room were becoming unbearable.

But close on the heels of the corporal, the quarter-master followed with treasure in the form of bundles of mail, which he distributed like alms to the N.C.O.s. They in turn took malicious pleasure in taking an eternity to untie the string. Mail was the one great pointer to morale and the Q.M., probably at the behest of the C.O., had held back the previous day's mail for this moment when spirits were flagging.

For J.H. there was a rare letter from Rhiannon, complaining that it was 'getting a nuisance to feed the dogs'. What offended him most was that she should dismiss the whippets as 'dogs'.

The sergeant seemed to take an age to reach F.X. but when he did there were two letters for him. F.X. turned them over, decided firmly which he should read first and tucked the other in his tunic pocket. He read the first without much apparent interest. It was from his father. '... Well lad it's time to sign off wishing you home soon all are waiting eagerly for the great day. Yours truly, Father.' Then even less for comfort: 'PS Have not seen Marian much lately. Your mother says she is avoiding us but I say that is just woman's talk you know how they are. Well cheerio for now.'

He stuffed the letter unceremoniously in his pack and with more engagement took out the second letter. Abstractedly he pushed the envelope along with his father's letter in his pack and set to reading this second letter.

J.H. watched the whole process and could not help wondering. 'Bad news from home, Frank?' he asked.

But F.X. was hardly present. 'No ... no, nothing special like ...' he muttered, then read over the letter again. J.H. guessed it was very special, and watched as F.X. folded it carefully, then reverently, it seemed, slotted it into his left tunic pocket. All that J.H. could guess was that the letter had disturbed F.X. and he longed to help but knew better than even to hint at it.

Once again, for a while there was peace.

This halt it was the junior officers who had the benefit of fresh air, for having finished their meal, the adjutant allowed them out, so long as they were within reach in the square.

Outside, without the noise of the Battalion marching, they could distinctly hear the distant small-arms fire, the more eerie because the normal sounds of the city were absent and the traffic – of horse, tram and train – almost dead in the bright light of early afternoon.

They strolled back and forth across the square and tried to puzzle things out.

'The Old Man's in there somewhere', said Saxton. 'That dispatch rider fellow holds the secret. What say we tackle him? Anybody seen him since we arrived?'

They all looked round. The motor-cycle was there, but there was no sign of the man.

'What about the sentries, then?' Saxton suggested.

'We can't exactly go to a private and be seen winkling information out of him', retorted Captain Harwood.

'Oh, come off it', said Saxton. 'Here we are, as dumb as they come, not a scrap of intelligence from the top-brass, and some sort of show going on in Dublin – and you think we shouldn't take a risk like that!'

'Well, yes I do. I mean, it would be awfully infra dig, don't you think?'

The captain was affronted by Saxton's bold habit of command, but did not have the answer.

'Oh, to hell with that. I'm going to have a go. Who'll go with me?' Saxton spoke impatiently. 'Shouldn't we all go, sort of extend our stroll a bit as far as the gate and pretend to be passing the time of day?'

'I think it would go down rather badly', Harwood insisted.

'Look here, Sir,' said Saxton with infinite patience. 'We've travelled here at the double, there's a hell of a racket over there somewhere. We've heard that destroyer having a jolly good go at something or other, and here we are, ready, I'd say, to be sent in to sort the bloody thing out. And what do we know? Damn all. And if I know the top-brass it'll be like that till we suddenly find ourselves with our bloody heads blown off by an Irishman... Remember, we'll have to lead. I say we have every right to find out anything we can. It's our lives they're risking, isn't it? Because make no mistake – this bloody march and that racket over there, whatever it is, mean trouble, and I'm not happy about it. So come on, who's for a gentle stroll as far as the gate?'

That convinced them. Nonchalantly, pretending to be engaged in idle conversation, with hands locked behind their backs in manly bearing, they strolled towards the gate. But halfway there, the adjutant shouted from the steps of the Orderly Room:

'Sorry, gentlemen. Could you please hang around a bit nearer so that you're within call?'

Back they went, strolling back and forth along the inner wall of the quadrangle furthest from the gate. The small-arms fire was quite distinct at times, but nowhere in the locality. The barracks seemed well removed from the trouble centre.

They were left in the air by the adjutant's proscription – and not a little agitated. Each knew that Saxton was right: come what may, officers would have to lead and, as ever, better the devil you know than the devil you don't.

Like the men, they were trained for trench warfare, the new orthodoxy of battle resulting from the Flanders stalemate. With revolvers drawn, they had led charges on fictitious German trenches over and over again, trying desperately to make bayonet charges sound real.

Since arriving at the barracks, Dobie had hardly spoken. Each rattle of gunfire upset him more and more. What he feared most was not personal harm, death or injury, nor the customary fear in officers of failing to perform well in front of the men in times of danger. Those were always present.

Here he was, having argued his way from pacifism towards militarism in the name of an ideal, Belgium, only to find himself facing the possibility of flushing out and killing Irishmen in Ireland. The past twenty-four hours had changed that moral position of his into an extremely doubtful one. Ireland! He was appalled.

Again, he tried to recollect anything he had ever known about Ireland and was brought up at once by the name of Cromwell. Oliver Cromwell had been responsible for occupying Ireland and cruelly suppressing Irishmen, even to the point of massacre, in the name of a doubtful dominion over the island.

Dimly, Dobie the idealist saw a parallel with the current German occupation of Belgium, but did not care to pursue the argument, telling himself that times and people, as well as circumstances, were different. But he was extremely uneasy. If Germany had no right to Belgium, did it not follow that neither Cromwell nor the English Government of the time had any right to Ireland?

Then he remembered words engraved in his mind, taught him by Nonnie's loving tutelage – words of George Fox the Quaker founder when confronted by the very man, Cromwell:

I (WHO am of the world called George ffox) doe deny the carrying of any carnall sword against any, or against thee Oliver Crumwell or any men in the presence of the lord God I declare it . . . and this I am ready to seale with my blood, and this I am moved to give forth for the truthes sake.

That was the absolutist pacifism he had learnt from Nonnie, from his father before her, from his schooling by example if not by polemic, and from his attendance at Quaker meetings.

Dobie would admit that his knowledge of Ireland and the Irish was little more than academic, however well his 'nutshell' lecture had gone down with his colleagues. In the past year, his mind had been fixed on the pacifist position in relation to Germany's occupation of Belgium, and this diametric change of direction to Ireland had given him no time to reconsider his position, except to acknowledge that Saxton was right. The army was no place to consider one's moral and political stance. Ireland was a political gadfly that had unmade more politicians than any other issue for more than a century. Had it been worse than usual of late? Not that he recalled. In any case, it would have had to be a vast deal worse to occupy any attention while the Western Front engaged all the headlines.

While there had always been a number of Irishmen in the other ranks, Dobie had never met an Irish officer, nor for that matter any Irishman. His impression however was that they were different somehow, a separate group often, although they mixed easily.

There was an incident he remembered now which marked that difference. A revivalist preacher had called at the camp; not an infrequent occurence in the weeks preceding embarkation, for what better opportunity to capture souls? Such preachers usually held their audience in thrall by sheer voice ... except for a little knot of Irishmen, who brushed rudely past the gospel singers, anxious to be out of reach and hearing of the preacher and his congregation. Not that Irishmen did not share their comrades' problems, though they appeared to be less afflicted when the Society of the Rechabites or the Band of Hope called to drum up sinners, to have the Pledge signed, and generally to call men to book.

How those Irishmen bustled past their comrades, trying not to be observed! While ordinary English or Scottish or Welsh lads, often first time away from home, could be easily persuaded to join in the messianic fervour of the Redemptorist preachers and the Pledge Societies, nothing would induce an Irishman to even watch from the rear as the hymns welled up to Heaven – 'Rock of Ages, cleft for me, Let me hide myself in Thee ...' The Irish could sniff the agony of the puritan conscience a mile away, and would have none of it.

If a Methodist miner had fallen for the demon drink, then signed the

Pledge in an agony of repentance, and then – worst of all in the purita-
nical scale of values – become a 'backslider', then the last to worry
were the Irish, who would have none of the agonising in the first place.
They drank or abstained as they saw fit without any prompting from
outside. Their inner concerns were otherwise ordered – at confession
on the first Saturday of the month. And then, by Jove, how they
mustered, as though at the crack of a whip, when the Catholic padre in
his black soutane came to stake his claim in the camp chapel. Their relations with their God were codified, more concerned with the relationship of God and man than with the latter's relationship with his
fellow men, in which Drink ranked as the devil, according to the
revivalists.

And reflecting on it, Dobie now saw the difference as greater than
appeared on the surface back in England, for here, on this other island,
he already detected a sharp contrast. Churches, big and small, pre-
dominated, and they had already passed several; not one chapel in
sight. Furthermore, the Calvaries and the Virgins outside the churches
were so unfamiliar as to shock. And that crowd swarming out of
church at Kingstown on an Easter Monday was so far removed from
anything that could happen in predominantly puritan England that he
felt he was – abroad – yes, abroad! Even the smell was different, and
under the familiar Britishness of so much else, there was an air of un-
familiarity that he could only put down to – and here he acknowledged a certain unwonted prejudice in himself – Popery, and
shuddered slightly at the un-Quakerly intolerance of his line of
thought. Yet the difference? Oh yes – how difficult for example to talk
to an Irishman – had he ever done so? He doubted it – could he talk as
easily to one as he could talk to, say, Harwood? – yes, old Harwood,
nice ordinary sort of chap without much to him, not the sort of chap to
excite much interest, not like old Litherland who had you helping him
in his alcoholic settlement at the drop of a hat; even so, you could just
go to Harwood and there was no barrier to clear before you began.

Because although he could not for the life of him remember, if ever
he knew, what faith Harwood subscribed to, if indeed any, there was
nevertheless a certain solid assumption about a chap like Harwood.
Dash it all, Harwood was ENGLISH – that was it – and there was no
need to go on about it any more. But, looking round him, THIS, whatever it was, was different, and he could feel it in his bones. It was not
that they were not being looked at, cheered, not that they had no audience to march their best before – it was in the air, and again he shud-

dered at the whiff of intolerance within himself. Yet despite the removal of the physical dread of Flanders temporarily, he did not see the present implications as anything but an agonising complication of his personal position. Why were they here? If he was just able to quell his own intolerance, were there not others who could not and would not? And what of the intolerance on the other side? He could imagine a situation in which the mutual intolerance could smoulder and burn and finally consume. Consume? Never, surely. Never. If there was intolerance on both sides, there were also areas of brotherhood. The very existence of so many Irish regiments in an army ranged against a common enemy for a start was evidence of certain communities of interest, whatever the politicians might exercise in the way of differences. And so many other factors brought the two peoples together. Surely, they must build on that, rather than allow the intolerances to smoulder. The Quaker in him saw the way, and the danger of departing from the way. Yet if they were here to deal with some sort of trouble ahead, the intolerances would spill over on both sides. He might not remember much of all the facts of history, but there was sufficient memory in him in addition to his reading for him to realise that when they did spill over, then there was violence. He hitched his belt a little for comfort, set his gaze firmly ahead, and tried and failed to put it all from him.

Were they there as an occupying force? He found it difficult to argue away from that now. Ireland was clearly a separate island, it had a different religion, deeply-rooted, not just 'established' which probably accounted for a good proportion of Cromwell's puritan violence. It had once had a separate language too, but he could not recall in full detail the various vicissitudes of politics and government in the intervening centuries, except that the two communities were different. There had always been an Irish Question, it was ingrained in British politics, and its non-solution involved occupation by one side, and opposition of various shades by the other. That the two communities had achieved a *modus vivendi* was obvious to the extent that the Irish battalions had been raised without difficulty and had given valuable service in France. Irishmen in both England and Ireland had rallied in their thousands, and he remembered the two comrades who had enlisted on the same day as himself. They were probably in the trenches in France by now.

But that did not mean that the evil of occupation against the wishes of the Irish people, or at least of some of them, did not still exist. As

142

Saxton had put it, it was all right if you were privileged, but if you weren't you either had your face ground into the bog or you conspired against the Government.

If indeed the British were occupying Ireland (and that seemed inescapable, however hallowed by time or Act of Union, or by the tacit consent of even a majority) how different from this march would be the Quaker approach.

Growing up for William Dobie had been punctuated by place names. He marked events by their geographical location and historical association. In the August holidays of '14, between school and university, the name Sarajevo had spelt a sort of doom that would be for ever associated with the hiatus between boyhood and manhood. Sarajevo — Sarajevo — and now for no reason greater than some temporary hiccup between digesting the dreadful events of the Western Front, he was in Ireland, possibly to kill Irishmen. He remembered that first week in August, and how different the Quaker stand would be. That week, after Sarajevo, old John Aiken had stood up out of the silence of Meeting and from the great beard that spread over his chest had read the words of William Penn at a confrontation with Red Indians:

The Great Spirit who made me and you, who rules the heavens and the earth, and who knows the innermost thoughts of men, knows that I and my friends have a hearty desire to live in peace and friendship with you, and to serve you to the utmost of our power. It is not our custom to use hostile weapons against our fellow creatures, for which reason we have come unarmed. Our object is not to do injury, and thus provoke the Great Spirit, but to do good. We are met on the broad pathway of good faith and goodwill, so that no advantage is to be taken on either side, but all to be openness, brotherhood and love . . . I will not do as the Marylanders did, that is, call you children or brothers only; for parents are apt to whip their children too severely, and brothers sometimes will differ; neither will I compare the friendship between us to a chain, for the rain may rust it, or a tree may fall and break it, but I will consider you as the same flesh and blood with the Christians, and the same as if one man's body were to be divided into two parts . . .

And he had then sat down, and not another soul had risen at Meeting to speak, because the curse of Sarajevo had reached even this room sanctified by the silence of the Great Spirit and words failed. Now the force of the words came back as he tried desperately to justify a position that had been unthinkable only twenty-four hours earlier as he

143

prepared to leave England for the Western Front.

'I still think this amount of force against the Irish is excessive, whatever they've done', he confided to Saxton. 'I begin to wonder if I can go
through with it all. Couldn't they just starve them into surrender?'

'Look here, Dobie, keep your voice down. That sort of talk can get
you into serious trouble. Why don't you drop it, man? I've told you
once before, once you are in the Army, old man, you've got to kill your
own grandmother if they order you to. Get that straight.' Saxton was
more than irritated, he was downright angry and did not bother to
hide it.

But Dobie's torment compelled. There was no escape: 'While I have
to agree with you in one way, there's a great deal of difference between
joining up to help clear Belgium of the Germans, then finding you
could be ordered to start killing Irishmen. Why, Saxton, you know as
well as I do that there's hardly a unit in the British Army without a
good proportion of Irishmen in it. Look at the number in our battalion
alone. What about the Tyneside Irish Battalion? And that's just one.
Why, man, there are whole battalions from Ireland itself. It's hard to
swallow an order to kill Irishmen.'

This time Saxton bordered on violence. He gripped Dobie's arm
and hissed: 'Keep your voice down, man. Don't you realise that if you
extend your argument, you'll be talking treason? I don't want to hear
it. An army obeys, and it obeys completely – it makes no sense otherwise. You can't pick and choose what orders you'll take, what enemy
you'll shoot or not shoot at. That's for the politicos to sort out. We
just carry out the orders. Ours not to reason, old man, so calm
down.'

'But Irishmen', Dobie persisted, his dark brows knit together.

'Yes, even Irishmen', Saxton replied. 'I don't see the difference, to
be candid, Dobie. The Government isn't going to send us here to give
them a Military Tattoo. Whatever the racket ahead, you can rest
assured it's Irishmen who're causing it. And if that small-arms stuff is
theirs, or half theirs, then there's only one way of stopping it: with
greater force. And if it's not Irishmen, then it would be Germans. I see
no difference either way. The Old Man was definite at that school: it's
Irishmen who are shooting, and I guess some of ours are shooting
back, which makes double the racket. In the end it could all amount to
nothing, a storm in a tea-cup. But whatever it is, we have to do as we're

144

told.'

But the adjutant had returned to shepherd them yet again. They were jumpy, but this time he was soon able to reassure them, for he was carrying mail.

'This has been held over from yesterday', he said mildly. 'Seems a good moment to distribute it, what?'

Dobie was thankful to be drawn away from his sombre musings. There was a letter for him and he spotted the bold hand before the adjutant passed it over to him.

'Dearest William Dobie...' He was able to smile.

'Good news, old chap?' asked Saxton, who did not have a letter and was prepared to share anybody's.

'Oh no, just – well, you know – some people have a droll way of putting things.'

'She must be a bit of all right, Dobie, to get such a smile out of you. We haven't had a peep out of you since leaving the hallowed shores.'

'She is', Dobie volunteered. 'Yes, she's all right', and he beamed.

Saxton was delighted to have guessed right. 'Come on then, share your spot of comfort with your comrades-in-arms.'

Dobie smiled on, but moved away like a boy with a favourite book. Once apart from the group he read: 'Dearest William Dobie, Now you have gone abroad I feel there is no need for all the restraint that society demands of women. Is that wrong, William? Surely not...'

How she plunged straight into the heart of the matter. In the most chaste, even required way they had proclaimed their love for one another. Yet the required restraints had also kept them apart. They had had so little time, so few opportunities to be alone together. Yet even there they were luckier than some, for their respective independence from parental constraint had allowed them opportunity for the meetings in town and above all in Wensleydale. That had been decidedly *risqué*, but he was thankful for it.

'... I think my favourite Shakespeare play is *Troilus and Cressida*. I know it's a sad play, of course, but it says the most beautiful things about love. And it's all so difficult that I can believe in it, their love, I mean. "Why tell you me of moderation". That's exactly how I feel. If there's no way in which you and I are Troilus and Cressida, thank goodness, even so, the play's sadness and its partings in such sweet sorrow reflect how I feel about you at this moment when the wretched war takes you from me...'

He did not know his Shakespeare as she did. But he had already been affected by her enthusiasm and this letter carried him far away from the grim parade square where his colleagues paced impatiently or read their letters.

'... There's a line from Troilus when he is confronted by Cressida: "You have bereft me of all words, lady". That's a bit like you, don't you think, William Dobie? Though I forgive you so long as you feel the same sort of love. Do you?

Boldness comes to me now, and brings me heart:-
Prince Troilus, I have lov'd you night and day
For many weary months.

'One day, you and I must go through the play. There's plenty of war for the men to skip off to from time to time! I remember our day in Wensleydale. That was beautiful, beautiful. But what a job to get you to kiss me. You don't regret it, do you?

I wish'd myself a man;
Or that we women had men's privilege
Of speaking first...
... My lord, I do beseech you, pardon me;
'Twas not my purpose, thus to beg a kiss.

'But I don't really have a single regret, even if you perhaps thought me a little bold. William, I wait only for the day of your return. This temporary parting has taught me one thing, that when we come together again we must make the most of it. There's one thing I can assure you of, that I won't go to another man, like Cressida. But that's quite another story, poor thing. She should have fought for women's rights...'

He hoped she would not fly off on that particular tangent. He could not help feeling uncomfortable about it, but did not know why. Perhaps that was the burden of simply being a man. But she left it and sailed on blithely.

'... I am full of plans for your return. We must seriously discuss our future. I love you and you love me, I know you do, so why shouldn't we talk, have a good gas about it, like proper lovers instead of meeting so secretly all the time? I suppose you will soon be in those beastly trenches. I can't imagine what they are like, but they must be awful. I shall pray for you all the time, but to whom I'm not sure, because I don't believe in the great bearded god who keeps things the way they are...'

Oh, dear, was this women's rights again, or just the world in general, in which case he was inclined to agree with her?

'. . . But I do pray. That's all we women can do, and I do. Now that we are parted, I begin to feel like all the other women. I feel the urge to knit. Shall I knit you something? Now that summer is on the way (or at least is supposed to be, though I'm freezing at the moment) shall I knit you some winter woollies? You've no idea what it's like just waiting helplessly. I try so hard to be good about Caroline, seeing she gets some sort of education, which is more than I got – although at least, old Babs who used to look after us saw that my English was decent. I can't add two and seven and I don't know where Berlin is, but I'm grateful for being taught to read and write. And I'm grateful too for what Babs made me read. Poor Babs, she died much too early. I could do with her now, to help me with Caroline, who isn't the easiest! Still, Aunt Venables next door is a great help. But I do wish she knew something about *men*. You have to know the enemy to defeat him! . . .'

Always back to that; Dobie wondered if he would be able to stand up to it indefinitely. Might it not get just a bit shrill as time went on? Then once again he beamed as he remembered her diatribes against male domination, and her humour withal. Yes, he could tolerate all that, so long as it was she, with her smile, her impetuosity, her beauty; yes, her beauty, for he felt as never before her particular beauty, the great diadem of dark hair shot with gold, and the laughing eyes.

'My God, some girl you've got there', Saxton shouted across the yard. 'Come on, Dobie, let's have a glimmer.'

But Dobie turned away, still smiling.

'. . . Enough of that nonsense, William Dobie. The day will come when you men will be our equals. In the meantime, I leave you with a few more words from Cressida:

. . . . but I was won, my lord
With the first glance that ever – Pardon me –
If I confess much, you will play the tyrant.
I love you now; but not, till now, so much
But I might master it: – in faith, I lie.

'And I do love you, William Dobie, and I do lie if I seek to master that love. So there you are, all restraint gone. Should I be ashamed of myself? Now what about you?

Love and blessings,
Laura.'

He read it over again, word for word. Saxton was right, he had all the luck. No man deserved such a love letter, least of all he. And yet he felt a sudden confidence in himself.

147

Then yet again, the adjutant was rushing out of the barracks. Was this it, the orders, whatever they were? The adjutant shouted – there seemed an urgency that sent their hearts plummeting. Dobie rushed to join his comrades. Yes, this was it. The adjutant was all bustle.

As he joined the group, Dobie stuffed the letter carelessly in his tunic pocket and felt bad about this rough treatment. The adjutant was really flustered. This was action of some sort.

Dobie frowned, as though in pain. Had the Great Spirit failed him – or he It?

PART THREE

PART THREE

Colonel Marsh had finished his lunch, delicately dabbed at his moustache with his napkin and intimated to his colleagues that he was ready to recommence operations.

But first, his opposite number had something to say.

'The problem,' said Colonel Saunders of the local garrison, 'is to know where these Irish are. We know they're in the General Post Office, of course – and in that mill. But judging from what we've experienced in Sackville Street, they're swarming like flies in all sorts of places. We've flushed them out of the south-west area of the city, the Castle area, but we can't be sure of what lies between here and the city centre. So far, nobody's been through that area all this week. Rumour is rife. Now you're here, Colonel, may I suggest that you send a patrol into that area first? You could feel out their strength, and if it's all clear, you can then concentrate on the river. If not, you'll have to clear it before tackling the river with any sort of force.'

But Colonel Marsh was impatient of such vacillation. He had got into the rhythm of movement. Not twenty-four hours before, they had been in camp; indeed, he had only just received the order.

The general, knowing his Battalion to be nearest readiness, had chosen them, and here they were, just a day later, across the sea and ready to engage the enemy. He saw it as an expeditionary force and was proud of the speed with which they had arrived in Dublin. Now that they were on the move, they would continue to move.

He had seen enough of stalemate in France, and he had not performed particularly well within its necessary constraints. Here, in Dublin, there were no constraints – the local garrison was weak, as he saw it, lacking in initiative, too long home-based in the comfort of town barracks. The initiative was his, and he would resist any suggestion of stalemate, of becoming stationary and deploying patrols.

'I think we can deal with it, Colonel', he said. 'I think if we keep the Battalion intact and in full marching order, we'll put the fear of God into anybody in our way. We're a little below full strength, but six hundred men marching down a street is a sight to stir the heart if

151

they're on your side. If not, God help them is all I say. So what I propose, sir, is to march out of here as a Battalion, continue along this road and up to the bridge leading to Sackville Street. This side of the bridge we halt, link up with what local forces you have there – and I'm still not clear *what* you have – and organise the best line of approach from there.'

The colonel did not suggest, he proposed and disposed. His tone was clipped, military, commanding. His impression of his opposite was of softness and immobility. He had established his command at once, over their initial handshake and the glass of whiskey. He had hinted at his experience of France (without detail), then gone on to describe how he had whipped the Battalion into shape for France. This Irish operation was to be a mere interlude. Their presence would be enough, provided they were quick and decisive. He was anxious to get back to France and found the present exercise a tedious interlude. Cautious patrolling was not called for, would only betoken undue respect for the rebels.

Without allowing Colonel Saunders to demur, he asked Major Dean-Forbes to bring in the adjutant.

When the adjutant came in, the colonel spread the city map on the table between them.

'First, I want the Battalion on parade on the square as soon as you get out of here. Next, I want it to march out in good order, no slackness, mark you, along this road here, towards the bridge. Understand?'

'Yes, Sir.'

'It's perfectly straight, till you come to the final bend round Trinity College. At the gates of the College, clearly marked, here, I want you to halt. I myself shall drive up then and consult with local forces to work out the best line of attack. I don't expect any trouble on the way. The Battalion is sufficient show of strength to deter any troublemakers. I gather the main force of rebels is concentrated just over the river. Colonel Saunders informs me their firepower is confined to small-arms, so we should be all right up to those gates, provided you keep just out of sight of this spot, just south of the bridge. We must assume it's still under rebel control. That's all, Mr Forsyth, off you go, and see that it's a smart turn-out.'

And that was it. Their fate was sealed. Whatever the 'something' at

Loos – or Mons – that had eventually put Colonel Marsh in command of the Battalion, it did not show. His command was absolute, sure, unwavering. The die was cast.

The adjutant stressed the smart turn-out. 'A' Company was assembled near the gate, ready as usual to lead the Battalion. CSM Green had got the message. He cajoled and bullied them into shape as he walked up and down their lines, shouting.

Now, in the open again, hastily adjusting straps and settling down to the relative silence for the order to march, they heard the intermittent rattle of small-arms fire in the air. The sergeant-major's bullying alarmed them. Toes shuffled in boots to ease blisters – for the men sensed that a limp now would bring down fires of coal on their heads. The CSM's tone demanded a full and strict and tidy parade turn-out – and the reality increased their alarm.

One last irritable shout before the order to march: 'Settle down, Roberts, will you?' For F.X. felt ghastly. He had developed what he suspected was a large blister under his left big toe. He was afraid of the rifle-fire ahead, and his thoughts were still with Marian.

In his left-side tunic pocket he felt the letter.

The envelope had disappeared, but of the letter, already he knew every word by heart. He took the risk of being bawled out by CSM Green, feeling that with the obvious danger ahead he had a right to this talisman which he still failed to understand. He knew every word by heart. But that is not the same as understanding its import. What *did* Marian mean? What was the letter about? Since she was asking if he understood, it was obvious she expected him not to, or why should she ask?

As the Battalion wheeled out of the barrack gates, F.X. grasped the letter tight in his left hand, as though to wring a meaning from it. He was afraid, because all round the city was silent except for the ring of their boots on the tarmac and cobbles and the small-arms fire in the distance. It was always some way ahead, out of reach. Otherwise, the silence was palpable. He was afraid of the silent city, of Marian's letter, of Father McNally. And because he was afraid, he felt something he had not felt before: he felt *young*. What had happened between Marian and himself, what was happening now, was not for him. He was too young ... He wanted to protest, to run, to return to innocence.

153

He did not formulate it into thoughts or words, but as his hand clutched that letter, his resentment took the form of images of days spent in innocence. He had never done that before, never lived in the past, it was a new experience. Days bathed in sunshine, days with Marian, days on summer trips to Mablethorpe; those were days spent in the present, never in the past. Clutching the letter was clutching at lost innocence.

The CSM was shouting his head off as they wheeled through the gate. Their step was so awful as to be almost human.

'"A" Company, pick 'em up now – left, er right, er left er right er ...' – at the top of his voice, followed by a lower mutter of, 'You shower o' creeps, you, what's this, Sunday School trip, heh?', then loud and clear again, 'Left, er right, er left er right er...'

It fell on F.X. like the birch on a condemned man; it seemed unnecessary, superfluous. Like the rest of them, he was marching as well as he could. The Army had not prepared them for marching miles on hard city surfaces, had told them nothing and left them to guess the worst. They had been flung into a strange, silent city after a restless night of non-stop travel. There had been unnerving sounds of rifle fire ahead and the shock waves of naval gunfire; all this, with most of them dwelling on personal problems in a moment of danger. The best that could be said of them in military terms was that they numbered six hundred and were armed with Enfield rifles.

The cumulative shock of it all, all wrapped up in less than twenty-four hours, even the crossing of a stretch of water without the great khaki welcome of comrades in France to break the spell of leaving the relative comfort of camp in Catterick and England's secure shores, all had the effect of reducing them from a cohesive force trained for ritual violence to a rabble of individual men whimpering for something lost.

Even the CSM was falling into that rhythm. He was not confined to a rank, to a set place in the mob; he could change pace, stand still and cast a beady eye over their performance as they passed by, for their performance was his.

And later, after the unthinkable had happened, and he had time to reflect, he would remember this. Where was he, precisely, when it happened? He would like to think it had been at the front, but he was sure he was not.

He knew he was the first to *see* what happened at the front, but he was not *at* the front when it did happen.

Their performance, in drill, in inspection, at parades and on ma-

154

noeuvres was his responsibility. On that part of them he had made his mark, and success could elevate him eventually to that most privileged rank of regimental sergeant-major. That was why he was now up and down, front and rear, with an eye on the whole Company.

He could not answer for their performance in action, nor was he expected to. The best drilled men could occasionally fail at the first hurdle, when real bullets were flying. Nobody knew that better than the CSM. Whatever made men heroes, it was not necessarily a smart turn-out or a capacity for marching at a good pace and rhythm. They helped, of course; without them, you had a mere rabble. But no amount of it could inject that last military energy and excitement that would rout a weaker enemy, or withstand a stronger one.

As the CSM visibly slackened into the loose rhythm – or lack of it – he knew he had done his best. Nothing, he knew, could replace the old country and city spirit of the old Territorial Army, of which he had been a member until sent back from the trenches and promoted to training this new rabble who came from all over the place.

Men from the same locality in one Regiment stood together, had enjoyed summer manoeuvres together before the War – a whole month away from work and the domestic round in camp on the moors round Catterick, or in the pines round Aldershot. They had been good; and, with the Regulars, they had been most of such Army as Britain could muster on the outbreak of war.

Those men had been sacrificed in the slaughter of the first two years of war. And their sacrifice had apparently achieved nothing, except to hold the enemy at tremendous cost. The present stalemate in France would presumably provide the platform from which the trainees of the New Army, like his own Company, would go into attack and roll back the Germans.

Likely bloody story, thought the CSM, slackly surveying the poor dressing and the ragged step. God help Britain, God help the British Empire if it depends on this lot!

He was unlikely to achieve promotion to RSM with this lot. No general could extract such obedience in his minions, or extend empire, as absolutely as an RSM. So CSM Green halted, bawled and smartly quickened pace at their side, and took up his post just short of the front rank. Only so could he keep an eye on all the Company, while Lieutenant Dobie and Sergeant Forster marched up front, leading, but not quite aware of the rabble behind.

For they were a rabble. He was even allowing himself to fall into their rhythm. In the first place, there was nobody to express their performance to, no cheering and admiring populace lining the street as they passed by. The streets were empty. In the second place, this senseless march over cobbles and tramlines was no way to show off a Company. The men were stumbling, finding difficulty in keeping a good dressing. Frankly, he could not blame them. Nobody seemed to give a damn. Lieutenant Dobie could not know a good marching step if he saw one, and Major Dean-Forbes was way back, travelling with the colonel and H.Q. So why bother?

The CSM lost interest, and was even seen to turn his head once or twice, showing an interest in the neighbourhood. Without a word from him, the men became even slacker and the march a shambles, until even Lieutenant Dobie, picking up a brief glance from Sergeant Forster marching across the other side of the front rank, decided that the sound was so unlike marching that he was justified in breaking step, waiting for the CSM to catch up with him, and having a word with him. The CSM was mooning just then. He was shocked and angry with himself when he saw the lieutenant awaiting him. He could take it from the major, but from a raw recruit like Dobie it was too humiliating.

'Pick it up there, come on now, left-er-right-er-left . . .' he screamed at the ranks. He kept up the screaming right up to Dobie's ear, as though he were not there, so intent was he on regaining the right step.

The lieutenant, recognising the snub, decided to stand his ground and cast his eye over the men as they passed. He knew, and he knew that they knew, that only the CSM could instil regimental ardour into them, but he had to make a show of it.

Where he eventually stood was crucial. He too would remember that for a moment – *the* moment when things happened – he was not at the front.

Yes, they were bad indeed. Yet he did not care. He too, like the men, had marched seven miles on little sleep, on unsuitable surfaces built for heavy horse and dray traffic, not for army boots. He longed for a bath.

It was the first really warm spring day. The sun was well round now, high on their forward left and beginning to have an effect. The trees were breaking bud, and the heat was so dry, you could almost hear the cracking of bud-tips as leaves pushed their way out into the light after a tardy spring.

The sight over the men's heads of a magnolia exploding with

flower-buds put Dobie in mind of Nonnie. Each year, they had greeted spring together by solemnly processing down the long walled garden to the magnolia in its sheltered corner. Quietly, and without unbecoming fuss, they admired it and thanked whatever gods may be for the return of spring. And lest they be construed as worshipping the bare tree with its pale waxen bloom, they would pass on to other things.

Poise, restraint, and a certain spiritual decorum in all things – like the magnolia at this stage, thought William. At once he corrected himself, for however pure the bloom in its white and pale magenta perfection, it could hardly be described as restrained; it was positively unrestrained in its theft of space and attention during its brief period of full bloom.

He was making a poor show of regimental spirit. As, hastily, he turned left, with most of the Company ahead of him, he saw the road rising slightly over a bridge. That would be the canal the colonel had pointed out. It marked off the centre of the city from its inner suburbs. The noise of falling water confirmed this surmise, and he quickened step to try to get up front and lead the men over the bridge. That would amount to the moment of entering the city.

But his gazing at the magnolia had left it a bit late, and the front rank was almost at the approach to the bridge before he started. He saw the opening made by the canal. The street ended well before the bridge; there was quite a break before it began again at the other side. It looked more like a real city ahead, the houses were taller, less like inner suburbia.

The gap between them worried him. A road ran each side of the canal at right angles to them, widening the gap. On the map, that gap marked by the canal had appeared like a moat round the inner city. Since there was trouble in the city, that gap marked the beginning of the danger area. Dobie walked faster.

That was all he was thinking of – the gap, and the urgent need to be up at the front – at the precise moment when the unthinkable happened.

The CSM had passed him, still bawling his head off – the ranks were marching loosely and untidily – when it happened.

At that precise moment, the first few ranks froze where they were.

Sergeant Forster was flat on the road on the hump of the bridge, the front rank likewise. The positions were difficult to take in, so sudden-

157

ly different were they. In a flash, from the upright marching position, they were prone.

The second rank was broken too, with three men sprawled on the road, one on top of another, his head turned skywards in a blank stare that terrified what remained of the third and fourth rank.

Here Moffat, Pearson and Simpson stood thunderstruck. The ranks behind them, still only half aware of the crack of rifle fire that had burst into the front, pushed forward. The fourth and fifth ranks, horrified, held their ground till the entire Company shuffled, too puzzled to comprehend what was happening, all of which was quite outside any regimental drill they had learnt. They did not so much halt as just *stop*, for want of forward space.

Sergeant-Major Green, halfway down the Company, had heard it. With his practised ear, he detected the whine of flying bullets. He too was shocked and came to a standstill, not so much at the noise as the sudden decimation of Sergeant Forster and the three forward ranks.

He was the first to realise they were dead – or should be – at that range. He glanced at the windows across the canal and guessed at once. As the Company slithered to a stop, he tried to pull his regimental wits together.

Lieutenant Dobie was further behind, catching up, still contemplating the gap created by the canal. His mind had not quite registered the fire over the scrape and rattle of marching boots. For a second or two, he was impatient of the shuffling halt as the ranks collided with one another. His mind was slow to come to terms with this new development, of ranks colliding just when the colonel would expect the best possible performance on entering the city proper.

He quickened step still further, somewhat impatient with the CSM who was evidently puzzling things out. But it was too late.

As the whole Company stalled and came to a stuttering halt, and the ring of their boots died momentarily, a second burst of fire smashed into the next rank. Only the CSM could tell where it came from. The rest did not realise that the shooting was coming from *somewhere*: all they saw and knew was the sudden stop, the piling up of ranks, above all the sprawling figures on the road before them.

As they stopped and puzzled for the few fatal seconds, as the CSM darted forward at a crouch, and the lieutenant quickened his pace impatiently, this second round of bullets found standing targets.

Moffat saw Simpson slowly spin towards him, his legs folding and a ghastly hole pulsing blood from his forehead. Clasping Pearson by the

158

hand, he shouted:

'Christ, out of here, look out . . .'

In one leap, dragging the unresisting Pearson with him, Moffat cleared the parapet on the right side of the bridge and was in the canal fifteen feet below in one movement.

As the 'old sweats' know, it is those few seconds that mark men for life, one way or another. It is then that men are alive one second and dead the next, mere sacks sprawling over a road or in a field and beyond all earthly help. It is then, for the survivors, that the pulse leaps suddenly and men do things without thinking; sometimes the right things, but sometimes the wrong ones. It is out of their hands, which way they turn and what they do. But they do them, one way or another.

Only in the rarest cases, of a sort of mental and physical paralysis, does a man freeze like a rabbit before a stoat – and stay frozen. At such moments of the totally unexpected (for all the training schemes in the world cannot simulate the live engagement, the feel of real bullets flying, of comrades falling round you dead or bleeding terribly), at such moments, it is every man for himself. Each suddenly retreats into his own particular encapsulated world, like a hermit crab, and cuts and runs for his life.

It is only those who hear of the bullets by proxy, so to speak, those at the rear, who think they can assess the situation and produce a rational solution. Those at the front do not act – they react.

Moffat's leap was a two, at most a three second reaction. A split second later, Pearson was in the canal with him, though whether of his own volition or by Moffat's helping hand he knew not. As they plunged over the parapet, their rifles spun off their shoulders and away from them in a wide arc. They were not out of their depth, but spluttered in four or five feet of water, clawing frantically at each other in an attempt to find their feet. For the second time in two days, Moffat was sodden.

They were shocked and very frightened, yet at once Moffat knew that they were out of it so long as they stayed down there where the line of fire was well above their heads. They had achieved a breathless, sodden safety. And Moffat, as ever quick to assess an advantage, began to shout in the direction of the parapet, calling his comrades to join him and Pearson. But in the confusion above, no man heard him.

At the same second on the wide bridge, the fourth rank turned in-stinctively, as though ducking away from a sudden jet of water, bent

159

double and tried to stampede to the rear, only to bump clumsily into the bewildered fifth rank, and the sixth, so that the two Robertses, from glancing across rank to each other, bumped almost head-on in the stampede. That made for another second or two, and it was then that F.X. fell in sudden agony and quite helpless, clutching his thigh, falling and hitting his head against the parapet where the bridge curved into the nearside canal-road at right-angles to their own main road. He fell into safety, his thigh shattered, knocking himself unconscious as he fell, and then lay limp.

But of that J.H. knew nothing as he dodged and ran for cover.

The rest of 'A' Company scattered then, back along the wide, exposed road; a few through garden-gates of houses flanking the main road they had just marched along in barely passable order.

One or two, unlucky, were caught struggling with a recalcitrant latch and fell where they were. Others, darting about like hares, scattered along the grassy canal bank on the near side, not knowing where to find shelter, so remorseless and searching was the fire. Finally, the survivors scuttled behind a low parapet, little more than a kerb that divided the grassy bank of the canal from the road.

Even then, bullets sputtered off the granite and pinned them down so effectively that they could only lie prone, the packs on their backs showing for a target.

Still, men bunched and bumped into one another on the bridge for those fatal seconds. The CSM's keen eyes, spotting the slightest cover of the bridge parapet and marking the source of the rifle-fire, caught sight of a school building, the last in the street they were about to leave. He shouted at the top of his capable parade voice:

' "A" Company – this way – follow me – all of you!' He dashed at a crouch, brushing Lieutenant Dobie as he turned, quickly, supple as a schoolboy, and darted back, to kick through the double-gates of the school-garden into comparative safety.

With bullets still flying and finding another three men, they followed, speeding, some of them crawling across the garden in desperation, as though to sink into the ground, to a recess in the building that appeared to be out of the line of fire. They were not thinking, but simply fell into the recess because the CSM had gone there. Others scattered about the school-garden and into the shelter of the low railinged wall facing the canal, and found themselves trapped, unable to move further as bullets cracked into the cast-iron railings above their heads, or into the granite wall.

160

It had all taken a few seconds only. No man, not even the 'old sweat', the CSM, knew quite what he was doing. Their eyes dilated with fear as they crouched and shuffled for shelter in the recess. And all the CSM could think was that, by this instinctive retreat, he had saved what he could of his Company.

If he had pushed Lieutenant Dobie aside in the blind rush, what matter? It was no time to dwell upon the niceties of rank. That could be explained. But where *was* the lieutenant?

Without pausing to think, the sergeant-major dashed, crouching, back to the gates across the little garden, ignoring the flying bullets. He knelt cautiously behind the shelter of the gate pillar, and peeping out, registered with horror Lieutenant Dobie facing 'B' Company and desperately trying to stop the oncoming ranks by waving his arms. He had forgotten the shouted order to retreat or to about turn, and was gesticulating ineffectually, like a civilian, as the bullets flew round him, though unbelievably not finding him. CSM Green could only scratch his head.

He shook himself at once, shouted loud and clear:

'"B" Compan-y -about-turn!'

And, indeed, it worked. They stamped, turned about on the spot and were almost facing the rear, ready to march back in the direction they had come from. Just then, the rifles from the other side of the canal seemed to redouble their fire, and another six men fell as they were turning.

The CSM saw it all clearly, right before his eyes. He kept his head, called again above the din:

'At the double, "B" Company, pick it up!'

They held together somehow and were off, to a kind of safety and a possible collision with 'C' Company not far behind even while the rifles over the canal were being reloaded.

But the CSM could not worry about the collision of Companies; with every passing second, he began to register details.

First, the lieutenant, who (he could hardly believe his eyes) was still standing there, oblivious of his own danger, an obvious target with his Sam Browne, pips and revolver, gazing across the canal to the parapet where Roberts F. X. lay sprawled and bleeding profusely. The CSM guessed what was passing through Dobie's mind. Again, he shouted:

'Leave it, Mr Dobie, leave it! This way – and keep your head down!'

As, instinctively, Dobie turned, the CSM also registered the exact source of the trouble. Over the canal, in a position commanding a full view of the bridge and the wide main road down which they had marched, there it was, a large house, the first of the tall four-storey houses that continued into the city. All the window-panes were broken, and he could see, quite clearly, the gleam of rifle-muzzles in four of them or more.

Another glance, and he took in the casualties of both 'A' and 'B' Companies. That was enough. He swore and snatched at Lieutenant Dobie as he came up, still living his charmed life, and pulled him roughly into the shelter of the gate-post. As though to stop all movement, the sergeant-major pressed hard on the lieutenant's shoulders, and at the same time took in quickly the location of his men.

He guessed that quite a few were cowering behind those flights of steps opposite, having seen one or two who had failed, now lying dead or wounded on the pavement. He glimpsed others, desperately sheltering behind trees alongside the canal and under the canal parapet. Then he cast a cold eye again over the bodies lying out on the road.

He leaned forward, only just exposing the top of his head, and looked towards the bridge. Drawing back, he met the shocked lieutenant's eyes.

'This is as bad as I've ever seen, Sir,' he said hoarsely. 'And, by God, I've seen some sights, I can tell you.'

Lieutenant Dobie could not speak. He was slower than the sergeant-major to take it all in. He realised only that he was lucky to be alive. His belt, pips and revolver would mark him as an officer, and he had lingered long enough and well within range to be picked off with ease.

As the CSM roughly bundled him into comparative safety, he could not even thank him. But in the few seconds of getting breath, their eyes stayed on each other, and their whole world changed at once. Two men who in normal circumstances would never have met, still less spoken to each other, knew that in the ensuing hour or two they would have to conspire and act in concert if they – and the remaining men in their charge – were to survive a situation as sudden and cataclysmic in its danger as men were ever likely to meet.

The bullets continued to spit and fly down the road before them, spattering little spuds of earth behind them in the open stretch of garden between them and the relative safety of the recess in the school building where some fifteen men had gathered.

'Ach, Sir,' said the CSM, 'you've all the luck in the world, standing there to be shot at and still here to tell the tale, heh?'

The lieutenant came out in a cold sweat as he remembered. Then the CSM, still crouching and keeping careful cover, turned round to face the school-building.

'I'm crossing this garden to the men. Watch how I do it and wait. When I signal, follow on in the same way and don't linger. Got me, Sir?' Dobie nodded.

The CSM braced himself, then sprang out of cover and dashed across the exposed garden, flinging himself in a dive into the recess. Ever cautious and cunning, he waited, staring across at the waiting lieutenant. After thirty seconds, he waved frantically, afraid to shout lest he be picked up over the canal.

Dobie sprang, dashed and flung himself as he had seen CSM Green do it. He found his voice. 'Do you hear shouting?' he asked.

The sergeant-major quietened the men around them and listened.

'Yes, Sir. There's still some men alive out there. I suppose they had the nous to find good cover somewhere. That's what it seems to be about.'

'But why should they shout?'

The CSM cocked an ear again.

'Ach,' he said disgustedly, in a tone the men knew only too well from the parade square, 'some idiot in the canal! That's fine. And shoutin' his head off. I suppose he thinks he's at Cleethorpes and we can chuck him a bloody life-belt. Fine, heh, fine!'

The CSM was taking a liberty with his language, and the men took comfort from that. They recognised the irony in the voice, the twisted humour at the expense of one of themselves, and they felt safer. And they were.

The sergeant-major and Lieutenant Dobie were getting better every minute. The lieutenant was even thinking it out.

'Sergeant-Major, we're safe here, aren't we? That rifle-fire comes from the other side of the canal, yes?'

'It does, Sir', the CSM replied patiently, realising he must give the young lieutenant time. It was his baptism by fire, after all – and a hard one at that.

'Then let's think it out properly while we're safe here, and see what we can do.' Desperately he tried to maintain rank before the CSM and the men but his eyes had not registered clearly all the details that had passed before them in the few brief minutes of the engagement. His

163

brain switched madly from one incident to another. But he could not focus his impressions. Nothing remotely like this had ever been required of his brain: to register hostile rifle-fire, men falling, the direction of the danger and the means of avoiding its staccato violence. It was as though nothing in his previous life had ever happened, though mad images of Laura kept flashing across his mind as he tried to adjust. He found it difficult to place her, to remember her clearly, and the images gave way to some new menacing noise that was now his *real* military education. Laura had existed – praise God – but neither she nor anything else in his previous existence related to this sudden horrible reality. These few minutes of cringing under fire became the whole of his life.

Not half an hour before, he had been reading Laura's uninhibited love letter. That letter had the effect of dismissing his cogitation on his position in Ireland. Love of that nature transcended all, and he had marched as far as the magnolia, the canal, with Laura in his mind – and Nonnie. Now he was lost, and all that was lost. None of it might ever have existed. Now all was shattering, explosive, hateful violence and *this* was life, *now*, and the suddenness and the force of it cancelled out all past and future. He was dimly aware of blood flowing on the road.

'We're in this garden,' he went on, still choking for breath, 'out of the line of fire so long as we're in this recess, aren't we?'

'We are, Sir.'

'Are there any men elsewhere in the garden, do you think?'

'There's a few under the perimeter wall, Sir. They've been trained to keep their heads down. If they don't, it's too bad.'

'Facing the canal?' The CSM nodded. 'My goodness,' exclaimed Dobie, 'we've got to get them in, they can't be safe there!'

However much the facts of his former existence might be rubbed out by this sudden hell, still his nature came uppermost. He was not satisfied about the men's safety. His mind worked along different channels from the CSM's.

Here the CSM was not satisfied. 'Look here, Sir', he said, and despite the present desperation of their position, hemmed in by raking fire, he took his time. 'It's like this. There's an enemy post over there. I don't care who the hell they are, but they're the enemy. Now, when you have an enemy, Sir, who's getting at you, you either have a go at him as opportunity occurs, or you take up proper defensive positions. What you don't do is nothing, heh? Well, them men at the wall is in the best defensive position of the lot, and they can return fire. See? That's war, heh?'

'I don't think we ought to risk any more casualties.'

'Look, Sir. There's more than a few men at the wall. Look at it as a whole. There's more men outside, some in poor cover along the canal, and they're pinned down unless we can pin the enemy down in turn. So forget them at the wall. You see, Sir, unless you can provide concentrated fire from a well-sighted firepost, you'll never help those men out there. And some of 'em will be wounded, bound to be. One thing goes with another, don't you see, heh? By luck, we've got maybe ten men at that wall, out in the open but safe – so long as they keep their heads down... They've got a clear view of what's opposite. They're all we've got so far. You'll never help anybody without their covering fire. One thing goes with another, you understand. See?'

The CSM was practically haranguing the lieutenant. Dobie was shocked, first to be so addressed by an inferior in front of the men, and secondly, because he realised the inferior was right. Thirdly, because he had no answer. 'One thing goes with another' – he mulled it over. How absolutely perfect. *One thing goes with another* – that was the secret of the engagement, of any military operation, whether offensive or defensive. One thing goes with another! It might have even helped him in his struggles within himself.

The black brows knit as it sank in. Of his ultimate objective, the safety of every man he could reach, he had no doubt. It was right enough. It was the means he had got wrong. Their assailants in that house were no Germans, and even now, with so many of his men dead around him, he could muster no feeling about 'the enemy'. Rebellious Irishmen they might be, but his mind was set, almost exclusively, on the safety of his men at the moment.

Regardless of politics or opinion in Ireland, the rifle-fire from the house over the canal was a threat to *his* men. It had already killed some of them and would kill more unless he could do something about it. He could never cut his way through the political jungle; he lacked the blind conviction of the extreme argument. So he had no particular feelings about those Irishmen firing from across the canal, certainly not the simple, straightforward hostility implicit in the CSM's utterances.

Unlike the CSM, the last thing in his mind was an attack-and-destroy movement that might cost more lives, be they British or Irish. What was foremost in his mind was the fate of those men out there, whom he knew by more than names by now.

He *knew* the Roberts boys, Moffat and his cronies, Yudkin, Liddell and the rest of them. In fact, from a few daily parades, from reading their letters and censoring them, from observing them at odd moments of his mooning, he knew them better than they might realise. And in spite of the sergeant-major's reasoning, he was still unhappy about the ten or eleven men exposed at the garden wall.

And so, if indeed one thing went with another, they must improve their defensive position. He looked at the stout door of the school set in the centre of the recess.

'Yes, Sir,' said the CSM, 'I see what's in your mind.' He nodded to the three men, then to the door.

'Come on – all together – a good kick with your feet at the middle', he said, pointing to the lock on the double-doors.

They kicked in concert – once – twice. At the third kick, the doors burst open with a splintering of wood, and the men rushed in with relief. Inside the small entrance-hall, they waited for the lieutenant and the CSM.

Without waiting for orders from the lieutenant, the CSM took command at once. 'All right. Now, listen. The fire is coming from over the canal. You'll see a house over there. See those classroom windows?' He pointed inside the left-hand room. 'They face the canal. So, carefully, two men to each window and keep your heads down. They'll soon spot you. Then wait till I tell you to aim and fire. I'll show you first, in case you've forgotten!'

Turning to Lieutenant Dobie, he said: 'So far, so good. So long as they keep down, they're all right.'

He knew how the lieutenant's mind was working. But there was more to think about than that.

'I'll go in myself and fix things up, Sir. I'll be back in a jiffy. Then we can think it out, heh?'

Dobie could only shrug his shoulders and watch as the CSM went in towards the men under a series of little Gothic windows that lit the classroom.

'All right', he heard the sergeant-major address the men still crouching under the windows. CSM Green went to a tall cupboard which he opened. He took a pile of text-books from inside in his large, capable hands and, in one deft movement, dumped them on one of the window-sills, without exposing himself at the window. He arranged the books in such a way that the sill was covered, except for a small gap leaving a fire-port. Then, taking a rifle from one man, he raised himself carefully, pushed the rifle muzzle through the fire-port, gave a savage push to break the glass, then quickly withdrew. Rifle-fire at once pitched into the windows, sending glass slivers over the men crouching by the windows.

'Now, all of you, do the same at each window. Make a fire-port like I've done, then keep down till I give the order to fire.'

Compelled by his familiar voice of command, the men set about the task and learned with him to ignore the bullets that flew and smashed into the room behind them.

Keeping the rifle he had borrowed at the ready, the CSM waited a full minute.

'Now, when I rise, do as I do. Take a peep along your rifle, take a bead and aim for those windows opposite. Fire when I shout!'

Cautiously, they followed his movements as he took one port, aimed, then shouted: 'Fire!'

A dozen rifles firing at once poured bullets into the house over the canal. Down they all ducked at once as the answering fire smashed again into the windows and scudded about the hard-walled class-room with a menace that sent Dobie to the floor in the little hall at the entrance.

Not all the mental preparation, nor all the assault courses and lectures on tactics at OTC, had prepared him for this. Far from preoccupation with the practicalities of defence and attack, his mind was fixed firmly on a few salient images during his dash back to this relative shelter from the searing danger out in the open on the bridge over the canal.

Above all, he was linking his recent interview with Roberts F.X. with the man's present plight, out there bleeding in the doubtful cover of the parapet. Dimly, he saw a debt he owed, and a way of paying it. Then he would return for some of the more endangered of the wounded he had glimpsed on the road.

But first – for he was working up a conscience, even a guilt, about it all – they were *his* men. He must discharge his responsibility to *his* men first and foremost.

He left the CSM to his war-games and opened the door to go outside again. In the recess out-of-doors he was still safe. He put out his head to the right, in the direction of the canal, to see what he could of the men hiding under the school wall. Waiting for a second or two to assess the hostile fire, he dashed across the garden and dived into the low shelter of the wall, bumping into Liddell as he did so. A bullet smashed grittily in the granite above his head.

'All right, men,' he addressed them hoarsely, out of breath, 'see that recess over there? Watch me dash for it, then follow one by one, as quick as you can. You'll be safe in there.'

He lifted himself in one movement from his prone position on his stomach and dashed back. The men followed without a casualty. Lieutenant Dobie was well satisfied with this first positive move. Eleven men were safe.

'Well done', he said. 'Now, when we enter this school, take every care. Bullets are flying all over the place. Stick to the walls. All right. Now – one at a time.'

But just as he was about to enter and lead them in, the door opened and out came the CSM, carrying a rifle. In answer to his questioning look, the lieutenant said: 'Another eleven men safe, Sergeant-Major.' There was something tidy about it.

'Safe? Safe? Nowhere's safe here, Sir!' Sergeant-Major Green did not bother to conceal his impatience. 'Nobody'll be safe anywhere until we can get some more answering fire!'

But at once the CSM realised his position. He could not give orders over an officer's head, especially in front of the men. 'May I suggest we leave these lads here a bit, Sir. Then we can go inside and sort things out like, heh?'

Dobie's heart sank. Under the sergeant-major's tact he sensed that this first little military manoeuvre of his was incorrect. 'Very well', he replied.

The two went into the small entrance-hall, closing the door behind them. Within that inner safety, the CSM once more searched his officer's eyes. He detected no signs of cracking. He was satisfied, but still impatient.

'Look here, Sir. We're not acting together, are we? We're in a spot. We've got to get at them fellows over there until help comes – if it comes. We can't just sit on our backsides and wait, can we?'

'Yes, I see that. But there are men in danger out there. We've got to help them, get them in somehow.'

'Yes, yes. But we won't get anybody in so long as those fellows have the freedom to fire at will. Now, take that wall you've just brought the men from. I was just going to go out and arrange more firing positions from that wall. D'you see what I mean?' He waited, then continued, 'Now you've brought them back. There's no room for any more rifles

168

inside the school. These eleven will just have to hang around. That's no good, Sir, don't you see?'

'All right, I see what you mean', replied Dobie.

He was still reluctant to risk lives, but he realised his best tactic would be to listen to the 'old sweat' and follow his advice. And out they went again.

The CSM harangued the men, described how they must dash back, one at a time, and fall on their bellies at a position behind the wall again. He led first, and yet again they followed without a casualty. Again, CSM Green arranged fireports by instructing each man to take off his pack and place it on top of the wall and hard against the railings.

The eleven packs were separated by small gaps. Once again, the sergeant-major demonstrated the use of a fire-port, took aim, fired and ducked.

'Right now, that's your job until further orders. Just keep on firing at intervals, then keep down. You're safe so long as you don't do anything daft, eh?'

He dashed back, this time not without harm. The bullets seemed to have found him, and the earth spat up all round him as he ran at a crouch.

'Hellfire!' he gasped as he dived into the recess and bumped against Dobie. He saw the anxiety in the lieutenant's eyes. 'Ach, it's nothing', he gasped again as he examined the damage. He had lost his cap, probably shot off, for blood flowed from his scalp. He felt no hurt, but put up his hand to feel the wound and was satisfied.

'No, Sir, only a scratch.' He pulled out a handkerchief, wiped roughly at his scalp. The bleeding eased at once. It could be ignored. He was more worried about his little contretemps with Dobie. Officers tended to remember things afterwards, and his sergeant-major's badge had been too hard won to give up easily. But as he searched the young lieutenant's eyes, he was relieved.

It was bad enough not getting the proper instruction from an officer – bawling him out for not doing so was tantamount to insubordination. At his rank, that would be a serious charge.

But he knew that with Dobie there was little risk. The lad had made a mistake, had acknowledged it like a man, and was prepared to forget it and get on with the job in hand.

Of one thing, however, the CSM was uncertain. Having arranged such defensive positions as he could – and twenty or so fire-points – he wondered what was on the lieutenant's mind.

In the few minutes since the first hail of bullets, the CSM had observed enough to realise that out of 'A' and 'B' Companies, Lieutenant Dobie was probably the only surviving officer. No sign of Lieutenant Saxton. Until such time as help came up from the rear, he was in charge. And help might take an eternity. And so, the lieutenant being in charge, what were his intentions?

CSM Green was satisfied from their dash through the bullets that the lieutenant did not lose his head under fire. No sign of hysteria whatsoever. But the lieutenant was thinking only of safety with regard to the men. Although the CSM would not accuse him of saving his own skin (indeed, there was a stiffness and stubbornness about the rarely smiling face that led him to believe otherwise), there was little doubt that where the men were concerned the lieutenant was more worried about their safety as persons than about their effective deployment as soldiers. In his eyes this was so clearly wrong, he was prepared yet again to express his impatience and risk the consequences.

He tried to think, assess the situation. How did the Company stand, for a start? There were a dozen men in the school, another ten or so out there at the low wall of the school-garden. But what of the rest?

From the few brief castings around with his sharp trained eyes, he tried to visualise the whole situation. They had been marching up this wide street, troubled only by tramlines. They had approached a gap, where first a road crossed their main thoroughfare, then a canal, then possibly a second road along the canal at its far side too. He was not sure. At any rate, there was quite a gap before the housing started again. That gap was the danger area.

The first houses on the far side overlooked that entire gap *and* their approach. That much he knew. There were the small gardens, gated entrances, a sort of parapet this side of the canal, trees – all scant shelter for those lucky enough to scatter. And, of course, some were *in* the canal, how many he could not tell.

Worst of all, there were the casualties, mostly on the slight hump of the bridge. To a former townsman turned military, there was something sacrilegious about casualties lying on a tram-route. Nothing held up a tram between stops, everything gave way. But the tram-wires overhead were silent, no sign of an approaching tram.

As to 'B' Company, they were mostly in the rear, though he guessed that they too might have scattered before the hail of bullets, probably cowering behind garden-walls further back.

'C' Company, he was sure, was intact. There had been time for them to see the trouble ahead and retreat in good order, if indeed they had even started before the bullets started flying.

'Right, Sir,' he said, 'we've arranged fire-power at the windows in here and at the wall out there. We have about twenty men back in action, heh?' And he wiped a fresh trickle of blood from his brow with an impatient gesture. 'Now what?' he went on. 'You must remember we're not here for our safety. One thing goes with another, heh? For a start, we've got to get communication with H.Q. somehow, haven't we? If H.Q. mount an attack on this bloody lot over there, they'll want to know how we're fixed. This is the front, if you see what I mean, Sir. Maybe they'll want us to provide covering fire. And there's ammunition to think of if we're going to be pinned down any length of time. We'll need to link up, no doubt about it, Sir.'

It was so far removed from the textbook that Lieutenant Dobie could only follow. 'You're right, Mr Green.'

'There's another thing, Sir. Since we're here in this school, at the front if you like, H.Q.'ll want to use us for observation – for intelligence, like.'

'Yes, yes . . .' said Dobie with some hesitation in his voice. With all the will in the world, he had so little to contribute. 'So what first?'

How odd, he thought, that the Army put such emphasis on drill, on kit inspection and clinical rifle-range practice, yet never seemed to develop those practicalities that the CSM had so delicately employed in arranging fire-points while under fire himself.

He had been fascinated as he had watched the sergeant-major's quick movements, how the men, under his ready instruction, had organised themselves into an effective observation point and advance firing positions under their own defensive parapet of school-books and army-packs. The very doing of it was affecting morale. From cowering defensively, they were now working things out, exchanging advice, and learning all the time how much could be done within the constraints of their prone position. When he saw one man, having arranged his pack as a parapet to his satisfaction, quietly place his rifle in the gap between packs, draw a bead on the house over the canal and fire with professional deliberation, he knew they were no longer civilians, but soldiers.

As far as these little practicalities were concerned, the Army's apparent philosophy was that you could only learn the hard way. But what a cost it all was. Dobie's mind returned to the dead and dying out on the bridge.

He recalled dimly that one or two had fallen on top of each other, like sacks. Yes. But how could eventualities like this be codified, put in books? He had to peep out of the recess, even though the bullets continued to fly, spitting into the grass of the small garden.

Even as he watched, he saw a man collapse at the wall as he was rising to aim and fire. He was appalled. He braced, ready to dash, to help, to do something, anything but just crouch in safety and observe. The CSM's big hand held him back.

'No, Sir, leave it. They've got to learn. No point in you joining the poor sod. The men'll settle, you'll see. I've seen this many a time. I know it's a sorry sight, a man going down, but it makes you so bloody mad, you're better for it. That's war, Sir . . . They'll learn.' But Dobie knew he meant, '*You*'ll learn'.

With the experience of trench warfare in Flanders behind him, CSM Green knew all the tricks: how to secure effective cover, how to deploy men and fire-power, how to measure enemy fire, to assess each different noise, each element of danger or of relative safety. Dobie knew the CSM regarded them all as mere amateurs. They were amateurs.

Sergeant-Major Green, in his turn, was thinking that Lieutenant Dobie, freshly baptised to it all in this unprecedented and quite unexpected Irish situation, would have to be taught. The lieutenant seemed willing to learn however. In rank, Lieutenant Dobie was his superior, who normally could not be addressed until he himself spoke. That was all very well in barracks. Here, in action, or out in the trenches, it was different. In experience (and that counted), the CSM was far the superior, and in this sudden débâcle, with men lying out on the bridge and the road, others half exposed on the canal bank, experience counted more than rank. The sudden reversal of role seemed natural to them both.

But even as they were both working it out, there was a concerted burst of fire from the Irish position and the CSM dashed across the garden to the gate-post again.

Sensing the added urgency, and by now practised in dashing at the crouch, Dobie followed.

Without the usual caution, the CSM looked out, to have a clearer view of the road as it approached the canal. Quickly, he withdrew, putting his hand on Dobie's forearm.

'Damn and blast', he hissed. 'The colonel's thrown in "C" Company. Bloody shambles – absolute bloody shambles!'

172

After the first burst of fire into 'A' Company, with as many as thirty officers and men lying dead in as many seconds, and after he had sent 'B' Company hurtling back with his timely 'About turn – at the double', CSM Green knew even as he shouted the order that he did not have the right to do so and that, furthermore, he could be charged later for beating a retreat in the face of the enemy.

King's Regulations were holy writ, inviolable. Or were they? There came a time when common-sense violated them – common-sense was often quicker. And here was a case in point.

As he saw the captain, subaltern and company sergeant-major of 'B' Company fall to the second hail of bullets, he knew the Company was advancing without leaders. There might be a sergeant or two in the rear Platoons, but there was no time to re-deploy the Company's command.

So he just bawled, and in so far as it sent them back, albeit with further casualties, it worked. Instinctively, he knew that 'B' Company's 'forward march' would be suicidal.

He could not worry, therefore, about being charged – though questions would be asked in a routine enquiry. That was when he would keep 'mum'. Whoever had sent 'B' Company back, they certainly would not find out from him, and he doubted if anyone in 'B' Company would be able to remember – or, rather, would have the nerve to remember.

There was a tacit code – that order to turn about, contrary as it might have been to possibly quite a few King's Regulations, had saved lives, and that code would wrap the entire incident in a cocoon of obfuscation such as only the Army was capable of.

The CSM dismissed it from his mind, knowing that the precious badge of rank on his forearm was safe on that score. He had been too preoccupied with Lieutenant Dobie and 'A' Company to dwell overmuch on such legal delicacies.

'B' Company, then, under his coruscating parade voice, had turned about automatically. Even as they picked up their feet 'at the double', more men fell; then they broke and scattered in the direction they had come from and almost into the van of 'C' Company still marching stiffly towards the bridge. Bullets continued to fly after them, and as they scattered, more men fell. The rest ignored the oncoming 'C' Company, fled into gardens, cowered behind the flights of stone steps leading to elegant front-doors high

173

above street level; and a few rushed into the school-garden, brushing past Lieutenant Dobie and CSM Green at the gate-post.

Thus 'C' Company found itself exposed. Captain Harwood, its commander, now had a clearer view. He saw the bridge ahead, vaguely took in that there were bodies lying over its surface and on the approach road. At once, he called the Company to a halt. He was puzzled and went over to his subaltern, and they both consulted CSM Betteridge over the other side. Then the captain instructed the CSM to turn the men about and run at the double back to a side-street, there to re-deploy.

But the nervous consultations had taken their toll. Too late, they all realised. For they were within range of whatever hostile fire it was that came from the canal area. Even as the order was given and men began to turn, bullets found their mark and men fell. The retreat thereafter was more a rout, and Captain Harwood ran quickly with his men, fearing to lose them. By sheer will-power, he and CSM Betteridge managed to line them up in some sort of breathless order in the side-street, just off the main road.

'B' Company, Captain Harwood realised with dread, was leaderless and had virtually disappeared. It was obviously time to consult H.Q., to answer for what was in fact a retreat in the face of the enemy. Unlike CSM Green, Captain Harwood could not dismiss this from his mind. To be charged with it in Flanders could be understood if never pardoned. But to be guilty of it in Ireland – Ireland! – no, he would never live it down. He felt desperately alone.

They had no contact with 'A' Company, which had taken the brunt of the fire. 'B' Company had marched into trouble, and in the mix-up with 'A' Company – and then with his own – had practically vanished from view into gardens and heaven knew where. So Captain Harwood felt entitled to see his depleted 'C' Company to some sort of order in the safety of the side-street.

He left the subaltern in charge and decided to face the music personally. He was about to stump off to the barracks when he saw the scout-car emerging. He waited for it to come on, then waved it to a halt.

Colonel Marsh popped his head out impatiently, then got out altogether and showed extreme irritation with the captain. He found

174

him incoherent and jumpy, and was not prepared to believe Harwood's tale of disaster. There were those who enjoyed bringing bad news; if they did not have enough, they would embellish it somehow. Captain Harwood, the colonel decided, was a prime example. He had to acknowledge that there was trouble ahead, but was more than doubtful if the captain had gone about it in the right way, or had appraised it correctly.

'Speed's the thing, Forsyth', he shouted to the adjutant, ignoring Captain Harwood completely. 'Speed! That's what it needs. So what first? I understand 'A' Company's sustained casualties and scattered. 'B' Company's run for it – pah! – and 'C' Company is here with us, ready. Very well.' He now turned to Captain Harwood: 'Whatever it is that's holding things up ahead, it's got to be moved before they can settle in. Speed's the thing. So charge that bridge by Platoons . . . send in No. One first, cover with No. Two, and push No. Three and No. Four behind them. Is that understood?'

And that was it. It was meant to be enough, a quick assault on the enemy before they had time to know what was hitting them.

Even as he received the order, Captain Harwood felt the inadequacy of it. But in the face of what had been in reality the retreat of his own Company and the rout of the other two, he was in no position to argue.

He looked across at the adjutant for help, but met only the cool, implacable military bearing, non-committal, which while not unsympathetic, was far from helpful.

Captain Harwood had had no time to appraise the situation, to reconnoitre, to locate the hostile fire, or to consult with forward elements who had taken the brunt of whatever caused the hold-up.

It was clear the colonel was more concerned with the hold-up than with the casualties. He had not even seen them, much less worried about them. Charge with No. One Platoon! Captain Harwood was astonished. Charge? Charge what?

As he returned his gaze to Colonel Marsh, the latter pre-empted him.

'Now get on with it, Mr Harwood. Speed is the answer to a thing like this. Get stuck into them. Clean them out, then we shall carry on to the centre where we're needed. All right?' he said briskly, dismissing the captain.

Captain Harwood went over it as he returned quickly to his standing Company of terrified men. He had an idea that, as soon as they emerged into the main road again, they would be within range. He knew the rifle-fire was coming from somewhere ahead, but ahead from what? 'What on earth ...' he muttered. 'Charge, what ... ?'

He went back to CSM Betteridge, who did not bother to hide his puzzlement. But the captain merely transferred to him the implacable stare that the adjutant had given him. There could be no argument about the order: No. One Platoon, in two lines, on either side of the road, to charge. 'To charge what?' the CSM's eyes asked.

Captain Harwood continued with the instructions: 'No. Two Platoon to give covering fire.' 'From what position? – At what?' the eyes questioned. 'No. Three and Four in reserve', the captain continued. All right on paper – a captain, two subalterns, and a CSM should be feasible, he thought – but without conviction.

The officers and CSM fussed a bit, aware of the colonel's impatience – 'Speed is the thing!' – and felt frightfully ineffectual and unconvincing in front of the men. Each knew they had no choice.

As to the charge, however it went and at whatever objective, Captain Harwood would take a line of twenty-five men, CSM Betteridge the other.

The sergeant-major deployed the two lines at opposite sides of the side-street, ready to charge out into the main road. He did the same with Nos. Three and Four behind them, then sent No. Two out to take up positions in the main road to provide covering fire.

The men were puzzled and frightened, but the CSM merely transferred the all-operative military glare.

There was no fire from the canal area. Both sides had quietened down. In the lull, it was possible to hear the moans and cries of wounded men. But as the fifty-odd men of No. Two Platoon trotted out to take up positions they had not yet seen properly, there was a furious burst of fire immediately and eight men fell before the rest could scuttle into gardens behind the walls and flights of steps, still too far away from the canal to be effective covering fire.

Even so, all knew that the colonel insisted on results from this initiative. Captain Harwood gave the signal across the road to the CSM, registering while he did so the further disorder of No. Two Platoon ahead. He was far from convinced of No. Two's cover. But it was too late.

The two lines trotted on, avoiding bodies of No. Two Platoon with both feet and eyes, on past the gardens and steps and the cowering men of 'A' and 'B' Companies, on and into the air, light and menace of the canal area with its burden of dead and wounded men. Captain Harwood, on the left and on the side away from the school, saw the lock-gates just above the bridge at the closed position, holding water deep and level above them – and in the few seconds as the bullets began to spit and fly, he veered slightly left to avoid the bridge and chose the narrow cat-walk that ran alongside the timbers of the lock-gate. It proved an irrational choice.

They bunched fatally. Captain Harwood frantically negotiated the cat-walk, followed by a corporal and twenty-four men, with CSM Betteridge running at the right-hand parapet of the bridge with his twenty-five men. There was no covering fire as they ran. As the machine-gun fire burst murderously into them, they were the unluckiest victims of all. Captain Harwood gained the far bank with only ten men left.

He was frantic. Once over the lock-gate and on the bank, he wove left and right, uncertain what direction to take, still ignorant of the source of the firing. Then, instinctively turning right to join up with Betteridge on the right of the bridge, he fell, staggered on a few steps, then rolled so heavily and terribly that he pitched further right, plunging over a low wall and tumbling down the steep bank, ending up at Moffat's and Pearson's feet at the edge of the water, still sheltering under the high arch of the bridge.

The survivors of the two columns ran on into the streets beyond, cut off but unharmed only because the Irish now had enough to mark in No. Three Platoon which was already running through the non-existent cover of No. Two and into their sights. This time the aim was so sure that not one man gained the far side of the bridge. As men fell on top of bodies already there, the survivors of No. Three, only twenty, plunged back to join others in the gardens. No. Four, advancing behind them, lost a subaltern and a dozen men, then scattered. The few minutes had been carnage.

Lieutenant Dobie and CSM Green, watching helplessly from the gate, were horrified. Dobie in particular was appalled when he saw Captain Harwood running with his men across the cat-walk over the lock. Whereas 'A' Company had marched cold into the trap, the captain ought to have known by now what they were running into. His eye-brows met in sheer disbelief at what he saw as senseless Army heroics. He saw Harwood as a fool contributing blindly to the pile of dead and wounded whom a few moments before he had considered rescuing somehow.

He was anxious to organise help and was puzzling it out when Harwood and his men fell in the mad rush across the canal. He watched with horror, his head too far out for safety, as men fell with a splash into the brimming water of the lock. It was so quick, he was unable to count how many fell. Twenty? Thirty? – it was difficult to tell. A few splashed about frantically, either unharmed or wounded lightly enough to swim. Bullets whipped up the water surface, and he saw two men go still. Others found refuge under the shelter of the lock-gate, a most uncomfortable place for cover. Bodies drifted in the flow like so much flotsam.

'Shambles, bloody shambles!' CSM Green shouted to the lieute-nant. 'What in God's name are they trying to do back there? Look at that lot. Christ almighty, does that bloody colonel want to murder us all?' He was referring to the survivors scattering for cover and being picked off one by one. Some were screaming from the bank. 'We've got to get in touch with H.Q. somehow, Sir,' he went on, 'they can't know what's going on back there, sending men in like this. Why don't they think?'

The cries of the wounded were pitiful.

'We'll never get out there to help them now,' said Dobie, 'unless we get organised somehow. H.Q. you say? Very well, Mr Green, let's do that. Send a runner.'

'No good sending a runner. They'll take no notice, the mood they're in. There's no time to explain. I'd best go myself, Sir. I'll go back and try to stop any more nonsense. I'll find H.Q., wherever it is. I'll aim for the barracks, maybe meet the stupid buggers on the way. We've got to stop this, heh?' By now, all language of rank had faded between them.

'It seems the only thing to do', said Dobie. 'Somebody's got to tell them. This is unbelievable. Look at those men out there. They can't have an inkling what's going on at H.Q. Yes, you go. I'll be here if there's any message back.'

'Now, don't do anything silly, Sir. That's no-man's-land out there now, you understand? There's a chance if you hug a wall, but out on that road, no. That's *kaput*.'

'All right. I'll stay right here. I promise you.'

The boyish dependence of it did not strike him. The CSM's authority was that of experience; it brooked no denial. Of experience, he himself had so little. The only casualties he had ever seen were Litherland's poor topers on a Saturday night in Stepney – and Laura.

As the thought flashed madly, he had to keep back tears. Experience, and experience – innocence, and innocence. Oh, Laura! Innocence and experience ... And he bit his lips as he watched a man lying wounded out on the road, helplessly banging his flat hand on the cobbles, trying to raise himself and failing.

The CSM bent low, to minimise exposure, and, hugging the garden-walls, dashed off on yet another breathless run.

As he watched and waited, Lieutenant Dobie battled with himself. He saw the man, all too clearly, not twenty yards away, still banging the road with the palm of his hand, in agony, unable to lift himself or crawl to safety. He knew the CSM was right. To cross that stretch of open road, just there, was suicide. That would be of no help to the man, and one more man lost. That was the no-man's-land he had heard so much about, where to move was to die.

He held back the sobs of anguish as he watched helplessly. What in the name of God that is within us all, he thought, would Nonnie make of all this? Could she even imagine it? How she would weep and pray if ever she came to know. She must never know, not this, in Ireland of all places ... How could she ever understand *this*, after all his talk about Belgium?

Then F.X. – Francis Xavier – lying out there, possibly dead. But Dobie, remembering his moment of gazing out in the open across at the man, had the feeling that F.X. was not beyond help even now. What had been in his mind, only yesterday, that had made his inarticulate plea for help so heart-rending? Lieutenant Dobie had to hold himself back again, but with difficulty. The tears were very close; not from fear, strangely enough, but from waiting, the frustration and indecision.

Watching the man banging his palm ineffectually on the road, his first image of Laura came passing over his fevered mind. What had all this to do with his life twenty-four hours earlier as he wrote the note to her to go with her letters to him? How could one reconcile this with a life such as that implicit in this latest letter of hers?

'William Dobie ...' he heard her voice through the crack and whine of bullets, 'William Dobie ...' What had that to do with Lieutenant Dobie here, crouched under a gate-pillar, waiting, watching a dying

179

man out on that road, wondering if Roberts F.X. over there by the parapet was still alive with his personal problem unresolved for want of communication between them only the day before?

Unable to bear the sight of the man any longer, he turned and made a dash back across the garden to the recess, to the company of men cowering there – and even so, felt the betrayal of it. But he knew that CSM Green was right. Here, of all places, the heart must not rule the head. Perhaps when the CSM got back, they could work things out.

Then he remembered the sergeant-major had given him a job to do. He entered the school and encouraged the men to do the best they could. He could not resist raising his head dangerously at one window to look forward. He could just make out Roberts, still lying there at the corner of the parapet. Now that he knew the direction of the bullets, he knew F.X. was safe from them for the moment.

The men beside him were tired. The fatigue of it all, on top of the march and the night's voyage, had drained them. Only the sergeant-major could galvanise them. Affecting an urgency of action he did not feel, Dobie trotted at a crouch along the wall, out to the recess. Still, the strange silence lingered. Collecting himself, he made the now familiar dash back to the gate-post, to keep the road under supervision and to await the CSM's return. Trying to dismiss from his mind the man thrashing in pain out on the road, he saw Laura for the first time again as he was lifting her gently off the road, with Litherland helping, her dark hair dishevelled and her eyes dilated with fear, or was it defiance?

That man on the road, in terrible agony, hitting the ground with his hand like that. He must be helped soon – very soon.

Lieutenant Dobie crouched, and turned his head towards the gate-post with a sudden appalling tiredness. Roberts F.X., that man on the road, and violence abroad such as he had never imagined possible. He resisted a temptation to slidedown by the gate-post and just sit. But in resisting, he realised how poor a soldier he was among these raw recruits manning their hastily made fire-ports.

It was all wrong for him. Even more, he was all wrong for it. Yet he had to do something – anything. Out of his fatigue, he tried to clear his mind. But that, if anything, was even more tired than his body. Ten minutes – twenty? – he did not know. He tried to focus, but the long, slow procession of his life now resolved into three alternative images that flung about in his head, like butter slopping about in a churn: Laura, the man on the road, and F.X. He fought with it, resolution churned with memory. 'Shock,' he whispered to himself, 'shock – nothing wrong – only to be expected ... yes...' Resolution and memory fought and became stronger. Shock, he thought, and knew as he diagnosed it that he was all right.

The man thrashing the road with his hand was bleeding – like F.X. He would die soon if help did not come. Dobie crouched low, looked hard to see if it were just possible.

Sergeant-Major Green was a long time returning. If things quietened down, they could use the other classroom for a casualty-station, get the medics up, the doctor ... it could be done. Wasn't the CSM running up and down this very minute? But the medics were probably still off-loading their motorised ambulances and medical supplies at Kingstown. They would hardly be expecting casualties on this scale. And so, that man would die. Dobie found that he too was banging his flat palm against the gate-post in his anguish of spirit.

No, the CSM would not be more than a few more minutes. The first job was to prepare that room for casualties, then send a runner to fetch medics. If they were still in Kingstown, as seemed likely, then they must find a local doctor, an Irish doctor. Why not? Doctors were bound by their Hippocratic oath not to discriminate between those who needed their care. Perhaps a white flag then? But it could not be relied on. That needed a mutually arranged truce, and they were far from that. Well, then, why not take a chance, go out, bring F.X. first, then the man with the thrashing palm? Oh, that was unbearable, a man in such agony and so close by ... But it was no-man's-land.

When, finally, he got F.X. in, he would make sure he got every attention. And he would try to deal with his domestic problem, for that was clearly what had brought F.X. to his room a day before, troubled as ever he had seen a man troubled.

Although in the CSM's book he had proved a poor soldier, something about the 'old sweat' assured him it was understood between them that useless though he might be as a tactician, the sergeant-major accepted his proper compassion for the wounded outside and would help him organise help in a soldierly fashion.

The main thing was to get F.X. in alive – then overcome his shyness about that letter – but only after the wound had been attended to. If it had taken this engagement and a severe injury to F.X., at least it had opened him up. When the CSM returned, he would see to F.X. at once. That was a top priority.

The men were very quiet. Everything was quiet, as though both

181

sides were waiting for the next move. Only occasionally now, there would be the snap of a bullet one way or the other. Even the man out on the road was quiet – dead? Dobie gazed, tried hard to focus on the man's hand, still stretched out beyond his head as he lay face down, his cap flung a few yards away from him.

The way the man lay, absolutely limp, the sheer inertia of his every part, told the lieutenant that the man was dead. Had he gone to help him, as seemed the one sensible, Quakerly thing to do, he too would be dead by now, for the man lay in the most exposed area of the road in the tramlines.

Dobie's knuckles were white as he clenched his fists. Resolution, yes – but for WHAT? – something, anything. But he knew that to have helped the man would have been the wrong resolution. That would have hindered rather than helped. Whatever he was to do must be constructive and no burden to others.

Lieutenant Dobie braced himself as he heard the running of feet. He put his head out the fraction necessary to look back up the road. It was the sergeant-major. He would have answers. Something could be done now.

As not one Platoon commander returned with the scattering of men who got back as far as the side-street under the blistering stare of the incredulous Colonel Marsh, the impression the Battalion conveyed was that of a rabble. As the result of the engagement gradually dawned on him, the colonel was furious. It only strengthened his determination. Blazing, he turned to Major Dean-Forbes:

'Dean-Forbes, I want you to go back to barracks and get those damned locals out here. Tell them I want a field-gun of some sort, and quick. They must know what they've got. I want them, too, to help us sort this lot out. They must surely have known about this. I'll have a thing or two to say about it. So get along and be back sharp. Tell me how things are, about the field-gun especially.'

The major set off at a quick pace, though not at the undignified 'double'.

'And tell them,' shouted the colonel, 'it's not men I want, it's that gun. And themselves, of course. I'll have a thing or two to say about this, I can tell you.'

As he thus transferred blame, the colonel was still near the scout-car bonnet, just in the shelter of the side-street. He moved forward carefully, assessing by the sound that the hostile rifle-fire was safely far enough away; some two hundred yards away, he guessed. Far from absolutely safe, especially from ricochets from the road-surface; nevertheless he moved on, into the middle of the road, fuming. Ahead, he could see men crouching at either side of the road, afraid to budge, and useless as covering fire.

'Get back here, you men!' he shouted. But not a man looked round, nor even budged, so fixed was their terrified gaze on the canal area.

Taking out his field-glasses, the colonel swept his view over what he now regarded as a battlefield. He thought he counted perhaps forty or fifty men lying out there on the bridge, or near it. He could see others, probably wounded, crawling desperately to find cover under the parapet. Then, raising his glasses slightly left after the canal, he spotted the house over the canal.

Since the road bent slightly left there, that house occupied a strategic corner-view right along their own approach. If its occupants were looking, they would be able to see him clearly. He thought it would be a waste of a bullet at that distance; they were too clever. The colonel's blood boiled at the audacity of those rebels. Granted that, in the end, they were in a suicidal position, that house was nevertheless perfectly placed for its purpose of holding up just such a force as his, perfectly placed for an ambush. It had caught his Battalion like rats in a trap. The main road actually funnelled his troops right under the guns of the rebels. Each of his Companies had received a mauling (he looked at his watch), a mauling in a brief twenty minutes.

That house enraged the colonel. He would bring it down stone by stone if necessary. No Irishman would hold up *his* Battalion. He was expected at the city centre. This obstacle would be cleared and the Battalion, however depleted, would arrive there as scheduled.

Colonel Marsh had reached one of those moments of anger when the irrational takes over. He gave one great whack of his cane against his polished leggings and started striding forward. Against all regulations, he would strike the first man he came across crouched miserably inside a gate-post. He could not hold himself. He strode, he accelerated, was near enough to a man, when a bullet cracked against the granite setts and flew on behind him. A sharp nick of granite hit his legging and disfigured its polished surface. It stopped him in his tracks. Blazing, but not moving, he looked hard towards the house over the canal.

'By God!' he hissed between his teeth. 'By God, I'll cure that lot, if it's the last thing I do!' And he turned deliberately, walking back to the scout-car without haste. He had faced bullets as Company Commander in '14 and '15, and it would take more than a few Irish rebels to shake him. Settling himself, he moved out again sufficiently to scan the canal.

He put away any thought of moving back what was left of the three Companies – his entire Battalion – and redeploying them for alternative action of some sort. There seemed no way of doing it, no plan presented itself, so he preferred to keep such thoughts away from him.

Returning to the scout-car, he paced up and down, flicking his swagger-cane against his thigh, fuming, impatient, but glad not to have to make any further decision until Colonel Saunders came up – if he came up. The colonel had an uncomfortable feeling that Saunders might refuse. After all, had he not recommended caution, patrols first?

Colonel Marsh was not senior to Saunders in any way, only fresh from across the water with a War Office telegram in his pocket.

After five minutes pacing, he saw Colonel Saunders and his captain walking briskly down the side-street with Major Dean-Forbes. He had been right to send the major, he reflected, and bracing himself, returned to the car to await Saunders's arrival.

'Were you unaware, Colonel,' he asked as the party neared, 'that the canal crossing would be opposed? Major Dean-Forbes has told you, I take it?'

'Yes, I half expected something,' Saunders replied, 'but when or where I couldn't be sure, of course. Otherwise I'd have told you. I did, you may remember, recommend patrols. In my opinion it wasn't safe to risk a whole Battalion in such circumstances.'

'I dare say, I dare say', Colonel Marsh went on testily. This cautious man, risking nothing, irritated him. 'Well, patrol or no patrol, we now know what we know. They're there ... I don't know how many or what weapons they have. Looks like small-arms only to me. It's their position that's so strong.'

'Have you had no information from up front?' Saunders queried. 'They might be able to be a bit more precise.' He found Marsh's tactics, or lack of them, rather hare-brained and reckless.

'Well, no, not exactly. Hasn't been time, has there?' Colonel Marsh sought to change the direction of the conversation. 'We can flush them out if we can have that field-gun. Could you provide such a thing, Colonel?'

184

'I've already sent a motor-cyclist with the dispatch. You understand our telephone system has been tampered with. The gun should be here in half-an-hour. It's in reserve further west along the canal at the next barracks.'

'Ah, thank you', said Colonel Marsh, conscious of losing the initiative and anxious to re-establish it.

He was determined to deploy the field-gun himself if possible, and was not keen for Colonel Saunders to reconnoitre the canal area in any way. When he saw CSM Green approaching, crouched at the double, he guessed that he had urgent information, so, anxious not to share too much with Saunders, he went ahead to meet him.

'Your cap, Mr Green. Where's your cap?'

The sergeant-major checked himself just in time before giving a salute. Hatless, in front of the CO! And about to salute! Shows you what a bit of action does to your presence of mind . . . he thought.

'I'm sorry, Sir. Lost it ahead, Sir.'

'Lost it, Sergeant-Major? Lost it? What d'you mean?'

The CSM allowed his impatience to show, just a fraction.

'Yes, Sir. Shot off by the enemy, Sir.'

But the colonel had no time for excuses, and even less for the smear of blood on the sergeant-major's forehead.

'This is a pretty set-to, Sergeant-Major. What's the hold-up?'

The CSM outlined the position as best he could. Patiently enough, the colonel questioned each detail, determined to remedy what he saw as more bad luck than bad management. In a way, he was glad of it.

They were committed – and he preferred that. The house, fortified to an extent he was still unsure of, and his Battalion were now locked in combat. He could not retreat – that was unthinkable. And he could not advance until he had cleared that house. The situation was simple. He was determined that the tactics would be equally simple.

Once they had the field-gun, things would soon resolve themselves. He could manage the rest. Before returning to Colonel Saunders, he took out a small pad and pencil from his tunic-pocket and made a note of what CSM Green had told him in the way of casualties.

He was startled to hear of the loss of the officers of 'B' and 'C' Companies.

'Only Second-Lieutenant Dobie left, eh, Sergeant-Major? What's he doing? Where is he?'

'He's holding the schoolhouse this side of the canal, Sir, facing the enemy fire. He's arranged effective fire support from every window in the school. But we can't move, Sir ... it's suicide. They have a machine-gun. What we need is artillery ... pound the place to rubble, Sir, that's what we need.'

'I've arranged that, Sergeant-Major. Should be here in half-an-hour.' The colonel paused to think, to take it in, to get things in his little notebook. 'So we have Lieutenant Dobie. That's one good thing, anyway; an officer in the forward position.' The CSM took the liberty of looking skywards for a moment. ('God help England!') 'Tell Mr Dobie to hold on', Colonel Marsh was saying. 'Tell him I have artillery on the way, and to keep a runner at the ready. I'll send forward whatever orders I have for him. You got all that, Sergeant-Major?'

There seemed the vestige of a possible plan of tactics to build on the CSM's information. 'Effective fire support', the sergeant-major had said. Well, that was something. Once the field-gun arrived, he would build on it.

'Very well, Sergeant-Major, off you go. And my compliments to Mr Dobie. Tell him to stand fast. He might be mentioned in dispatches yet.'

'Yes, Sir.' And off went the CSM in his crouching run. 'Jesus,' he muttered under his breath, 'I'll be a Chelsea pensioner long before my time at this rate. "Stand fast", he says. Doesn't know 'is arse from 'is elbow if you ask me! Couldn't organise a piss-up in a brewery, 'e couldn't.' He was little wiser and only too aware that as he ran fast, he was the sole target at the moment.

He felt a stabbing pain over his chest. He was ready to drop, but bobbed and wove desperately along the street towards Lieutenant Dobie, more anxious about what the lieutenant might do next than about anything the colonel might have in mind – if anything.

The sergeant-major had not stopped moving since the first hail of bullets. He was fit for a man of thirty-eight who liked three or four pints most nights of the week. The spell in the trenches in Flanders had kept him on the move. There was never a minute's rest and if you survived the diet and the German shells you were bound to be fit.

Back in Blighty, the parade square and the constant bracing of shoulders, the smart military gait, and the route-marches and exercises on the moors had kept him in trim. Yet as he trotted back up the road, circumventing the occasional body and weaving all the time to avoid presenting a target, he clutched his chest and knew that a turning-point had come.

'I've been looking', said Saunders.

This found Colonel Marsh off balance. He was still digesting the CSM's intelligence and would rather Colonel Saunders neither confused the issue nor went mooching about for his own information.

Resisting the glare, Saunders continued doggedly: 'I've been looking at the bridge. You've sustained more casualties than I'd imagined. That's not just rifle-fire. They must have a Maxim or something. You'd be surprised what they pick up. It's a dirty market, second-hand arms. We've even found an old Gatling in one house this week.'

'It could be.' Colonel Marsh was shaken about by opinion and had only partly registered the CSM's information. Running into a few rifles was one thing, but a machine-gun was quite another matter. He sensed the criticism implicit in Saunders's opinion. He preferred not to discuss it further and made much play of reading the map spread over the bonnet of the scout-car.

He was irritated beyond words when, of all things, a road-sweeper came along with his little cart, the man who did the rounds of the city after the horses. No military engagement was going to suspend this vital service. The little man, his ragged overcoat held in with a length of frayed rope, contrasted sharply with the well-tailored officers. They were near a cross-road so there was the usual concentration of the man's raw material, and he was obviously a fastidious craftsman. He worked up to the officers round the scout-car, then straightening up, asked politely: 'Would ye's ever move, now, and let a man finish his bit o' work?'

And they gave way, not without the thought that if they were engaged flushing out Irish rebels over the canal, where did this sudden irruption of an Irishman with a brush, shovel and handcart leave them?

So the man continued out into the main road, where it seemed a truce was being observed by his compatriots, since he took particular care and left the road clean of any trace of a horse without a single ricochet to disturb him.

Colonel Marsh returned to tracing routes on the map, bridges, possible strong-points. He would use the half-hour, he decided, to memorise what he could of the city's lay-out. He had nothing more to say to Saunders, who seemed to him a commander without a command. One advantage he presumed Saunders might have over him, and that was some experience of what could only be described as street-fighting, even if it had been only during the previous three days; unless he had been sitting on his backside in that office of his, letting others think it out, which would account for the presence of rebels so near a British Army barracks.

The last thing the colonel would do was ask any more advice of Saunders. Not that he *had* asked – or taken – any. If street-fighting had to be learned, he would learn now, though he had to admit to himself that in no respect whatsoever did it offer any of the circumstances, positions or formations that he had ever learned of the art of war, either from books or lectures, or out in the field.

For a start, how was one supposed to deploy a Company in this mess? There was no way, it seemed, of forming men into an effective fighting force that could strike at the enemy, no reserve trench in which to line them up under cover – no trench or enemy line to charge.

Attack? In line ... or by wave? Nothing seemed to answer. Furthermore, 'B' Company, cowering behind the flights of steps, provided about as effective a covering as Boy Scouts with bows and arrows. He knew from bitter experience how far you can push men when the going is rough. He knew that only by mustering them in a trench, serving them the ritual tot of rum that was supposed to put fire into their bellies but mostly failed to, then by whistles and shouts getting them 'over the top' behind their Platoon commanders in one collective line, would they move at all, knowing they were watched from behind by Military Police with revolvers, ready to goad stragglers or to book them for cowardice in the face of the enemy, a charge answerable with death by firing-squad.

But Colonel Marsh would not ask his opposite anything. If the men were confused, absolutely out of their depth in a situation for which they had not been given any training, what they could not know was that their commander knew less about it, for he had even more to unlearn.

On his side, Colonel Saunders had much to tell the colonel, even where his own men were in relation to the engagement and what they were doing. But he found Colonel Marsh's manner dismissive, if not downright rude, and was prepared to allow him to make what mistakes he would. Nothing he would say would alter things with this man. He had tried, and his advice had been spurned. He would not speak again until Colonel Marsh appeared prepared to listen.

His own men, few enough for an emergency like this, were spread out thinly in the south-east approaches to the city centre. The breakdown in the city's telephone system was a nuisance, but only to be expected. It would be some time before the one Signals Company could provide communications with other forces approaching from points all round the city. So he held his peace as they waited for the field-gun. The gun-carriage would have to skirt round a bit, to avoid trouble, and might take a little longer than the half-hour he had forecast. But at least the waiting provided a truce for the combatants on either side of the canal. As Colonel Saunders scanned the scene through his field-glasses, he was shocked at what he could assess only as carnage. He could only just forgive the first blunder; he had warned Colonel Marsh, and the warning had been ignored. He had advised patrolling first before committing the entire Battalion in this approach to the city centre, and this too had been ignored. So the Battalion had moved into the trap with a pathetic inevitability.

Yes, he might find it in himself to understand the colonel's initial error; fresh from England, ignorant of Ireland and its particular problems and ways . . . yes, it could be understood and forgiven – just. But as he viewed the bodies lying on the bridge two hundred yards ahead and the many scattered around on either side of it, he found it hard to understand or forgive the second wave. It smelled, almost, of criminal negligence.

Major Dean-Forbes had let that bit of information slip. And Colonel Saunders, from the initial poor impression he had received of the colonel, now found him – yes – criminal in his wastage of lives. What the major had said was rather hard to imagine, but now he was able to fill in the picture himself. Machine-gun or no, he felt the colonel was using a sledge-hammer to crack a nut. Three Companies against – what? – perhaps a dozen, at most, surely, two dozen Irishmen. That position on the canal could so easily be turned: there were other bridges that offered a crossing, and not all could be defended like this one. In fact, there were so many, both above and below this one, that he knew he had no choice but to go back to Colonel Marsh, however much he disliked re-opening the conversation. There were men's lives to think about, and personal feelings had to take second place. But it took quite an effort. He lowered the field-glasses and returned to the scout-car.

'Colonel, you realise that house over the canal can easily be surrounded and isolated', he said quietly, holding himself in before the colonel's glare. 'There are several bridges between here and the next barracks upwards and another below, on the way to the flour-mill.' Steadily, he faced Colonel Marsh's rising apoplexy and continued doggedly, 'Don't you think you should pull back what you can of your Companies and reassemble them at the barracks, leaving some men to cover that house? Send one group further up this secondary road to the next bridge up the canal, another group over the bridge below, and filter through side-streets to surround and cut off the house. In fact, you can choose any bridge you like. That way, the artillery will be more effective when it arrives. The rebels will have more than one way to face, and their line of retreat will be cut off.'

'Colonel Saunders,' Colonel Marsh found it difficult to speak, 'Colonel!' He was finding it even more difficult not to shout. 'It seems to me you've had most of a week to organise and do precisely that with your own forces, and now you have orders for me after a few hours in Ireland. I think you...'

'I was not giving orders, Sir, I was offering a suggestion, so to speak. If you...'

'Look here, Saunders. This is my Battalion and..'

'Your second wave has been expensive in lives – think of that. And the other bridges are only a stone's throw away. You could...'

'If you're afraid of casualties, you might as well give up soldiering. My experience in France leads me to...'

'I cannot claim the honour of service in France, but nobody in their senses would...'

By now they were both shouting angrily at each other. Major Dean-Forbes listened with fascination. He had it in mind that, without being dishonourable to his own commander, he was being ably exonerated by Colonel Saunders from any responsibility for the disaster up the street. He dared not look at either colonel, but from Saunders's tone it became increasingly clear that he was laying the blame personally on Colonel Marsh's shoulders for not being more circumspect, for spurning local advice, for not patrolling a potentially hostile area before committing the Battalion, and above all, for stubbornly and wantonly sending a second wave to almost certain slaughter.

The colonel had not asked for the major's counsel, and he had not offered any. But the present exchange between the two colonels was sufficiently acrimonious for Saunders to see that Major Dean-Forbes's advice, if any, would have been ignored in any case. The major, like everyone else in the officers' mess, knew the colonel had come direct from France; he did not know the reason.

He knew only that senior officers were not returned from France without a reason. Indeed, the shortage of officers was so great that the cause must have been grave, very grave. Yet he held the rank of lieutenant-colonel, so it could not have been anything smacking of cowardice or drunkenness, or of ordinary corruption such as embezzling mess funds or whatever.

Judging by the colonel's behaviour so far on this fairly simple operation (for however bewildering a city situation compared with a field one, it could be easily resolved with a little thought – Colonel Saunders was making that abundantly clear), the colonel's return must have been insisted on in France for some military blunder.

That he was not an easy man to get on with could not be the reason; Battalion commanders were not supposed to be particularly likeable. They were looked up to as autocrats at the mess table, their word was law, and it was enough for a CO to favour vintage port for them all to have to like it, or to be virtually blackballed.

Remembering poor Dobie, out there, alone, the one surviving officer Platoon commander in 'A' Company, he reflected that the young lieutenant's somewhat stiff-necked attitude in the Mess was rather commendable, given a man like the colonel. Quietly, he rued one or two of his more blistering exchanges with the young lieutenant.

'Senses? Are you accusing me of insanity, Sir?' shouted Colonel Marsh.

'No, Sir, I'm not. If you find my language a bit strong, I beg your pardon. Shall I say that I think . . .'

'I'm not interested in what you think. I asked you to repeat what you said.'

'Look here, Sir, if you keep on sending men over the bridge, you'll only . . .'

'Am I mad, Sir, or am I not?'

'Since you press me, yes, I think it's mad to send men in as you've done.'

'Thank you, Colonel Saunders. This is my operation. May I ask you to return to your desk in the barracks and let me get on with my job? At least, I'm doing something . . .'

'I've no intention of leaving the scene if my artillery is being used.'

'I'll handle it myself.'

'No, I'm afraid you won't.'

'Dean-Forbes', shouted the colonel, though the major was only a few yards away and the colonel was well within hearing of the sullen

191

men standing slackly on the pavement. 'Do you hear? I'm being refused artillery support. Will you note that, please?'

'I'm not refusing,' Saunders persisted quietly, 'indeed, I have called it up for you. I insist only on being present to see that it's properly used. Judging by what's gone on so far, I need to.'

'D'you hear that, Major?' the colonel screamed. 'It is being implied that I'm not fit to command, by people who were so incompetent to deal with a local situation of little military consequence that I've had to divert my Battalion from training for France to put it right!'

'That's a completely false appreciation of the situation, Sir. You know as well as I do that the same call from France has left us so thin on the ground that we were doubly vulnerable to insurrection.'

'Insurrection! Insurrection you call it! A few rebellious Irishmen occupy a few points in Dublin, and you're stumped. Well, I am not, Saunders, I'm not. Get me that field-gun and I'll settle this in quick time. Are you going to give it to me, or are you not?'

Major Dean-Forbes was not altogether surprised by the argument, only by its heat. Like all officers, he had seen enough officers' messes to know that the most senior of men could quarrel over a minor military tactic. But this was out in the field, with men's lives committed. One of these two antagonists was going to be found culpable over this business and, equally so, the other would be vindicated.

He knew that he had to choose, then and there. His moustache gave trouble. He adjusted it with a touch, then looked Colonel Marsh straight in the eye.

'Could I have a word with you, Sir?'

'Yes, what is it?'

Major Dean-Forbes felt justified in nudging the colonel's elbow. But he had judged the colonel's position accurately enough to get away with it. He pretended to be taking him by the elbow to view the canal again from the edge of the main road, as though to re-appraise the situation.

'I think perhaps we ought to allow Colonel Saunders to look after the gun. It's his command, after all.'

Colonel Marsh seemed past reason. He glared. This one suggestion could make or break the major, and they both knew it. A thwack of the swagger-stick on the thigh. Then the colonel blazed:

'Very well, Dean-Forbes, he'll stay. And on your head be it if he makes a balls of it!'

As to that, the major had a thought or two. But he held his peace.

Indeed, no more need be said all round, he thought, since the ring of horses' hooves came from the Kingstown direction.

The team of four hauling the carriage looked superb. They were at full rein, with a trooper riding the right fore-horse. As they dashed up, they made a show to stir the faint-hearted.

They drew to a halt with a clatter of gear and harness, the crew were down in half-a-minute, the gun was round, the horses led to the rear and all cleared for action.

At once, bullets ricocheted off the road-surface. But the gun-crew were trained for it all and shielded themselves shrewdly as they worked.

Colonel Saunders, without even looking at the colonel, dashed over to the gun-crew. The troopers set about their duties with the indifference of specialists to other forms of life, such as the little knot of officers at the scout-car.

In very little time, the first shell thudded into the house over the canal. The sound, while more familiar to the troops crouched in gardens and side-lanes, shocked most of them for a second – then a thin cheer rang out as they realised the gun was theirs.

Bricks and mortar fell in a cloud of dust off the house. Methodically, the shells raked each window of the house. It was as though a strategic demolition were taking place. Where there had been windows, there were soon gaping holes. The brickwork had fallen in one case to the extent that the floor was exposed.

For the gun-crew, working over open sites, it was as easy a job as they were ever likely to get.

As the sergeant-major ran back towards Lieutenant Dobie, the silence over the canal was uncanny. The men at the low garden-wall were tired too. They just lay flat behind the shelter of the wall and railings and, like the lieutenant, waited – for what, they did not know.

There was no doubt now in Dobie's mind that the man out on the road was dead. He had been quite still for many minutes. He might have been asleep, except that his stillness had an awkwardness about it, as though he had been caught in a moment of rigour.

Lieutenant Dobie's head lolled. He was losing all sense of time, of place, even of circumstances.

The odd thing about war (again, as the 'old sweat' will tell you) is that fewer men die because of the enemy's antagonism and hate than from their own momentary lapses of concentration. Sheer physical exhaustion and mental stress affect judgement in men neither trained nor accustomed to it. It is a thing you have to learn to cope with. It cannot be taught.

Lieutenant Dobie, his mind slopping about between past and present, and fatigued beyond anything he had ever known or imagined, was about to act irrationally. He could endure the frustration and pity no longer.

But nothing concentrates the mind of any rank like an approaching sergeant-major. Just as his feet were about to move in some impossible direction, Dobie saw the old campaigner bobbing along the wall, the strain of running showing on his face, but determined as ever. Old Saxton might delineate Dobie as a 'stand-off half to life', but nothing had prepared the lieutenant for this sort of tackle as the CSM flung himself into the gate and bundled him, so to speak, unceremoniously into touch.

'Sorry, Sir, very sorry. Run off me feet, heh?'

'That's all right, Sergeant-Major. Now what? The men are desperate, you know. Did you tell them back there?'

'Oh yes, Sir. They're sending artillery. That'll settle 'em. Just you watch.'

It was then that the renewed concentration of his mind fixed Dobie's eyes on the man on the road. It was not a private – it was an officer, a colleague. He had been so hypnotised by the hand thrashing the road in pain that he had not taken it in.

'Saxton!' he hissed at the CSM. 'It's poor Saxton. And I didn't bring him in. We might have saved him, he's so near.'

'Ach, no, Sir. You couldn't do anything for anybody in that spot. You'd only have joined him, that's certain. Don't fret, Sir, you couldn't have done a thing – *not* a thing, mark my words. That's war, Sir. I know.'

Yes, the CSM would know, if anyone did. But the sight of the debonair Saxton, so easy going in his conversation, but so firm in his definitions of duty and treason, and now lying awkwardly out in the tramlines, was too much. Lieutenant Dobie's mind had wandered. Now resolution firmed. There was nothing he could have done for Saxton, he could see that – nothing, except die with him. And that helped no one.

But there was plenty else.

One after the other, the lieutenant and sergeant-major dashed back

194

into the recess, and then into the school where they could assess the CSM's news, if any – and CSM Green rather doubted if he, or anybody, was any the wiser. Indeed, except for the possibility of a field-gun arriving in the near future, he had little to tell.

He had sensed the tension between the two colonels, but that was not a thing he could discuss with the lieutenant. For any good his errand had done, he might not have gone at all. He saw that Lieutenant Dobie searched his eyes for more; for orders, for a message of relief for those men lying on the road, quite a few needing only to be brought in to be saved. But the possibility of the impending arrival of a field-gun was all the comfort the CSM had to bring.

And he knew that as he said it, he had nothing more in the way of initiative, nothing left to hold the young officer in check. The rest was for Lieutenant Dobie to resolve.

The sergeant-major retreated just that little, to get his breath and to ponder on the tightening over his chest. He would cut down on the beer – it was bound to be that. He did not look the lieutenant in the face again.

As Moffat squelched forward through the clinging weeds of the canal to reach the body of Captain Harwood sprawled on the bank, he knew no bullets could touch him. Whatever instinct had led him to leap wildly over the parapet, it turned out to be right. The bullets flew overhead, but here, down below a steep bank, they were out of reach.

'Dead!' he shouted to Pearson above the splashing of water over the lock-gate above the bridge. 'Dead, dead as a door-nail, poor bugger.'

Since they fell into the water, which was further than they had guessed, they had plunged about through mud and clinging weeds, from one end of the bridge to the other, as though in a tunnel, puzzling it out. Then, as it dawned that they were in what amounted to a ravine, they knew they were safe so long as they stayed down there. The whole canal, from the bridge downwards, was theirs. They were too deep for a bullet to fly anywhere near.

'Did you see old Spider go down?' asked Moffat.

But Pearson was too shocked to answer – first, by the raking rifle-fire, then by the plunge into the water. They were both entirely soaked.

Moffat started searching methodically for the rifles. One by one, he fished them out.

'I'll get some bastard for this. Old Spider ain't gonna die for nuffin!'

By now Pearson could, just, find words. 'Not with them things. Wet, mate.'

And Moffat flung the rifles back into the water.

Now he plunged across to the body of Captain Harwood again, and with shaking hands took the officer's revolver out of the polished leather holster. With a sort of simian care, he turned it over and over, trying to work it out, till he found what he supposed was the safety-catch.

'Wait here, Pug. Here, get yourself dry on the grass. Nuffin'll touch you, Pug, just keep where you are.'

Moffat scrambled up the steep bank. It was topped by a low wall. It marked the end of his cover. He edged up, inch by inch, until he could just see the chimney of a tall house. Inch by inch, he raised his head, more and more of the house coming into view. Then he saw, so clearly he could hardly believe his eyes, there at the first window, a man clearly visible, keeping cover by the side of the window.

The man edged forward, took aim across the canal, fired and darted back into the room.

'I'll get you, you bastard,' whispered Moffat, 'I'll get you.'

Carefully, he aimed the revolver at the opening where the man had appeared, and waited. He knew nothing of trajectory, nothing of ballistics – he just aimed along the short barrel as he had been taught in rifle-drill – and waited. And waited, his finger on the trigger.

The man moved. For a second, he appeared at the window. Moffat took every care with his aim and pulled the trigger. Nothing happened. Moffat cursed, lowered his head, and again with simian movements tried every little knob or button on the gun.

He thought he must have put the safety-catch on rather than off. Now he could not remember in all his tinkering whether or not it was changed. Still seething over Simpson's death, he took up position, aimed and waited. The man moved again. Moffat gave him time to present a full view, aimed with elaborate care, then pressed the trigger.

With his elbow incorrectly crooked, the crack and recoil jolted him unduly, and he did not see the result of his shot. He took position again. The man seemed not to be there any longer. He waited – he could not be sure. Had he killed, or not? One for Spider? He could not be sure.

He raised his head a little and found another window. Again, the momentary appearance of a man, his aim, his fire – and away, out of sight. Moffat waited, aimed. The man came out again. This time,

Moffat was prepared.

Arm straight, he pressed the trigger – and watched. The man slumped on the sill, then slid into the house.

Exultant, Moffat clambered down the bank with chimpanzee leaps.

'Got one, Pug – one for Spider Simpson! And mebbe another...'

He stuffed the revolver into his tunic-pocket. 'Come on, Pug, this 'ere canal's safe as 'ouses! Let's get out of 'ere an' back to the others, an' tell them.'

He led the bedraggled and vacant Pearson along the bank down-stream, always at the bottom of the ravine, away from harm. They came to another bridge. Judging the firing to be well away from them, Moffat clambered up the bank, encouraging Pearson as he led. In-stinctively the street urchin, Moffat followed a devious route until he recognised the gates of the barracks.

Then, as he saw the colonel and his group along the side-street round the scout-car, he ran forward, forgot to salute in his excitement, and addressed the colonel direct:

'I know where we can fire from, Sir, perfect, safe as 'ouses it is. Done it meself, got one of 'em.'

'Who's this man, Major?'

But Moffat was not so easily put off.

'I tell you, Sir, I know the place. I'll take you to it if you want. You could get 'em one by one, I tell you. I got one, mebbe two. Clean as a whistle, I did.'

'Put this man in irons, Major!' shouted the colonel, incensed at the direct address of this private in a wet uniform.

'Oh no, you don't,' replied Moffat with all the assurance of the suc-cessful warrior. 'Come on, Pug, outa here!' And he dashed off again before any officer could move.

Again, by street instinct and the noise of small-arms fire, he found his way to the school by a back-route. He and Pearson scuttled round the building, flung themselves into the recess, then through the door where Dobie and the CSM made sense at once of what Moffat had to say.

'My rifle's wet ... in the canal, Sir', said Moffat after breathlessly retailing his story and describing the excellent firing position on the far bank of the canal and how to reach it unharmed. Dobie had no answer for lost rifles and looked at the sergeant-major.

'Never mind that,' replied the sergeant-major, 'we'll give you another. Leave Pearson.'

'Pug, Sir? No good without me.'

'No, leave him. I'll look after him. Go with Corporal Dinsdale – he's got ten men. Go back the way you came, then leave it to the corporal. He'll arrange the fire, heh?' And suddenly, irrelevantly, he remembered he owed Moffat a fiver. Then he amended his conscience; that'll be the day, he muttered inwardly, this boy's having the time of his life! He patted Moffat on the shoulder as he sent him off with Corporal Dinsdale – from a sergeant-major to a private, that was more than a debt cancelled. It was an accolade.

'Well done, Moffat', said Lieutenant Dobie, anxious to keep in on the act.

And so, the only rational action of the day from the British position took place. Not all the shell-fire was going to root out the Irishmen. They were too determined, too fired by an ideal, to be frightened off by the blunt assault of a field-gun. But to mount their own fire between shells, the Irishmen still had to expose themselves for a few brief moments.

They were relatively safe from the fire directed from the schoolhouse, it was just too far and too random to be more than a threat. But Moffat's position was right under the house, and Corporal Dinsdale was wise enough to accept Moffat's tutelage. Carefully, they picked their targets and had more effect than the rest of the Battalion and the Artillery together. It was only a matter of time before Colonel Marsh could finally march his Battalion, some two-hundred and thirty short, towards the city centre.

Back in the school, Lieutenant Dobie and Sergeant-Major Green watched as the heads of Corporal Dinsdale's party came into view under the wall on the far side of the canal.

Even the British Army has a limit to its tolerance and that, thought the CSM, was saying a lot. He had gone 'over the top' in his time, but reckoned he had never seen such a bungling mess as this.

There was no more fight in the lads, he mused, as he darted about from one position to another, not only making their defence-and-assault positions more effective, but giving a word or two of the old soldier's comfort to men he knew were fretting about friends lying dead or wounded outside.

From the window, he watched as Moffat and Corporal Dinsdale

with his troop picked off the Irish positions one by one. He knew by now that the 18-pounder could fire all day, and the Irishmen would still be there. It would take more than one field-gun to demolish that house. Moffat's was the only answer – to pick off the assailants one by one as they exposed themselves to fire along the main road.

Moffat's position was just right; only a Mills bomb could winkle out Moffat, Dinsdale and his troop. He noted with relief that the Irishmen seemed to have overlooked that sinister weapon for getting behind walls and into trenches. From their position under that wall, Moffat's party of men more or less equalised the Irish position.

The sergeant-major, quietly totting up, reckoned that nearly two hundred were casualties; and more would die yet, or sustain wounds, so exposed were men out there, still under inadequate cover.

As Dobie and the CSM watched the systematic destruction by shells, the lieutenant decided the time had come to assert his rank.

'Now's the time, Mr Green. We can get some casualties in. Those people over there won't show their faces while these shells pour in. There'll be nobody alive in there soon if this goes on.'

'I wouldn't rely on that. Men can time shells. I know, I've done it meself – until it comes sort of automatic.'

'Maybe, maybe. But we've got to get them in. Some of the wounded will bleed to death for want of a dressing. It's inhuman to leave them out there.'

Roberts F.X. was very much on Dobie's mind. The firm conviction that he was alive out there gripped him: a life to be saved, not allowed to seep away minute by minute on the open road.

But the CSM was not so easily moved. One life can cost another – that too, he had seen before.

'Ach, you've got it all wrong', he said with duly controlled patience. 'More men will die if you send them out after casualties now, I can tell you. You never know, the colonel might have a move up his sleeve. There must be more bridges to cross than this one, and he might be awake by now. So don't send any more men to their death. Not for a while, anyway.'

'Very well. I'll do it myself. Roberts out there is the worst. He's trying to move, can you see?'

'Ay, Sir, I can see. But leave him for a bit. Wait for the next assault. You'll see. The colonel will re-assemble the Battalion after the gun's softened up the position. He was having it out with the locals while I was there.'

But he could see the lieutenant was determined. There was something about the face, the brows, that defied argument. He knew that the lieutenant was going; that while he would respect the advice not to risk men, it did not apply to himself. Nothing would stop him.

'Mr Green, I'm going out by the gate. I'll skirt along the wall, then dash across the open to the parapet. It won't take a second. If Roberts is alive, I'll get him back to the gate. Then you and the men could deal with him. Yes?'

'I still think you shouldn't, Sir. It'll take more than a few shells to silence that lot over there, you mark my words.'

'Nobody can live under that pounding', said Dobie. 'I doubt if there's anyone alive in there by now. And Dinsdale is making his mark as well.'

The boom of the field-gun continued remorselessly. The pall of dust over the house shrouded the Irish positions as the shells thudded into it with a deafening detonation.

Still, the CSM detected the occasional whine and crack of a bullet. The Irish were bent on a show of defiance, he knew, however little they might be able to see and aim effectively. He had seen just such defiance before – and was not deceived. It was a common enough experience in Flanders. The German sniper who held on day after day under the most appalling shelling, and still survived to pick off the occasional jay-walker. But how to convey this experience to a greenhorn like the young lieutenant?

'You'd be surprised, Sir. I've seen snipers take a lot worse pounding than this and still find life and soul to notch up one or two of ours.'

'No, no... Nobody can survive that. Just look – it'll soon be rubble.'

'They'll survive. I tell you. Just wait and see. They're still firing. Mark my words.'

'Well, then, they must be heroes.'

'Depends on whose side you're on. They're no bloody heroes as far as I'm concerned!'

'Heroes are not the prerogative of one side or the other.'

That was beyond the sergeant-major. He was steadily losing what patience he had left and was about to shout his head off. Then he rued it. He saw the determination in Dobie's face. Quietly, he pleaded once more:

'Don't go, Sir, it's madness.'

But with a lunge, the lieutenant was already off.

The sergeant-major shouted to the men to mark what windows they could see over the canal and redouble the fire.

Back in the school, he watched from a window. He was just in time to see the lieutenant dash across the canal road to Roberts. The luck of the devil, thought the CSM as he noted that not a single bullet flew. The shelling, if not finishing the Irish, was keeping them quieter. And Moffat with Dinsdale's little party keeping them away from what windows were left.

Dobie was breathless as he reached F.X. The bridge parapet where it turned the corner in a descending curve provided adequate cover. He had no qualms about turning F.X. over, since he was lying with his face down. Then Dobie saw the wound, high in the groin, bleeding profusely. He looked into the man's eyes: they were glazed, full of hurt, the eyes of innocence. A few weeks previously he had been still at the family hearth – now he was baptised in fire and lying out in the open with a painful, gaping wound.

There appeared to be some bone damage, as well as the torn flesh. But, though weak, F.X. was conscious, if unresponsive to every manoeuvre of the lieutenant.

Dobie took a shell-dressing from F.X.'s tunic-pocket, slit open the wrapping and pressed it to the wound. Then, clumsily, he tied the bandage round the thigh.

He felt strangely calm as he went about the whole business, as though in the eye of a hurricane. Although Roberts groaned as he lifted the injured limb to get the bandage under, Dobie was so intent on the task that he was suddenly far removed from the violence above and around them. As he tied the tapes of the shell-dressing, he checked its effectiveness and was satisfied that he had staunched the bleeding.

Then, as he sought to grasp F.X.'s left hand to heave him over his shoulder for a dash back to the school-gate, he saw it grasped a note. As he turned to release it, the hand only held tighter.

'Let it go, Roberts,' Lieutenant Dobie hissed, 'I want to hoist you up on my shoulder and make a dash for it. We'll soon have you right. Come on, let it go.'

But Roberts only held it more tightly. Dobie pulled hard at the paper, and it came away.

'Answer it, Sir. Will you? Answer it...' Roberts's voice was hoarse, resigned.

'What is it? A letter?'

'You'll see, Sir, you'll understand, I know. Answer it for me, will you?'

'I'll try.' Hastily Dobie pushed the letter into his tunic pocket along with Laura's. Then with a pang he realised Laura's was not there. Oh God, great God! Not Laura's letter of all things. Losing that was a sort of sacrilege. He was so angry with himself that he wasted precious minutes searching for it on the ground. Even as a bullet cracked against the granite parapet above him he hesitated and looked around. That letter from Laura mattered. He knew he was safe enough under the parapet. Had he dropped it in the barrack square, or on the way to the canal? He searched frantically in his pockets again, but there was no sign of it. He was furious with himself. He made sure Roberts's letter should not suffer the same fate and pushed it firmly home. It was by now a matter of conscience; conscience demanded every care. Resignedly he returned to the task in hand. He heaved Roberts on to his shoulder, still in the crouched position.

Forgetting the CSM's advice to wait for the next shell to explode into the building he tried to rise. He was shocked at the dead weight of the man. He had not realised a man could weigh so heavy. Roberts groaned with the pain as Dobie staggered drunkenly. Nevertheless, while the dust and rubble fell away from the building and bullets whined in the air, Dobie continued to roll and heave until, with an almighty effort, he got to his feet.

Through the school window, the sergeant-major, now careless of cover, saw how exposed the lieutenant was and shouted at the men to redouble their fire. As he saw Lieutenant Dobie hesitate and appear to search for something, the sergeant-major cursed: 'Hellfire! Will the man ever learn? I told him to time it. What a time to look for lost property. Likely lost his bloody watch!'

Angrily, he smashed at the window with his rifle butt to enlarge the opening. Regardless of the risk, he rose, cupped his hands at his mouth and yelled: 'Wait! You're too late now. Wait for the next shell!'

But it made no impression. As the seargeant-major saw the lieutenant rise painfully with Roberts across his shoulders, he shouted again to the men to keep firing.

Dobie struggled off-beam with F.X. on his back. He lurched this way and that across the open road and kept hoisting F.X. up, as though there were all the time in the world. It was all obviously more than his strength could take. But he was determined. And he would return for more men once he had F.X. inside. That was the proper, the only, human thing he could do.

He battled on, rolling like a ship in high seas. But he was succeeding. The CSM could see the sheer determination on the bent head. And then, Dobie went out of view.

But looking back, one or two of the men, still lying out in the shelter of the low wall alongside the canal-bank, could see. As the lieutenant and his burden reached the corner of the school-wall, they saw him stretch an arm to the wall for support, then gradually slither down, slowly, still determinedly it seemed, as though to rest, with Roberts F.X., still semi-conscious, high on his shoulder. Then, appallingly, they both lay sprawled, spread-eagled, F.X. across the lieutenant.

The sergeant-major waited – waited and wondered. Then, shaking himself, he turned from the window and ran back to the entrance-hall. There he paused, never so impulsive as to risk his life carelessly. He bent, dashed across the little garden, feeling naked without his cap which still lay to his right in a too exposed part of the garden, and he crouched at the gate-pillar. He put his head cautiously round the edge of the post to see what he could of the canal area.

He saw the trouble at once. There, at the end of the school-wall, the lieutenant was sprawled, F.X. spread-eagled over him.

'Quick, one of you!' he shouted at the men huddled in the recess. But they were 'B' Company, not easily moved by the CSM of another Company.

He dashed back once again, grabbed the first man he dived against.

'Right, out you get, the lot of you!' He glared at them. 'Go on, over to the wall, and help "A" Company. I want that house plastered with fire!'

But they were slow to act. Still holding his 'volunteer' by the collar, he gave a savage kick at the nearest man.

'Out you go, go on. I'll have any man on a charge if I find him sitting on his arse any longer. Out, the lot of you!'

The anger in his voice shamed them. They ran at a crouch over the garden to join their comrades from 'A' Company.

'Now, you', he addressed the frightened man under his grip. 'Come with me, and quick.' Together, they dashed over the open ground to the gate.

'There's two men lying wounded just round the corner. I want you to follow me. Catch the hand of the first man, I'll catch the other hand, and we drag him in. See? Straight over the garden into the entrance-hall. Understand? No stopping, heh? Just grab and in with him. Then the same with the second.'

But with the noise of shell-fire and bullets still flying from the canal direction, the man—a stranger to him—showed no sign of moving. His eyes just stared. So the CSM pushed him out and followed.

Once out, the man ran, saw F.X. lying and clawing the ground as he tried to crawl off the prone lieutenant, and together, he and the sergeant-major grabbed at F.X.'s hand and started to drag him. Fear increased their efforts. They ignored F.X.'s groans, and in one agonising motion they dragged the protesting man through the gate, across the garden and into the open doors of the school.

Pausing only a moment to recover their breath, the CSM grabbed the man again and they ran back to Lieutenant Dobie. As they bent to catch a hand apiece, the man yelled and fell. Startled, the sergeant-major grabbed him again, then saw the man's forearm hanging limp and blood already pumping through the sleeve.

'All right, laddie, run back as best you can. I'll manage.'

The man recovered his wits, rose and staggered back towards safety in the school.

The sergeant-major knew he had only seconds before he too would be marked. Remembering the lieutenant's struggle to lift F.X., he stuck to his original plan of dragging him in. The lieutenant was 'out', so he grabbed both his hands and, staggering backwards, dragged him, breathlessly, to the gate-post. He heard the bullets lashing the pavement, but he and the lieutenant were not easy to mark against the wall.

He rested a moment in the cover of the post, then again dragged Lieutenant Dobie, across the garden this time, and with a last supreme effort, got him through the doors, where he laid him beside Roberts F.X.

Then everything went black. He lay back against the wall of the entrance-hall and tried, urgently, to cope with the unfamiliar twilight of consciousness. He willed himself to focus on the lieutenant, wanting to do something. But he could not move.

Consciousness came and went in waves as he fought with himself.

Slowly, he came round. But something told him he would never be the same again.

He went about it with military deliberation – one: lift one hand, and down; two: lift the other one, and down; three: flex a leg; four: flex the other. Repeat. Slowly, his head cleared. With a final effort, he got to a kneeling position and bent over the lieutenant, lying face downwards.

With all the strength he could summon, Sergeant-Major Green turned the lieutenant over and looked down at the pale face. And the sergeant-major bent closer. But he knew.

He knew, with all the field-craft of the old soldier, that the lieutenant was no longer with him.

There was no mark on the lieutenant as the sergeant-major, still incredulous, searched gently with his hands over the tunic. He tried to lift him, but had no strength left. And the blackness came over him again.

He hung on, desperately, to keep up, not to slip sideways on to the lieutenant, and as he clawed his way back to full consciousness, he could only think how badly he had done it all, dragging the lieutenant like a sack of potatoes. He would have liked to have carried him in, as the lieutenant had carried 'Francis Saviour'.

Then, all at once, it was as though a light had been turned on. He was alert again. Turning to the classroom door, he recognised one man to whom he could put a name.

'Roberts!' he shouted.

John Henry, startled, dropped his rifle and ran to the entrance-hall.

'Ach, lad, how many times have you to be told to carry your rifle with you everywhere? No, don't get it now. Give me a hand to lift the lieutenant.'

John Henry blenched as he looked at F.X., and then at the lieutenant. He bent down and gingerly raised the limp torso. Again, the sergeant-major ran his fingers over the back of the tunic, then came upon the small tear near the spine.

'Poor young sod,' he murmured, 'must have got it when he was hitching Francis Saviour higher up on his shoulders. His luck ran out. Should have been dead long ago, the way he stood about after the first lot o' bullets. Just like him to die carrying a man in.'

Still, the semi-conscious states rippled over the sergeant-major – yet he hung on. There must be no weakening in front of the men. Now that the young lieutenant was gone, he was in sole command until that lot back there thought something up and relieved them. So, with fumbling hands, he straightened out the lieutenant's tunic. Anything, to keep going. He seemed to be in a trance as he murmured on at the same time.

'Ah yes, neat and clean,' he went on, 'neat and clean, heh? I'll say this for the lieutenant, 'e was always one for being neat and clean.' Then a thought occurred. He would see that the lieutenant was spick-and-span before his last journey to the rear, whenever that might be.

'Who was his batman, Roberts? Get him to tidy the lieutenant up a bit.'

'Roberts, Sir, Frank Roberts.'

The sergeant-major took some time to take it in.

'Francis Saviour, heh?' he said quietly. 'I've always wondered what his mother could have been thinking of . . . Well, she owes a lot to the lieutenant, God bless 'im.'

There was an infinite patience in his face as John Henry looked at him.

'Put him down, Roberts.'

For John Henry, the little entrance-hall was sealed off from the rest of the world – and from time past and time future. And here was death, in a tiny enclosed space, with the sergeant-major still on his knees and looking strangely quiet, and with, outside the door, a world of violence raging.

He took it in that Lieutenant Dobie was dead, but registered no particular feeling. He wanted to look at F.X. lying parallel with the lieutenant, but not nearly so clean. Both trouser-legs were matted with blood.

But John Henry could only look at the sergeant-major, almost as Sian looked at himself with her large whippet eyes, waiting for the next move.

Then the snap: 'Move, man!' the sergeant-major shouted. 'Don't sit there like a fanny. Shell-dressing!'

John Henry at once fished out a shell-dressing from his tunic-pocket. Together, they turned to F.X., who was now unconscious.

'He'll be all right,' the sergeant-major mused, 'but the poor lieutenant made an awful bloody mess of this dressing.'

Carefully, he unfolded the old dressing from F.X.'s leg and skilfully applied the new dressing in such a way that the bleeding stopped. He then pulled off the left sleeve of F.X.'s tunic and through the shirt injected the needle of the little morphine ampoule he had pulled out of his

206

own pocket.

From his experience of casualties, the CSM guessed that F.X. would survive if he could be moved to a dressing-station in the next hour or two. The wound was bad enough, but not crucial; it was the profuse bleeding that might tell against him if he went too long without attention.

He returned to Lieutenant Dobie; closed the staring eyes under the serene black brows.

'Ach, the lieutenant, of all people . . .' he whispered to John Henry. 'He wouldn't have harmed a fly. If Francis Saviour lives, it'll be Mr Dobie he owes it to. Poor young sod,' he mused as though John Henry were not there, 'he made a terrible bloody soldier, but an awful good man . . . All right, Roberts, stay here and look after Francis Saviour.'

The sergeant-major had not seen the lieutenant die. But he had seen that last stubborn effort, and as far as he was concerned it was not going to be wasted. It was all part of soldiering, which for him was simply an intermittent succession of such incidents strung together, with the parade-ground and the sergeants' mess as preparation for them.

He found himself staggering as he went into the classroom. Carefully, he ripped blankets from two of the men's packs and went back. He took every care of F.X., covered him with one blanket, then turned to the body of the lieutenant, straightened out the limbs and reverently draped the second blanket over him.

Leaving John Henry to look after F.X., he returned to the men at the windows, took John Henry's rifle, aimed and fired. There seemed nothing else to be done.

This was the front-line, and that was what you did at the front-line. As with Flanders, even if the bullets went nowhere, it was better than just waiting. And you never know your luck.

EPILOGUE

The days warmed after the Easter week, and in spite of the War – and for a few because of it – people exulted in the sun. These weeks of May passed relatively quietly, for the build-up to the great offensive on the Somme was on the way, but not yet complete.

There was a lull of sorts in the stream of telegrams from the Western Front. For a week or two after Easter, Ireland appeared on the front page of the national newspapers. Insurrection – executions. A few people were nauseated by the summary executions and protested against them. If anything would unite the Irish people to revolt against British dominion, they claimed, those executions would.

Miss Pomfret, her hands clad in heavy gloves against the thorns, was training some burgeoning roses against the sun-drenched north wall of the garden. In spite of William's absence, she was almost content in the spring sunshine.

She watched with a certain misgiving as several cabbage-white butterflies sunned their wings in the captive warmth of the garden. Then she smiled. The thought of Nature's bounty crossed her mind.

William had missed the magnolia this year. That was sad, but perhaps, as he had opined in his letter, all would be over by Christmas. Next year perhaps. She felt lazy and, taking off her gloves, she moved to a chair on the terrace, where a book lay invitingly.

But its pages did not compel her attention, and she dozed.

She was startled when Mary came to her, yet she knew at once. It was the telegram that had been always at the back of her mind since his last letter. She saw that Mary too had guessed, but dismissed her as calmly as she could.

She held the little buff envelope in her hand, unable to control the trembling of her hands. She rose and passed through the french-window into the darkness of the drawing-room. Distractedly, she looked for the paper-knife, found it on her desk and slit the envelope with extreme care. She read the telegram slowly, word by word. Then she sat down.

Why so long...? April 26th ... Why, oh *why* so long? All these

211

days she had presumed him to be alive, and he had been dead since April 26th, they said. Why, oh why did it take so long to tell her?

She folded her hands over her lap and sat straight, head bowed a little. April 26th... It was the thinking of him alive when he was already dead that distressed her at first.

Gradually, her eyes got used to the light in the room after the bright sunshine outside, and only now did she notice that a parcel too had arrived. Mary had placed it on the desk. This she opened more frantically, since it could conceivably contain something to refute or qualify the telegram which only said, after the usual regrets, that Second-Lieutenant Dobie had been killed in action on April 26th.

There was a letter with the parcel. She ripped the envelope open carelessly and quickly unfolded the enclosed letter.
'Dear Miss Pomfret,' it read.

'It is with great regret that I have to confirm to you the death of your', and here the writer seemed to have some difficulty with a word. There was a crossing-out, then, 'ward, Lieutenant William Dobie. He fell bravely during an attack on insurgent elements in Ireland...'

Ireland? She was confused. IRELAND...? Why Ireland? *To die for Ireland*? Something was wrong, clearly. Was he not in France? Her heart leant with hope. Had not his last letter said 'France'? She could not remember. Certainly, he had said 'abroad'. Perhaps she had read 'France' where he had not actually written it. Was there another Dobie?

She hesitated, put her hands towards a drawer to find his letter. But returned, instead, to the one in her hand. She knew by now the news was true. 'Second-Lieutenant Dobie was a valued member of the Battalion who quickly learned the habit of command. In the officers' mess he was respected for the independence of his opinions. On behalf of his brother officers, I send you our deepest condolences.

'I am sending herewith with his personal effects, a letter found on his person, which I thought you ought to have.
'Yours sincerely,
F. W. Dean-Forbes (Lieut. Col.)
Officer Commanding.'

It was only when her hands picked up the compass – from Darlington, she remembered – that she broke down. The tears shook her, and for a long time she was wracked by sobs. Then, calming herself, she looked

212

for the letter the commanding officer had mentioned. It bore no address and had obviously been put in a new army envelope. There was no knowing where it had come from.

'My dearest', she read and remembered how, in the postscript of his last letter, William had promised to talk something over with her. She turned her head to one side, her handkerchief to her eyes. She could not read for some time. Then, with an effort, she read on: 'I was glad to have your last letter and to know you are all right. I am writing this urgently. I will try to write again tomorrow, a longer letter. The reason I am writing this is that I'm very worried. I didn't want to bother you before, but it is well past my time. In fact, it's ages past. Do you understand what I mean? It means that what we did that night isn't going to be all right. I hope you understand. I don't know what to do. I didn't want to bother you, knowing how awful it is for you, but I have to tell somebody about it. I love you, my dear. All my love, Marian.'
Marian.'

Miss Pomfret broke down once more. She could not control her sobs. And after half-an-hour, Mary brought Cook and together they guided the distraught lady to her bedroom.